DEMONIC CRISIS MANAGEMENT FOR THE MODERN VAMPIRE

VAMPIRE INNOCENT
BOOK SIXTEEN

MATTHEW S. COX

DIVISION ZERO PRESS

Demonic Crisis Management for the Modern Vampire
Vampire Innocent Book 16
© 2022 Matthew S. Cox
All Rights Reserved
This novel is a work of fiction. Any similarities to actual persons living or undead,
demons, or ghost-possessed pieces of office equipment are coincidental. No portion of
this book may be reproduced without written permission from the author except for
quotes posted in reviews or blogs.

ISBN (ebook): 978-1-950738-54-0

ISBN (paperback): 978-1-950738-55-7

CONTENTS

INTO THE TINY NARROW CLOSED

Comfortable is a matter of perspective.

This box I'm presently stuffed into is on a comfort scale somewhere between being stuck on stage at a school talent show with a serious accidental wedgie I can't subtly fix and an adult trying to get into the back seat of a 1978 Toyota Celica. On the plus side, this is more comfortable than suffering the social obligation to climb up on that stupid saddle chair thing at the steakhouse Dad likes so the staff can sing happy birthday. Bad example. That's horrible. I'd rather streak Woodinville again than endure the spotlight of a bunch of chain restaurant employees being forced to cheerfully sing an insincere birthday wish to a total stranger while a few hundred other total strangers watch, all of them glad it isn't their turn up on the saddle chair.

Whoever came up with that idea, anyway? Society has enough contempt for aging without establishing a system of public shaming people for getting a year older. Wait, I wonder if Olmaz had a hand in it? He's like the demon lord of petty annoyances.

Anyway, back to comfort.

There are things I find comfortable. Surprisingly, my vampire existence is one of them. I say 'surprisingly,' because there hadn't been any choice on my part insofar as opting in to the unlife. Ashley, on the other hand, jumped in feet first, knowing full well what she signed up for. Sierra thinks it's a little bit creepy-clingy that Ashley literally wanted to die so she can spend forever with me, her best-friend-slash-sister-from-another-mister.

You know, I never liked that phrase. It implies Mrs. Carter had an affair. We girls really need something closer to 'brother from another mother' that doesn't sound so, I dunno, patronizing. Rhymes be damned.

Sierra's hardly in a position to call Ashley creepy, considering she's twelve and has actively sought out the opportunity to drink vampire blood. What girl her age would even think—oh wait, never mind. People who take the Goth thing way too far—or highly motivated Girl Scout cookie marketers—would likely not hesitate to drink blood if given the chance. Had some Goth kids in my class in high school. Fate has a weird sense of irony, doesn't it? Vampirism found me, Miss Follows Rules Girl, and not the kids who dressed up like faux vampires. Any one of them probably would've adored the chance to become a vampire for real.

Hmm. Maybe that's why it didn't happen? Like the way the police academies tend to reject overly gung-ho mall security guards with power fantasies. Perhaps if someone wants a thing too much, it's a bad idea to give it to them?

Anyway...

Here I am in a box.

It's a nice box. Padded even. No, it's not a coffin. Also no, vampires don't sleep in coffins. That's a total Hollywoodism. The enclosure I'm tucked away in right now is more of a concealed bed. Ashley and Chloe are in here with me. Yeah, there's not much room to move. Somehow, in our sleep, we migrated from both of us being on our sides facing each other with Chloe stuffed between us to me being on my back, Ashley on top of me, and Chloe kinda curled up like a cat by our feet.

Since it's unusual for vampires to move while sleeping, I'll chalk up the repositioning as the effect of us being jostled around in transit.

Yes, our hidden bed is in the back of Grandpa Sheridan's trailer. Remember last year when I talked about our 'last family road trip?' Seems it wasn't the last one after all. Not sure which is more persistent: Wright Family traditions or Dad's urge to do geeky and awkward things. Sometimes, I really do feel like we are living a National Lampoon's movie. At least my father isn't quite as clueless and inept as Clark W. Griswold. He tries, though. I have no doubt he does it on purpose since he loves those movies. Probably where the idea for road tripping as a vacation came from.

First thing I notice is the droning hum of the trailer tires on the road. Everything around me vibrates. Over the first twenty seconds of regained consciousness, I become increasingly aware of a myriad of rattling, clicking, tapping, and squeaking. There are times having the overly acute hearing of a vampire is unnerving. This is one of those times. It sounds like the trailer is going to shake itself apart at any moment. It's not. All these noises are faint. A normal person wouldn't really hear them.

The next thing I notice is music. Specifically, the not-quite-on-key tones of my family singing along to Tom Petty. They're not in the trailer. They're in Mom's Yukon, which is pulling the trailer. Sam and Dad are fearlessly belting out the lyrics without a shred of shame or self-consciousness. Mom sounds happy. Sierra's voice has a begrudging undertone that suggests she's participating out of guilt, not wanting to be the wet blanket but also not really thrilled about singing. Sophia is barely whispering due to shyness. Poor kid. She gets embarrassed if she hears herself singing even if she's alone somewhere. If someone else hears her singing, she practically faints. It is really strange—in a good way—she's adapted to being on stage in front of an audience for her dance class recitals. Of course, there, she doesn't make any noise, and she's one of a group, so *all* the attention isn't on her.

Ashley and Chloe are not singing.

Both are still sleeping. Even though they got lucky and turned out to be Innocents like me, they are still quite new. It took me around six months to be able to wake up regularly around 2:30 in the afternoon. I suspect Chloe might've woken up, shifted around, and gone back to sleep. Good chance it would've taken more than some highway bouncing to get her to curl up like that at one end of our 'bed.'

It's a good thing we don't need to breathe. Not necessarily talking about being in an enclosed space. More that Ashley is draped over me. We've slept together all the time—and I mean that in a strictly platonic, friendly sort of way. As in two kids sharing a huge bed on a sleepover. Co-sleeping with Ashley didn't usually involve clinging except after we watched an unexpectedly scary movie. Having her piled on top of me like this is a new thing. It would be awkward with anyone else, but Ashley's... well... Ashley.

This is no more awkward than having a giant cat sleeping on my chest.

I debate getting out of the box. Not like my moving would wake either Ashley or Chloe up. Simple touching or jostling isn't enough to disturb undead sleep. There would need to be malicious intent as well. Since I radiate the exact opposite intent toward Ash and Chloe, they'd remain comatose even if I moved their bodies around like lumber to climb out of this thing.

But, I don't.

Somewhere, I kinda remember hearing that it's illegal to be in a trailer while it's in motion. Might've been one of my grandfathers who said it. Maybe Dad. I don't know for sure if it *is* against the law for a person to ride in a trailer, but it does sound like a stupid thing to do. Like, if the trailer pops off the hitch and goes stray, anyone inside it is going to be in for a world of pain. Vampires, not so much. It'll hurt, but we'll get up. Unless, by some crazy circumstance the trailer goes off a ridge into an active volcanic lava flow. However, since we're not road tripping to Hawaii or the temple of an ancient Aztec fire god, it's a fairly safe bet to assume this trailer is not going to end up in lava should we get into an accident.

So, yeah. People aren't supposed to be in trailers while they're in motion. Oops. My bad.

Well, Follows Rules Girl is just gonna have to suck it up this time. We are breaking the rules. I try to distract her by thinking about how that law only applies to living people. To avoid the risk of some nosy driver seeing me through the trailer's windows and calling the police, I decide to remain in the hidden compartment. To further distract my rule-following subconscious, I end up singing along with my family.

Into the Great Wide Open indeed. I chuckle, gazing around at the confines of the compartment. More like the exact opposite.

I start to get a hint of feeling maudlin again. Singing 'with' my family, but not fully 'with' them hits me like a metaphor for my new reality. Meh. Not really. They didn't banish me to the trailer. The sun did that. Can't really help my un-biology demanding sleep. Next time we come to a stop, though, I will join them up in the SUV.

It's nice my body is immune to muscle cramps. Don't have a lot of room to move in here.

Soon, the Tom Petty song is over and a track from Rush comes on. Only Sam and Dad try to sing along with it. Dad doesn't even try matching the singer's pitch. Sierra and Sophia can pull off the same high pitch, but neither of them know the words. Sierra is embarrassed that Sam knows the words. Apparently, 'Rush' is nerdy. She says this as if she isn't one of us. Dad likes Rush. A lot. I think it's a cult or something. Whenever he runs into someone wearing a Rush shirt or who makes a comment about even knowing the band exists, they'll talk for an hour about it.

On one hand, logic says I should prepare myself for the eventuality of losing my family. Unless the Forces of Evil™ destroy me, I will outlive them. Though, I'm not entirely sure about Sierra anymore. Sophia did something to her magically and keeps dropping subtle hints about her living a really long time. Sierra wanted the strength, speed, and endurance of a vampire—primarily so she could protect herself, and us, from the nonsense that keeps showing up to mess with our family. She did not, however, want to die nor become an actual vampire. Sierra also doesn't fancy the idea of being stuck as a twig-thin tween for eternity. Yeah, that is slightly less awesome than being stuck as a twig-thin *teen* for eternity. I exaggerate. I'm not completely a twig. I do have *some* shape, thanks to Mom's influence on our genetics. At her age, though... yeah. My arms and legs had all the shape of McDonald's drink straws.

Family... plus two. Ashley and Chloe are my vamp family. I mean, Ashley has always felt like part of the family. Now, we have Chloe, who is balancing on a knife edge between being another little sister and my daughter. Good thing I have experience babysitting the Littles. Being responsible for an eternal seven-year-old isn't the worst thing in the world. It's like I'm watching someone else's kid for a weekend—only that weekend happens to be *Groundhog Day* and repeats indefinitely. The world is *so* lucky I am who I am. We could so horribly mess with people. Like, imagine the grandparents walking in to find Chloe drinking some cleaning product from under the sink, not knowing she's a vampire and it's utterly harmless to her.

Yeah, bad thoughts. Neither she nor I are the sort of person to be so cruel. Grandma Sheridan might have a literal heart attack if she saw that. Although, I am not potentially above flying to another state we don't live in on Halloween and teasing people in a hotel. We could pull off some seriously creepy *Ring* type stuff. Ashley, sweet as she is, would be totally in on it, too. She'd want to video record the reactions. And hey, on Halloween, people would eventually dismiss it as costume stuff.

Ashley stirs.

Yes. I am saved from boredom.

"Ugh. What time is it?" She shifts to one side and wipes a hand over her face.

Okay, her half-awake, dazed Ashley expression is even cuter with her fangs half-extended. I can't help but snicker. It *is* taking some getting used to for me to process the change in her, but I'd be lying to myself if I said she didn't go through the same adjustment when it happened to me.

"Not sure. Sometime after 2:30." I fidget. "I could check my phone, but it's in my pocket."

Ashley looks around, realizes she's sprawled on top of me, then blinks. "Did we roll over?"

"Trailer probably hit a few bumps."

"Oh. Yeah." She yawns, even though the gesture is purely theater—albeit subconscious instinct theater. "Sorry."

"For?"

"Squishing you?" She begins attempting to move to my left.

I shift the other way. In a moment, we're once again lying on our sides facing each other. Not that it's necessary, but I can breathe again. This is kind of like how we used to lay in bed as kids and spend hours talking when we should've been sleeping. Only, back then, we tended to have more than four inches between our noses. It sounds intimate, but it's not. Our proximity is purely a function of confined space.

It doesn't take us long to fall into old habits and start chattering away. Only real difference is we aren't randomly mentioning various boys or talking about stuff that happened at school. Instead, we discuss vampires. Okay, so it's basically the same thing as talking about school, just with a different set of people. Ashley thinks Ashton James is 'super hot.' She already knows he's in a relationship with Henry Arnold, but neither one of us knows if the two are exclusive. Vast age does strange things to a vampire's mind. For example, Aurélie. As a mortal, she had no interest in other women whatsoever. After several centuries, she stopped caring about the 'outside wrapping' and gets attracted to the personality. Once an exceptionally timid and proper lady, she's done things in the bedroom most seasoned adult film actors would hesitate to try. I don't even want to know. I'm happy to leave it at rumor and vague statement.

Yanno what's weird? Thinking about Aurélie having sex—with anyone—is about as cringe as the idea of my 'rents doing it. Does that mean she feels like another mom or... big sis? I mean, she doesn't look anywhere near old enough to be my mother. I think she was twenty or so when she turned vampire. Back in her time, she passed as an established adult. People with modern sensibilities nowadays could regard her as a teenager. It's crazy how much she can control her 'age' by altering her mannerisms. Like, when she showed up to confront Malcolm Bishop—Tilloa's jerk of a sire—she overplayed the teenage attitude. Swear she came off as being like sixteen. Totally did it on purpose, too, to dig the screws in deeper. Malcolm thought he got his ass kicked by a kid.

But yeah, at the soirees, she's totally vibing in her mid-to-late twenties.

I gotta agree with Ashley. Ashton James *is* hot. I'm not tempted to do anything, though. He's got a boyfriend and I have Hunter. I'm happy, despite also knowing Hunter is going to get old and die on me. No idea how long it will take me to get over losing him, or what sort of things I'll end up involved with after he's gone. At least for now, he's a much-needed point of normality in my life.

Mistake. Mentioning him skews our conversation into the whole aging thing.

"It's gonna get weird, though, right?" asks Ashley. "Are you still gonna be with him when he's as old as Dad?"

Ooh. Talk about cringe. "Umm."

"Yeah. Umm." She laughs.

I hate to say it, but the girl has a point. If Chloe is stuck mentally at seven for eternity, it means that I am also stuck at the mental state I was in at the time of my Transference. Forever eighteen, as they say. I don't think it's going to be possible for my teenage brain to look at a guy in his thirties—or older—and feel anything but 'eww' in regard to sex. Will knowing it's Hunter change that or will the notion of having sex with him ten, twenty, or thirty years from now start to turn creepy, like I'm having fantasies about one of the teachers at school?

No, I didn't. Just saying.

It's not the same as a girl my age having *dreams* about movie stars. It's a good thing Vigo Mortenson—as Aragorn—cannot read minds. I'd die of embarrassment if he ever knew all the things fourteen-year-old-me fantasized about. Him and Legolas fighting each other to see who'd win me over… yeah. Super cringey but hey, I was young.

The important thing there, though, is in no possible world did I ever expect to actually meet him—or Legolas. Idle fantasies are completely different from an older guy who would totally be into *doing stuff*. Ick. Not calling Hunter a creep. It's just me he's in love with. But, hmm. Is he going to start seeing me as a kid? Will *he* begin to get weirded out at the idea of being with me romantically when he's past thirty and I still look the same?

The more I circle around this thought process—out loud with Ashley—the more it seems like I'm going to have to make a really crappy, painful choice. Either we bring Hunter into the world of the undead... or I ride this relationship out for a few more years and then erase myself from his head so he can go on with a normal life.

"You could enthrall him?" Ashley grins. "Kinda halfway between? Not making him a vamp and not losing him."

I overact rubbing my chin in thought. "Not sure doing that would end well for either of us. What if he got addicted? Long-term thralldom is likely to end with him ultimately becoming a vampire anyway—or going insane."

"Ooh. Yeah, that's not a good idea." Ashley cringes. "Huh... maybe when we're a few hundred years old, we'll wind up kissing."

"Hah! Yeah, right. Come on, Ash. You're like my sister. George R.R. Martin isn't writing my life story."

She bursts out laughing. "Or George Lucas... What is it with writers named George having siblings in love?"

We spend the next hour debating the intention behind the Luke and Leia romantic tension. Ash thinks he was trying to be edgy. I think he initially started off shipping Luke and Leia together, then someone told him it would be too predictable, so he changed them to siblings midway through the writing process.

Either way, big cringe.

Of course, this leads to us trying to figure out which one of us is more Leia and which is more Luke. We go in circles for a while before motion down by my shins stalls us to silence.

Chloe's awake. She doesn't bother yawning, simply stretching out of the ball she'd been curled up in to thrust her grinning face toward ours. Fortunately, it's obvious she *just* woke up and hasn't overheard any of our conversation about boys or other more adult topics. By obvious, I mean her features shift visibly from death to life over the few seconds it takes her to crawl forward. Even though color is difficult for vampires to see in total darkness, I've acclimated enough to differentiate the pallid, greyish skin of a corpse from a fully lifelike child—albeit a really pale one. She could totally do the Wednesday Addams thing without even trying.

Can't say I'm a fan of seeing her sleep, even if she isn't *too* corpselike. I totally understand now why Mom doesn't want to look at me during the day when I'm out. As 'corpses' go, Chloe doesn't appear bad at all… like someone who only lost their life a few minutes earlier. It doesn't make a whole lot of sense for me to be creeped out by the sight of death. For one thing, I *know* she's not really dead… not permanently dead, anyway. For another, I'm a vampire, too. Me being unsettled by the sight of other vampires asleep is about as dumb as a shark not being able to stand the sight of blood.

We have enough room in this compartment for Chloe to perch between us on her stomach, like a kid watching TV from the living room floor. Okay, the 'nose four inches apart' thing is a bit of an exaggeration. With her awake, the tone of conversation shifts from 'teenage girl drama with an undead twist' to cartoons and kid movies. Ashley happily keeps on chattering away, even commenting out loud the 'age' of our conversation has dropped from about sixteen to eight.

It's bizarre how natural it is for Ash. It's even crazier how unbothered I am to be stuck with nothing to do but talk. No movie in the background, no phone, no video game, nothing electronic going on right now. Is this what life felt like for Mom when she was a teenager in the Eighties? Sure, she spent a lot of time on the phone with her friends, but her phone was tied to the wall by a cord. I can't even imagine. She had to stay on her bed or sit on a chair in the hall the whole time they talked. Seriously primitive, right?

Well, okay, so what if I generally stay on my bed the whole time I am on the phone, too? Point is, I don't *have* to. Technology for the win, or something.

"Good thing there's no boy vampires in here," says Chloe out of the blue. "They'd fart."

Ashley cracks up with an uncontrollable case of the giggles.

Her comment came off as so matter-of-fact, I can't tell if she's serious. "Umm…"

She sticks her tongue out at me. "I know. Vamps don't do that... but boys are so gross, they'd still fart."

"Aww, man." Ashley cough-giggles. "A vampire fart would be so gross."

Listening to my friend and Chloe have a serious discussion about the stinkiness of theoretical vampire farts compared to ordinary boy farts is too much for me. When Ashley says something about how Paolo would fart literal dust, I laugh myself light-headed.

Another weird thing—time flies.

Before I realize it, our tangential conversation regarding how different Disney characters would fart stalls at the sudden realization the bouncing has ceased. We seem to have stopped. All three of us listen in silence for a few seconds until the rapid *whud-whud-whud* of the Yukon's doors closing confirms we are, in fact, stationary.

"Sounds like it's safe to get out," I say.

"Yay!" chimes Chloe before reaching over Ashley's hip for the latch.

The kid opens the mechanism and pushes the lid—the seat of the trailer's 'sofa'—upward. In an instant, the world changes from being cool, like air conditioning, to unpleasantly warm. The brightness in the trailer blinds me in a wash of beige and orange. I swear, whoever was in charge of interior design for the companies that made camping trailers in the late Eighties or early Nineties needs to go back to school. Beige and orange do *not* work together. It's worse when sunlight is pounding an exaggerated version of the hues into my overly sensitive retinas. My hearing mutes with a short whooshing chirp, leaving me feeling quite mortal again. Grr. I'd have to say this is the worst part of being a vampire: what used to be normal to me now feels like I'm nerfed.

Chloe clambers out of the box. Ash and I sit up and stretch more out of habit than need.

"Sam!" shouts Mom, outside. "Do *not* urinate on that tree."

Wow. I swear, the boy has no shame. We all knew this when he joined Dad in trying to sing along with Rush. The trailer door flies open. Sam scrambles up the little stairway, nearly tripping twice in his haste.

"Hey, guys," he blurts while zooming past us to the little bathroom in the back of the trailer. He's in such a rush, he doesn't even close the door.

I can't help but chuckle to myself listening to Dad outside trying to make a case for tree-peeing. He claims it's both 'natural' and will make it easier to clean the trailer when we're done with it. The less we use the septic tank, the less work it'll be once we're home. This, of course, gets a chorus of 'ewws' from Sophia and Sierra.

Mom emits the beleaguered groan she usually lets out whenever she's not in the mood to humor Dad being a dork. He is, of course, not serious about us using the woods for a bathroom.

Ashley is still giggling too much at Chloe's question whether or not the Little Mermaid would fart bubbles to talk. She gets to her feet, steps over the wall of our sleep enclosure, then stumbles outside, walking in a semi-drunken stagger due to day grogginess mixed with spending hours in a confined space. I follow with an equal degree of ungainliness, pausing to scoop Chloe up and carry her out of the trailer.

And... whoa.

I gaze around at enormous trees. They're seriously large. We seem to be at some sort of approved camping area—evidenced by a sign or two—but I don't see any other campers nearby. Trees are pretty thick and the sun's keeping me squinting, so there *could* be another trailer like twenty feet away and I'm just not seeing it. Dad, as excited as a kid going to Disney World, putters around to get our campsite set up. Sophia watches him, standing somewhat stiffly, as if she's afraid of bugs and such all around her. Sierra is neither impressed with the woods, worried about bugs, or terribly enthused about spending a week out in the sticks. She is, however, tolerating it without complaint for Dad's benefit. Well, mostly without complaint. Her face is doing all the complaining her voice isn't. I give her a shoulder squeeze, which earns me an attempted smile, then a mild bit of guilt. Can't read her mind right now but I'm sure her thoughts are something like if my vampiric butt can tolerate camping, she should stop moaning about no PlayStation for a week and enjoy some family time.

Sam appears at the trailer door, slouching with the relief of a boy who's held in the need to pee for several hours. As if on cue, he farts. This is not unusual in the least, not for Sam, not for ten-year-old boys. Blix, who'd been perched on his shoulder, pantomimes passing out and falls to the ground.

"Boys," mutters Chloe.

Ashley bursts into laughter again, which sets Chloe off with the giggles.

The 'rents exchange a glance like they suspect they've missed some manner of joke.

Sophia steps up on my other side. The three of us stand there gazing at the seemingly impossible gargantuan trees. Redwoods are epic.

Behold, nature in all its glory—or something like that.

Yay us.

2

PERFECTLY NORMAL
ABNORMALITY

C amping offers a clear distinction between childhood and adulthood.

I no longer have any temptation to run around the woods like a hamster on cocaine and am content to simply relax in a folding chair. This means I've crossed over into adulthood. Sam, Sierra, and Chloe spent a while releasing pent-up energy from a long car ride. Sophia neither settled on a chair nor did the running around thing. She cautiously explored our immediate surroundings, convinced she'd be able to discover genuine faeries.

Much to her disappointment—and Mom's relief—nothing unusual happened.

It's dark now. I'd say 'it's finally dark' but it hasn't been too long since we got here, maybe an hour. I am once again comfortable because the unnatural heat of being exposed to daylight is gone. Progress is good. Ordinary daylight—meaning not intensely sunny— doesn't hurt anymore. Wouldn't call it fun, though. It's not *painful* to me, but it is super uncomfortable, about on par with going to the funeral for some elderly aunt you barely knew and listening to her partially senile husband stray off his eulogy script to tell everyone how great his former wife was in bed before going into a needlessly graphic explanation of their lovemaking as recently as a month ago. All you want to do is run screaming for shelter, but it wouldn't be appropriate, so you just have to sit there faking a smile and tolerating it.

That's me with daylight, only much less *awkward.*

However, the sun's down now. I still can't see other campsites nearby, but I can smell and hear them.

Ashley's in another folding chair next to me. We've been doing the sarcastic-ironic thing joking about how people go 'camping,' but bring trailers with air conditioning, propane grill, portable power units to run their television sets and so on.

Sam and Dad have arranged themselves flat on the ground a short distance away, gazing up at the sky and talking about stars, constellations and stuff. It's a really cool, heartwarming sort of father-son moment they both adore. My kid brother is a cool little dude. He's unperturbed by the lack of video games and modern conveniences. Wherever he happens to be, he'll find a way to be content with it. It's not in him to patronize Dad, so when he sounds genuinely interested in ramblings about stars, it means he really does find it interesting to talk about.

Mom and Sierra sit by a little campfire. The older of my kid sisters has set aside her discontent at being surgically separated from video games enough to get into a whimsical conversation with Mom about how she could improve her overall happiness and work-life balance if she simply followed the practice of throttling everyone at work who annoyed her. Mom's been talking about some stuff that happened—mostly stupid things her co-workers did—and Sierra suggests inappropriate medieval revenges for each one. Her quote of the night is 'there's no office drama you can't fix with a good choke slam.' This guy Mom refers to as 'Terry the Toucher' has a habit of invading personal space during conversation until his arm or shoulder brushes up against the person he's talking to. The guy's name isn't actually Terry. They had to watch a sexual harassment training video and the poorly acted example creep in the video was called 'Terry the Toucher.' I think the real creep is named Brody or something similar.

Anyway, Mom must be in a good mood since when Sierra says 'stab that creepy shithead and throw the burning remains down an elevator shaft,' she doesn't even complain about language, simply laughs.

Mom either knows Sierra is totally kidding... or she's fantasized about doing stuff like that, too. Probably both.

Sophia hasn't strayed too far from the trailer. Camping is not her thing. Not here, not with the Girl Scouts, not with whatever generic youth camp thing the parents briefly considered sending us to. Considering the last time she went into the woods, she ended up encountering a wendigo, I can't fault her for being on edge. However, I suspect her present anxiety has to do more with bugs. She's sitting on the little fold-down steps attached to the trailer, staring platter-eyed into the woods.

So much for faerie hunting. Poor kid's too scared to leave the light radius of our campfire. Two years ago, I'd have chalked her nerves up to Sophia being Sophia, but now... I'm not so sure. Given all that's happened with our family lately, she might really be sensing something. Her gaze isn't locked on any one point, so she's probably scanning for danger rather than staring at the monster already here to ruin our vacation.

Chloe's still wandering around. She's getting kinda far away from us, though. Kids do that. I probably should call out and tell her to stay closer to camp. I'm shocked Mom hasn't already done that. If any of my siblings or I meandered as far away from the campfire as Chloe is now at the same age, Mom would've come running after us. Is this a case of the 'grandkid' getting away with stuff the parent never could, or is Mom trusting Chloe's vampire nature to keep her safe? Other than the swath of woods behind our house, the kid's never really seen genuine forest before. I don't think they have trees in New Jersey, just traffic and toll booths. Yeah, I know, Dad said South Jersey is like totally different or something. Might as well be an entirely different state.

Meh. Should I pester the kid? Honestly, if someone tries to kidnap her, they deserve what happens to them. Ugh... I should really be more responsible. Last thing we need is for a story about a little girl kicking some creep's ass to make it to the news. Way to be subtle, not.

"Chloe?" I call. "Don't stray off so far. Come back toward camp a bit."

"Okay." She alters course to tighten her circle, drifting nearer.

Sam chuckles. "You sound like Mom."

"It's inevitable." Mom examines her fingernails. "Sooner or later, the day will come when you have kids of your own and you will all sound like me... or your father."

"Sound like Dad? Kill me now," deadpans Sierra.

Sophia's expression throws off entirely too much guilt for no particular reason. Uh oh. She got guilty as soon as Mom mentioned them having children someday. Ack. Sophia, what did you do? I can't help but think about that strange magic ritual she asked me for help with. She did something to herself, but nothing happened visibly. Why would she be guilty about Mom bringing up the idea of grandkids?

Well, the kid is eleven. She's out of the 'boys are eww' stage and into the 'boys are icky, but I'm kinda curious about them' stage. Another two years and she'll be kissing Aragorn in her dreams. Got a feeling Sierra's going to dream about Aragorn, too... but rather than kiss him, she'll be chopping down orcs at his side.

It's kinda fun for a moment to daydream about what the future holds for my siblings. Sierra's non-reaction to the comment is her trying to play cool. I have a feeling that despite her seeming disinterest in boys or anything even tangentially romantic, she'll end up being the first of my siblings to have a serious relationship and probably kids of her own. It's always the one you think will be last, right? I'm worried about Sophia. She's so sweet and trusting, she's either going to find an incredible guy and be really happy... or she's going to end up being taken advantage of. I don't care if it's unethical. No man—or woman if she ends up going that way though I don't expect her to—is going to get near Sophia's heart without me first going elbows-deep in their brain. She's too trusting.

That guilty look she gave Mom worries me, though. Maybe I

should try to catch her alone soon and press her for more details about what she did.

By some remarkable twist of fate, we enjoy a couple hours of quiet peacefulness. This is either an apology from the Universe for recent events, or a sure sign my unlife is going to go completely crazy as soon as we get home.

"Speaking of crazy," says Ashley in a low voice.

I give her side eye. "Are you reading my mind?"

"Not exactly. I just kinda felt like you were bracing for chaos."

"Yeah." I exhale. "It's too nice here. Afraid something's going to go wrong."

She bites her lower lip. "Well, like the last time you went on a road trip, didn't you end up in some kind of demi-plane?"

"Oof." I cringe. "Don't remind me. I'm still not entirely convinced it happened. Part of me still thinks the brothers and I all had a communal dream at the same time."

"Uh huh. Sure you did." Ashley crosses her eyes at me. "You saw brownies and leprechauns, right?"

I facepalm. Really doesn't make sense for supposedly fictional vampires to be real, but all the other stuff is actually made-up. Sigh. She's got a point. It's as dumb as the flat-earthers thinking every other planet happens to be a globe, but Earth is a damn tile.

"All right. Maybe it wasn't a dream." I slouch in the folding chair. "Doesn't mean I have the desire to do it again. Just kind of expecting to be punished for this nice, peaceful vacation with chaos as soon as we get home."

"Don't be such a pessimist." Ashley grins. "I'm sure you won't have to wait that long for something weird to happen."

Mom stares at her.

"Don't jinx us," says Sierra, sounding bored.

"This is Bigfoot territory, isn't it?" Ashley taps a finger to her chin.

"Eep!" Sophia sits up straight. "No! Don't say that!"

Ashley twists around to peer back at her. "Why are you afraid of them?"

Sophia blinks, clearly unprepared for the question. I don't think anyone has ever asked her *why* she's afraid of things. For the most part, she's afraid of *monsters*, so the 'why' is kind of understood. "Umm..."

"Don't be scared." Ashley holds up a finger. "One, they might not even be real." She holds up a second finger. "Two, for all we know, they might be nice. Just big furry marshmallows."

I chuckle. "Oh, sure. Bigfoot wandering around the woods, looking for a hug."

"Staaaaaahp!" wails Sophia, flailing her arms. "You're gonna give me nightmares."

Blix babbles at Sam.

Everyone—including Mom—turns to look at him expectantly.

"What did he say?" asks Dad.

"Blix says they're real," replies Sam in a pragmatic tone, neither sounding impressed nor worried.

Sophia sucks in a breath. Everyone else gets quiet. A trace of 'whoa' lights up Sierra's eyes. She appears suddenly less bored with the idea of camping. In much the same way as Sophia had been pumped for finding faeries, Sierra kinda looks like she's going to go sasquatch hunting.

"What?" Sam sits up to look at everyone. "Dad and Sierra got shrunk to the size of GI Joe figures, and you're shocked to hear bigfoots are real?"

Dad pats him on the head. "The boy has a point."

Sierra gestures at me. "The last time we went on a trip, Sarah got into a fight with a giant troll. She's anxious for good reason."

I shiver at the memory of being broken in half. Having my spine snapped like a piece of kindling totally sucked. I'd almost rather repeat four years of high school. Almost. Hard call there.

Sophia whimpers.

"Are bigfoots mean or dangerous?" asks Sierra.

"'Bigfoots' doesn't sound right." Sophia scrunches her nose. "What's the correct plural of bigfoot?"

We all stare at each other—except Chloe. Chloe couldn't care less about cryptozoological grammar. She continues meandering around.

"Bigfeet sounds stupid," says Sierra after a moment, breaking the silence.

Blix chatters.

"Only dangerous if cornered." Sam looks off at the trees. "He said if we do see one, try not to stare at it. It's better to pretend like you didn't even notice him. They hate it when people start screaming or chasing them."

Like a tiny version of a college professor with wings, Blix continues to babble and chirp at my brother.

Sam waits for him to stop, then translates. "There are some places where they get territorial and might attack people to scare them away, but we're not near one of those places. If we do see a bigfoot, it's because we accidentally snuck up on it. Blix says they're usually pretty good at avoiding humans."

Mom shifts her stare to Dad. "Jonathan, you promised this would be a calm, quiet week."

"It should be." Dad scratches at the back of his head. "You heard Sam. If we spot a sasquatch, treat it the same way you do those sports parents who stand at traffic lights ambush begging people for money to support their kid's team. Don't establish eye contact and pretend you don't even see them."

Mom smirks.

"I'd rather run into a bigfoot than that troll thing." Ashley takes a sip from her canned iced tea.

"Ugh. Thanks, guys." I sigh at the stars. "I'd almost managed to convince myself to forget that ever happened."

"Just don't go into any strange caves." Sam smiles at me. "And if you do find a cave, don't step through an unknown portal."

"Right." I chuckle.

"No caves!" snaps Mom, doing a spot-on impression of Edna Mode from *The Incredibles*.

Sophia giggles.

"Agreed." I nod once. "No caves."

3

FULL SUPERHERO

We have a nice, relaxing evening and a simple dinner of sandwiches from the cooler Mom packed. Ash, Chloe, and I eat them as well, partly because Mom made enough for us and partly out of reflexively wanting to feel normal. Neither Ashley nor Chloe bat an eyelash at being handed conventional food. Hmm. How much of it is a case of 'because we can' versus the Innocent bloodline having an innate need to mimic an ordinary living person?

Chloe soaks up the attention of a loving family. It's as heartwarming as it is heartbreaking to watch her so happily sitting around a campfire with us eating sandwiches and being goofy. Her overenthusiasm makes me think too much about her past life. Seven is still young enough not to think of family time like this as 'tragically lame.' I started to do that around fifteen. Sierra was already there at eleven. My death experience (can't really say near-death experience, can I?) gave us both an attitude adjustment. Yes, we shall embrace the lameness of family time and smile while doing so.

Dammit. I sigh mentally while watching Chloe grin from ear to ear, turkey and bread crumbs stuck to her face. Why can't people enjoy stuff like this without first seeing tragedy? It's not fair. Oh...

wait. Sophia. She's always adored family time. The girl owns her lameness. And I say 'lameness' there with full affection. It's the sort of 'lame' that the popular girls like Bree Swanson look down on. I'm fine with being looked down on by people who peak in high school.

Anyway, bad Sarah. Out with the negative thoughts. Enjoy the moment.

I'm still ruminating on the chicken and egg problem—wondering if I feel this way because I'm an Innocent or if the Universe made me an Innocent because I felt that way—when the 'rents and Littles go to bed. I don't really need to understand it, nor is it nagging at me in some strange, undead, existential crisis way. It's merely something to think about for amusement the way philosophers debate pointless things. By pointless, I mean questions or ideas that knowing one way or the other which interpretation is more correct would not in any way change one's reality beyond simple understanding.

Knowing for sure if destiny is a real thing wouldn't change much. If it *is* real, knowing my fate is predetermined wouldn't allow me to stop it from happening. Knowing destiny isn't real also wouldn't have a significant effect on my life. In one case, it wouldn't matter what I chose because the same general end result would happen no matter what. In the other case, it's not as if my choices would be different. I'm always going to make choices based on who I am. And why am I wasting time thinking about such pointless things?

Maybe I really am bored.

Sophia's on edge. Poor kid's probably going to have a nightmare about bigfoot. It seems to reassure her a bit to have three vampires around who will stay awake all night and watch over the camp. I'm not too worried. Even if a bigfoot *does* happen to wander by, what Blix says tracks with reality. They'd spot signs of a human presence and run the other way. It's not like sasquatch only came into existence last week. They've been around for a long, long time. That people still consider them a myth is a strong testament to their commitment to avoiding human contact. Or, hmm. I wonder if the Persons In Black go around smoothing out bigfoot issues the same way they handle vampires. As far as I know, they don't have one of those little memory-eraser flashy things. I merely call them PIBs in reference to the movie as a bit of a joke.

As soon as everyone's asleep—we can tell by the sound of their breathing—Ashley shifts her gaze to me. "Hungry?"

"You know, anyone I bite tonight is going to taste like a turkey sandwich with a hint of icepack."

She snickers. "Hint of icepack?"

"Did you or did you not taste a faint trace of plastic on your sandwich?"

"Oh. That." She does a goofy eye-roll. "Yeah. They sat in a cooler all day. What did you expect? Adds to the ambiance of camping."

"Right."

"Or something." She grins. "There's a small town not far from here. West or northwest, I think. Crescent City."

I blink at her. "You have cell signal?"

"No. Looked at maps before the trip." Ashley pantomimes being a scientist scribbling formulas on a whiteboard. "You know Dad is methodical about every detail."

"Right." I chuckle. He is. And yes, Ashley calls him Dad.

It's kinda complicated, but not. She used to call him Mr. Wright as a kid. Yes, it's a bad pun even though he can't help it. Search for Mr. Wright, anyone? A year or two after her father left, she just kinda started calling Dad 'Dad'. I think it's partly an F-U to her father, and partly just easier. Not only is she dodging the pun by avoiding 'Mr. Wright,' it kinda started to feel overly formal at some point since she'd essentially become a part of the family.

"Ooh!" Chloe zooms over to us, standing between our folding chairs and bouncing on her toes. "Is it time to go eat? I'm hungry."

These two talking about feeding gets my stomach grumbling at me. I have no idea how a vampire body processes blood, but I'm inclined to say it has nothing whatsoever to do with any sort of standard biological functions. Makes no sense my stomach would growl when the vampy side of me wants blood. Then again, it makes even less sense for a person's blood to taste like waffles and syrup or, French fries, cheeseburgers, chocolate, hot wings, or whatever else my brain does to it. One of the first things a new vampire needs to learn is not to question the weird and just go with it.

Yeah, I know I keep violating that motto. Working on it. Just accepting stuff and moving on has never been my way. I need to understand the whys of everything. Used to get paper wads thrown at me in school sometimes when I kept asking questions.

"Sure. Food sounds good." I stand.

"Yay!" Cheers Chloe in a quiet, whispery 'shout.'

The three of us are far from scary monsters. I'm in my usual T-shirt and jeans outfit. Tonight's tee is anime based, the cast of Cowboy Bebop posing by a high-tech wall. Edward's upside down, legs sticking out of a giant vase. Ashley's rocking a pink dress (shocker, right?) and Chloe's wearing a cute purple panda sweater, a white skirt, and black tights. None of us have shoes on. The box we slept in would've been even more uncomfortable if we went in there wearing sneakers. As long as we don't try to go into any convenience stores, we should be fine. You know, the places with 'no shoes, no shirt, no service' signs. Ashley often jokes about going into one of those places wearing *only* a shirt and shoes to see what they'd do. She likes to mess with stupid rules as long as she's sure she won't get in serious trouble for it. Never once thought she'd seriously walk pantsless into a public store. Vampire-Ashley, however, might develop the confidence to try it… if we're in a city far from home we'll likely never visit again.

Eep. Better keep a close eye on her. I've noticed myself growing bolder and less fearful of mundane things since becoming a vampire. Good chance the same thing will happen to Ashley. She is liable to do some embarrassing or silly things once she's comfortable in her new reality.

Her idea to pop over to Crescent City is a good one. It's unclear if Dad will want to spend the whole week at this campsite, which is somewhere in the Douglas Park area, or move on Wednesday further south to the Del Norte Coast Redwoods State Park. There are a whole bunch of hiking trails, museums, and other sorts of things around here to check out, many of which are a prohibitive distance from where we camped. He said something about checking out the 'north stuff' for a few days, then moving to another camping spot. Even if we are going to be out of here in three days, it's still a bad idea to feed from people in a nearby trailer or RV.

Vampire rule one: create a safe distance between living area and feeding grounds.

Okay, maybe that's rule two. Rule one is most likely 'avoid the sun.' At least, for most vampires. There are some unreasonable people out there who view vampires as a scourge in need of destruction. They'd even want to destroy ones like me who go out of our way to be nice to mortals while feeding. Some of the hunters are fairly skilled at picking up on signs of vampire feeding despite us not killing anyone. Not that it's at all reasonable to think a hunter is watching a remote area of Northern California's woodlands for vampire activity, but... better to be safe.

The three of us leap skyward—after a quick look around to make sure no one is watching us. Once I've gone a few hundred feet into the air, it's pretty obvious where Crescent City is compared to our campground. West, and a bit south. There's an extremely tiny town not far north of us that appears to be framed on three sides by a river forming a very wide U shape. It's a bit too close and too small. Unlikely we'd have an easy time finding someone outside at night there.

We fly slightly to the southwest for about six miles. Crescent City is easy to see from the air—a patch of brownish-grey civilization surrounded by green. Not far to the northwest of the city, the runways of a small airport look like a lopsided X hastily dashed on a treasure map.

It's about twenty minutes to eleven at night when we arrive over the downtown area. Further southwest, a swath of perfectly square residential blocks stretches for another mile or so to the coast. Crazy how much like a *Civilization* video game the real world looks from high enough altitude.

Our goal isn't sightseeing or exploring or even having fun here at night. Yeah, as vampires go, we're tragically lame. We're the stay at home watching anime or playing video games all night kind of people, not the nightclub party animals most vampires tend to be. We're definitely not the Portland Lost Ones who routinely go around amusing themselves with chaos, like relocating people's garden statues, doing graffiti, or smashing rich people's stuff.

Ashley points. "There?"

I follow her finger to a large sorta-triangular area surrounded by road. A huge rectangle of a building stretches east-to-west across the top end of the area with a little gas station to the right. At the southern point, a much smaller—but also rectangular—building is oriented north-to-south. Parking lot fills the majority of the... umm. Can't call it a 'block' because the area's much bigger than a single city block. It's also not block-shaped.

Whatever.

Point is, three people are walking from the parking area south to the smaller building. They're kinda in the dark and a safe distance from any other observers. Two men and a woman. One guy is three steps ahead of the other two. It doesn't look like he's *with* the other two as much as merely going in the same direction. Man Two and the woman are holding hands. Good chance they know each other. Spontaneous hand-holding among total strangers is not a common phenomenon unless serious amounts of weed—or summer camp counselors—are involved.

"I'll get the guy up front," whispers Ashley. "You and Chloe can split the couple?"

Sounds so wrong, but we *are* what we are, right? "Sure. That works."

We swoop down like phantoms, our bare feet silent on the parking lot. Sometimes, my amped up senses catch me off guard. I'm so focused on remaining stealthy, the texture of the paving underfoot shocks me. Sight and hearing aren't the only senses, after all. Our sense of touch is crazy. The uneven surface feels like I'm walking on rough stones. A vampire could probably step barefoot on braille and read it. Our prospective targets remain totally oblivious to us dropping out of the sky, not reacting at all to our presence until after we fast-walk to catch up to them.

Speaking of rough stones, my attempt to walk into the guy from behind while pretending to be distracted looking at my phone is about as 'smooth' as gravel. Yes, I'm a rotten liar and a worse actress. The guy gives me this look like he knows I tried to do some kind of bump and grab pickpocket thing and he's not buying my 'innocent' act. Fortunately, I am a vampire and that comes with mental powers. His girlfriend isn't quite as suspicious of me. I send the guy to Derpville before he can accuse me of being a thief. Chloe distracts the woman with an earnest sounding lie about 'we're lost; have you seen our parents?'

Ashley, blunt and direct as ever, hurries after the stray single dude and pats him on the arm. "Hey, can I talk to you for a sec?"

He jumps, then spins to face her, throwing off startled and guilty vibes like we just barged into his bedroom and caught him masturbating. Weird, but I don't pay his abnormally startled reaction too much attention. He's probably on his way to the liquor store in front of us to rob it.

I bite my target. Sure enough, turkey sandwich seasoned with a bit of 'icepack that's been in the freezer for three months'. Chloe compels the woman to crouch down, gently pushes her hair out of the way, then bites her on the neck. One might say it's highly unsubtle of us to feed right out here in the middle of a parking lot. On the contrary, it works. The woman appears to be hugging Chloe. I look like I'm making out with this guy. Same goes for Ashley. Any normal, rational, person seeing us would never think 'vampires feeding.' This is exactly why the vampires of long ago switched from being obvious 'in your face' monsters to fostering the notion among mortals that vampires are only a mythological creature. Gone are the days of a vampire swooping down on an unsuspecting peasant at night—and causing the entire town to swarm into the woods with torches and pitchforks. In the modern day, where no one believes we are real, the increased time, effort, and risk of trying to lure our targets away from this parking lot to a secluded area isn't worth it.

None of us are super hungry, which is good for our victims. They won't really even notice any side effects from our feeding. Especially the woman. Chloe is tiny. She doesn't take much, even when she's seriously hungry.

"Uhh, Sare," says Ashley in a quiet, hesitant tone, like she's about to tell me she broke the windshield on Mom's Yukon. "You should take a look at this."

I detach my fangs from the man's neck, then seal the bite mark. "One sec." Back into his thoughts I go. He didn't feel me try to pickpocket him, but he also picked up on the severe fakeitude of my bump. Seems I walked into him a little too purposefully for it to come off as a true accident. Easy enough to alter his memory of the bump to be innocent, deleting his suspicion I wanted to steal from him. Well... to be fair, I did want to steal from him—just not money.

That done, I let go of the guy and step around him to where Ashley's standing beside the lone dude.

She gestures at him. "Look."

The guy's in his late twenties. Light brown hair, brown eyes, neither hot nor ugly. Looks like what most people would conjure up in their imagination if you said 'California stoner with little ambition in life'.

"What?" I ask. "He looks really average."

"No." She stares intently at me. "Peek into his head. We have a problem."

Uh oh. Worried we might've accidentally ambushed a vampire hunter, I dive in without hesitation—and regret it. The reason the guy jumped and seemed so guilty when Ashley tapped his arm is as plain as the red in her hair, right at the tip of his brain, so to speak. This guy is thinking about his two buddies, Nick and Curt, who are back at Nick's apartment with a woman they kidnapped. Apparently, she works across the street from where Nick works. He's been watching/stalking/spying on her for weeks after she turned him down for a date. Dude finally snapped and just grabbed her. This particular low-life in front of me is named Tom. He's pretty damn sure Nick intends to force himself on this woman, and probably kill her afterward in hopes of avoiding prison. Nick and Curt sent him out to grab some food—from the Pizza Hut here—as well as beer.

Son of a... So much for a quick and simple feeding trip.

This guy isn't on board with the murder part, though he doesn't seem to have any major issues with Nick kidnapping and raping some woman he never met. Doesn't look like Tom has any interest in participating. He's hoping not to get involved. Seems like he's taking his sweet time going to pick up beer and snacks while debating if he should just keep on driving and not go back there. He's not committed to just leaving because he's been in the apartment while the woman was tied up in the back bedroom, so he's not sure if he's already legally part of the crime.

"Well, shit." I let a long sigh slip out my nose.

Chloe peers around the still catatonic woman, giving me a quizzical eyebrow lift.

"Yeah. Exactly." Ashley folds her arms.

Ugh. This is bad. Not sure if this is more or less traumatic than the guy who wanted to go home and molest his stepdaughter. Traumatic for me, I mean. I don't like seeing this crap. To be fair, the thoughts rattling around in Tom's head are an order of magnitude less nauseating than the other guy. And of course, now that I've seen what's going on in his head, me walking away isn't an option. Whatever happens to this woman tonight is going to be on my conscience. Yes, I have an overdeveloped conscience. But, for reals... if I was still mortal and someone kidnapped me and left me tied up in their bedroom, I'd for damn sure want a random vampire to kick in the door and get me the hell out of there. Gah. I'm getting all kinds of anxious merely thinking about being in her place. She's gotta be freakin' terrified.

Seriously... I'm going to develop a complex about jumping into people's minds because of stuff like this. Can't exactly help it when feeding, though. It's not like I went deep-diving into his past. He's thinking about this situation right at the forefront of his consciousness. Unlike that freakin' creep who couldn't *wait* to get home and be alone with that little girl, this guy's fixating on these thoughts out of anxiety. He's not happy to be in this situation and is trying to process how his friend Nick could be capable of something like this. Alas, this guy is as likely to walk away and disappear as go back to the apartment and just sit there doing nothing while evil happens. Even though he won't personally touch this woman, I can't respect him. He's more afraid of being asked to help dispose of the body than what Nick might do to her.

Yeah, I'm invading his privacy hardcore, but in this case, I consider myself to have a search warrant.

Ugh, at this whole situation.

"What do you think?" asks Ashley.

"Well, I can't just walk away and leave that woman to end up as a five-minute tragedy piece on tomorrow's news."

She nods. "My thoughts exactly."

"What woman?" whispers Chloe.

"Sec, kiddo." I take her hand.

Ashley sucks at her teeth.

I raise an eyebrow at her.

"Pizza Hut," she mumbles. "Couldn't help it. He was on his way to buy pizzas. My brain filled in the flavor."

I shake my head. "Not what I meant."

"We're obvs gonna go get her out of there, right?" Ashley raises an eyebrow.

"Yeah."

"What's going on?" Chloe raises her voice a little, still sorta whispering.

"This guy's friend did something really bad." I shift my jaw side to side, trying to edit the story for seven-year-old ears. "His friend—"

"Kidnapped a lady," says Chloe, staring at him. "They got her tied up and everything. That's mean."

I resist the urge to facepalm. The kid's reading his mind. Crap. At least this guy didn't see anything more graphic than a woman in a T-shirt and sweat pants with dye-blond hair tied up on the floor of a bedroom struggling to free herself and attempting to scream past duct tape.

"You gonna save her and kick their asses?" Chloe tilts her head.

"Looks like it. Can't just walk away." I sigh. "Maybe I *should* get a spandex costume. With sharp fangs comes great responsibility or something."

Ashley chuckles.

I hold up a finger. "Shouldn't require much ass-kicking. I'll leave that to the cops." Grr. This is the natural evolution of Follows Rules Girl. Of course, what these guys are planning to do is hardly on the same level as staying out past parental curfew. But… give FRG paranormal abilities, she's going to use them to help people. Besides, it's not like we have plans tonight other than sitting around a campsite vegging out and talking. Some vampires destroy garden furniture for fun. Some have wanton sex and party all night. And then there's me. My idea of a fun night is staying at home reading, playing video games, or watching movies. Sigh. Yes, I know. I have no life. Well, duh. Literally.

Yeah, it can be inconvenient to see stuff like this in people's thoughts, but if I start ignoring it as 'not my problem' too many times, I end up being just as evil as the person doing the killing. This has to be the reason some vampires start to turn inhuman. Anyone who can become aware of a situation like this and callously walk away from it is already a monster. Undeath only adds to it.

"Okay. I won't be able to unlive with myself if I don't do something to help that woman."

Ashley nods eagerly. "Let's do it."

"What about those two?" Chloe points her thumbs at the couple.

"They aren't involved. Neither one of them even know this loser," I mutter. "Just got out of their cars at the same time and happened to be going to the same place."

"Okay. I'll take them off pause." Chloe pads back over to the couple who are still staring into the Eighth Dimension.

"Guess I'm going full superhero, huh?" I smile.

Ashley fake cringes. "Ack. No. You never go 'full superhero.'"

"Thank you for the *Tropic Thunder* reference," I mutter. The original joke in the movie is so cringe. No one uses the R word anymore. At least, no one with a functioning sense of empathy. I mean, I get that the character in the movie was supposed to be a jerk, but still. It's not a 'quotable' line as written.

"I'm serious. No spandex." She pats me on the rear end. "You don't have the butt for it."

"Hah." I shake my head. "No one has the butt for it. The way they draw them is so unrealistic and hypersexualized."

Chloe swivels to look at me. "What's hypa-sex-imalized mean?"

"It means some guys aren't taking girls seriously as heroes," says Ashley without missing a beat.

"Grr." Chloe stomps, her foot making a tiny clap on the pavement. "That's stupid. Girls can be superheroes, too!"

"We sure can." I feel lame as hell, but strike a pose anyway. "And I'm about to do just that."

"No capes," whispers Ashley.

I give her side eye. Not the most appropriate moment for jokes. Tom is 'reasonably sure' his friends won't do anything to the woman until after he returns with beer and pizza. Maybe Nick wants to get drunk to summon the courage to follow through with his plan. We really should stop dawdling.

Because Tom did not immediately call the cops on his asshole friend—sorry for the language, Mom, but extenuating circumstances —I consider him part of it. I feel no guilt stomping on his brain with a mental compulsion to bring us there. He zombie-walks back across the parking lot to a smallish green Toyota. We get in, me riding shotgun with Ashley and Chloe in the rear.

Really should ask her to take Chloe back to the campsite, but I don't want to waste the time it would take if she protests and argues.

The ride is super short. His apartment complex is less than half a mile away from the Pizza Hut. With slightly more finesse than a self-driving Tesla, Tom pulls into a space, shifts into park, and cuts the engine... then sits there. In front of us are two identical two-story buildings, separated by a wide sidewalk. Three elevated walkways span above the middle, connecting the balconies, one at each end and another in the middle.

I stare at Tom. "Take me to Nick's apartment."

He gets out of the car. I follow, as do Ashley and Chloe.

"Ash?" I stop and look at her. "Would you mind waiting here with Chloe? Don't want her seeing stuff she shouldn't."

"What shouldn't I see?" asks Chloe.

"Justin Bieber concert… Dr. Phil… anything with the Teletubbies," I mutter.

Chloe tilts her head. Not sure if she's confused or thinks I'm being a dork.

"Or you could wait outside and let me handle it." Ashley grins.

I make a contemplative face at her while Tom walks off toward a stairwell. "I could, but… I don't want you seeing stuff either. You're still innocent."

Ashley overacts childishly sticking her tongue out at me, then sighs. "Fine. Okay. I guess I don't really wanna see anything too bad, either."

Our friendship over the years has often followed the path of me kinda imposing what I want over Ashley. She's quite passive most times. None of it has been anything of real significance, more like what movie do we want to watch. Yes, I've recognized I do this to her. I've tried again and again to tell her it's okay to disagree with me. It makes her happy to make me happy, so she hasn't insisted on much. But here? I don't feel any guilt. If that apartment contains a horror show, I don't want her having that memory. Can't say I really want the memory of it either, but better me than her.

Here's hoping Nick is really a chickenshit coward and needed to get himself halfway drunk to have the balls to attack this woman. Gotta move. Tom's almost out of eyesight and every minute could count.

"Back soon. I hope."

Ashley raises an eyebrow at me as I trot off after Tom. "You're worried you might get hurt?"

"No. I'm worried this isn't going to be a simple five-minute fix." I grumble. "The faster we get out of here, the less likely we'll be noticed and possibly risk exposure."

"Oh." She nods. "Right. I'll be right here. Yell if you need me."

"Yell if you need me," parrots Chloe.

I rush after Tom, following him up a stairway on the right side and into a passage where the building is split at the middle of its length. Four apartments occupy the passage leading between the west face and the east. It appears Nick's apartment is the nearest door on the right in the connecting hall. Tom pulls out a key, sticks it in the knob, and opens the door. I psych myself up as much as possible into 'badass mode.' Hey, I've gotten into scraps with vampires. I've killed a five-headed nopeasaurus. Two mortal creeps shouldn't even rate on my anxiety scale. It's really not them I'm worried about. My gut's twisted into a knot of anxiety over what's possibly happened to this woman in the time since Tom left to get food.

Deep breath, Sarah… and into the apartment I go.

Okay fate. Please be gentle.

4

THE MONSTER ACROSS THE STREET

One hand at Tom's back, I push him ahead of me into the living room.

Beige carpet. Huge TV. Big couch. White walls. Minimal decoration. Black coffee table that might be glass. Empty chip bags and Pringles cans littered around. This place is like the next evolutionary step from a dorm room. Like, *this* is what happens when a guy goes from seventeen to thirty without mental development.

Two guys are on the sofa clutching game controllers. The TV is on my right at too sharp an angle to see the screen, not that I really care what game they're playing. The guys seem so casual and normal—like they don't have a kidnapped woman in the apartment—it's freaky. Based on my mindreading of Tom, I recognize Nick as the slightly older looking of the two guys. He's pale, with black hair and brown eyes. Despite being inside his apartment, he's got a dark blue wool cap on for some silly reason. Wouldn't call the guy overweight, but his face is kinda rounded and full. Curt's a little younger and has a bit of a tan. Dude's got a pronounced brow line and square chin, kinda reminiscent of Lurch from the *Addam's Family*, only he's not particularly tall.

Rapid-fire gunshots coming from the video game plus sirens and screeching tires make it pretty much impossible for me to hear anything else in the first ten seconds of being in the apartment.

The game pauses.

Nick and Curt simultaneously lean forward, an anticipatory gleam in their eyes.

"About damned time," barks Nick. "What took so long?" He pauses a second upon realizing Tom is not carrying pizza and beer… then leans back, head tilted. "Hey, man. WTF. Where's the food?"

"Duuuude," says Curt, sounding disappointed.

With the video game now silent, the grunts, thumps, and groans of a struggling woman become super obvious to me. The noises are coming from the only way out of this room other than the front door: a hallway leading deeper into the place.

Unconcerned with the three idiots for now, I give Tom a slight push—enough to make him take one step out of my way—then proceed across the living room to the hall.

Nick and Curt stare at me, turning their heads to track me as I go by, both seeming too stunned at my audacity to say or do anything until I reach the hallway.

"Hey!" shouts Curt. "Where are you goin'?"

"Who the fuck is this, Tom?" Nick jumps to his feet. "We sent you to get food and beer, not a random girl."

Tom, still lost to the mental fog I hit him with, says nothing.

Muffled screaming from a mouth covered in duct tape comes from behind the closed door at the end of the hall. I rush for it, zooming past a small kitchen, smaller bathroom, and what—at a brief sideways glance—seems to be a second bedroom.

Nick runs up behind me.

My plan to ignore him doesn't work out perfectly. He grabs my shoulder and spins me around, pushing me back against the wall and staring down at me. Dude is high-strung. Super anxious. Worse than those guys who showed up at the abandoned motel to sell drugs. Normal me would've freaked the hell out if a guy this wound up had me pinned against the wall. However, I'm no longer normal. This guy isn't a tenth as intimidating as half the stuff that lands in my lap these days. I do my best to intimidate him right back, though a significant height disadvantage doesn't help. Neither does being scrawny or having the face of a sixteen-year-old. Yeah... I'm not built for intimidation, I'm a surprise.

"Hey, bitch. Do you just randomly walk into people's homes?" roars Nick, blasting me with the smell of cool ranch Doritos and store-brand soda.

Thoughts of the woman he abducted—Leigh Bennett—are right at the tip of his brain. He's pretty sure I've heard the struggling and is presently debating whether or not he should kidnap me, too, or throw me out of the apartment and then 'get rid of' the woman. I look enough like a kid to him that he thinks the cops won't believe me if they come here and don't find a woman tied up in the back room.

"Hey, asshole," I mutter, then ram my knee into his groin. "Do you just randomly kidnap women?"

A muffled *crack* comes from his crotch as my strike lifts him a couple of inches off his feet. Nick crumples to the floor in a ball, both hands cradling his nuts. He struggles to breathe for several seconds. By the time he lets out a scream of agony, his face is bright red and all the veins in his forehead are swollen.

Curt, two steps behind where Nick hit the rug, stares at me. The confusion in his expression tempts me to look at his thoughts. He isn't consciously aware of *why* something seems wrong here. I don't think he noticed his friend go into the air or even heard bone break, but the way Nick is screaming doesn't sit as normal. I don't look big or strong enough to do that to him.

I mean... it's *not* normal. I hammered him with supernatural strength.

Yes, on purpose. I know it's stereotypical to go for the nut shot. But hey, what's the best way to stop someone from shooting people? Break their gun. Same logic applies to what this bastard wants to do to Leigh.

So, I'm upset. Follows Rules Girl is entitled to a moment or two of rage now and then, right?

As the two-plus-two equals six equation works its way to completion in Curt's mind, he decides I'm dangerous despite my appearance. His attitude shifts from wanting to rag on Tom for picking up an 'underage girl' to a need to conceal the crime he's a willing participant in, worsened by a subconscious fear he's gotten into an impossible situation.

Okay, so vampires do have that effect on some mortals. I don't usually radiate paranormal dread. It's kinda rare for Innocents to do it at all, but, like I said, I'm upset. Not hitting him with the proverbial full Monty, though. No, I'm not talking about nudity. I mean, no glowing red eyes and fangs out. I still appear normal. Maybe it's the 'mess around and find out' expression on my face or a girl who looks like a teenager calmly putting Nick down in one move and not seeming the least bit scared that's setting off this guy's weird-dar.

He looks like the nameless, expendable dude who dies in the first five minutes of a Stephen King movie at the exact moment he realizes he's dealing with an unexplainable supernatural problem.

Curt yanks a knife off his belt and extends it out in front of himself.

"Come near me with that thing, it's going up your ass," I say, my voice part snarl.

He blinks. "You're not serious."

I shrug one shoulder. "Nah. I just watch too many Eighties movies. They love cheesy lines like that."

"Into the bedroom." Curt points the knife at the door. "Get down on the floor."

Aww, how cute. He still thinks he's the one giving orders here. "I was going in there anyway, but if you think I'm going to lie down and surrender, you're even dumber than you look. And you do look pretty dumb."

He takes a step closer.

"Sit still," I say, glaring into his brain.

Curt does a spot-on impression of a department store mannequin.

"Good." I start to turn away, but stop myself and swipe the knife out of his grip. "Gimme. I'm gonna need this."

He stares vacantly into the Eighth Dimension.

Nick rocks slightly. He's gone from screaming to moaning out his nose. I step over him and clear the last twelve or so feet of hallway in three huge strides. The bedroom door is locked, so now it's kinda broken. I'm not patient. The struggling sounds stop abruptly as I barge in.

Amid an ocean of random clothes, free weights, giant protein powder jars, and sneakers, a late-twenties blonde woman lays on the floor by the foot of the messiest bed I've ever seen. She's hogtied, but still fully dressed in a shirt and sweat pants except for shoes.

Leigh sucks a breath in through her nose—several strands of duct tape cover her mouth—like she's about to attempt screaming, but she doesn't. Upon noticing the person who burst into the room is not Nick, not even a man, she merely stares at me, her expression a mixture of hope and unease. She's trying to figure out what I'm doing here, and half afraid I'm part of this—some twisted little psychopathic teenager wrapped around Nick's finger who's going to help him torture her. Eek. Chill, lady. You've been watching too much *True Crime*.

"Don't freak out. I'm here to help," I say in as calming a tone as possible. "Knife is for the rope."

She slouches, relieved… then starts crying.

A little too fast to be normal, I carefully slice at the ropes. Nick's voice drifts in the doorway. In between whimpers and gasps, he's telling me all about how he's going to wring my neck and so on. Yeah, yeah, sure you are… maybe three months from now when you can walk again.

As soon as I get Leigh's hands free, she reaches up and attacks the duct tape on her face. Good. I'll let her deal with that. I cut the rope off her ankles, then take a step back, more or less standing guard in case Curt snaps out of his fog or Nick somehow develops the supernatural ability to ignore pain as well as a broken pelvis.

Hey, a guy crawling on the floor can still be dangerous if he has a gun somewhere.

"Holy shit," rasps Leigh after pulling the duct tape away from her face. "That asshole's been stalking me for weeks. He wouldn't leave me alone."

She continues to rapidly talk about how he asked her out once, she said no because she just got a bad vibe off him, and he'd been obviously staring at her every time she arrived at or left her job. Complaining to his manager didn't seem to help. Alas, she didn't bother calling the police, thinking they'd either not take her seriously or give her a hard time like she's the one doing something wrong.

Okay. My work here is done. Now for the tricky part. I need to erase myself from everyone's memory.

I crouch in front of Leigh as she rummages her sneakers out of the random clothing all over the place. As soon as she looks up and makes eye contact, I dive in. Ugh. She's seriously freaking out. Can't blame her, though. The woman had already decided to fight as much as possible in hopes he'd skip past the sexual assault and go straight to killing her... with a small bit of hope he might just give up and let her go if she put up too much of a struggle. She'd been prepared to die tonight.

Son of a bitch...

I can't even.

We both end up crying. Takes me a few minutes to collect myself from that surge of desperate emotion coming from her. Okay, this is way, way too strong of an emotional impact on her mind for me to simply delete myself. Maybe if I had another hundred years of experience as a vampire it would be trivial, but gotta work with what's here. My initial idea of creating a false memory of her managing to escape on her own is not going to work. So, I do the next best thing and invent a random person showing up. Best to keep it as simple as possible, so I don't bother trying to come up with any sort of explanation for who they were or how they happened to know Leigh needed help.

Altering her memory of me is fairly easy. She'll remember a woman, older than me, with black hair, taller, more muscular, a real Xena Warrior Princess type. After reassuring myself Leigh will not be able to accurately remember *me* as the reason she got out of tonight alive, I go back into the hallway for the easier part.

As far as Curt and Nick are concerned, Leigh managed to untie herself and escape. Nick will think she's the one who leveled him in one kick. I give Curt an Eighties martial art movie inspired memory of her expertly disarming his knife and throwing him to the floor before bolting out the door.

Tom gets the same treatment. I delete myself, Ashley, and Chloe from his mind. I program him to return to the Pizza Hut and get the food he originally went out for. By the time he returns here, the police will probably be waiting for him.

That done, I collect Leigh, carry her to the living room, and set her standing by the front door like a mannequin. Her bag—and cell phone —is still in Nick's trunk as far as she knows. I don't see it the apartment anywhere. Might be better for the cops to find it in the car, anyway. Not that we need to fabricate details here, but it will help convict these losers. It proves he's involved.

Tom walks out, heading to his car.

I set Leigh up with a bit of mental programming: wait twenty seconds, then snap to life and run out of here screaming exactly as she would if she managed to escape on her own. The twenty-second buffer is purely to give me a chance to move away to a safe distance before the commotion attracts attention and other people see me.

All set.

Can't help myself. I zip over and punt Nick in the groin one more time. He emits a clipped squeak and blacks out. Oops. The authorities are going to have a little problem believing Leigh—who has mortal human strength—did this to Nick. I really need to control myself and stop kicking bad guys in the balls with the power of a forklift. Hopefully, they'll chalk it up to that 'moment of extreme duress' thing where they claim people can lift cars off their loved ones in defiance of physics or something.

Anyway... time to go.

I race out the door, jump off the balcony, and swerve up to fly over the roof.

Nine seconds later, Leigh explodes like a time bomb. She comes rushing out the door shouting for someone to call the cops, that she's been kidnapped and needs help. I'd say she sounds convincing, but she's not making it up. Playing with memories always makes me worry someone's not going to believe the story, but it's ninety percent real here.

She runs down the stairs to the ground level. A few people emerge from other apartments. Two guys who appear reasonably normal jog toward her. One's older, dad vibing. The other guy's in his mid-twenties and looks like an adult version of a boy scout, eager to help whoever he can.

I hover out of sight in the dark for a moment, watching the scene unfold until it's obvious both guys are going to help her. The rest of this mess is no longer my responsibility. Whew. Satisfied things will be fine here, I wheel around and fly over the building to the parking lot.

Time to collect Ashley and Chloe, then return to the sanity of our family vacation.

5

THE DIPLOMATIC APPROACH

Dammit.

Nothing's ever simple in my unlife. I have no idea who or what my simple existence has offended, but for reasons beyond immortal comprehension, anything I am involved with has to end up going off the rails. Makes no sense to me. As a mortal, my life had been all about following rules, doing the right thing, not getting in (too much) trouble. And yet, the Universe loves to mess with me.

Really, I shouldn't complain. My life was perfect. Good parents, a nice house, plenty of food, school, friends... nothing to worry about. All of my 'problems' were simple annoyances. Well, most of them anyway. I still happened to be a girl. Getting catcalled at age thirteen by grown men is more than a 'triviality' of a problem. Happens to most of us. No one likes to talk about it for some reason.

I dread the day it happens to Sierra or Sophia for the first time. That it's all but inevitable they will experience a creep in the not-too-distant future gnaws on my guts. Well, Sierra has sorta experienced it already, but not in person. People in the chat for her video games can get really rude. She's had to deal with verbal abuse already. Sophia's still inside her innocent rose-colored bubble where the world is a nice place and the worst it gets is sort of 'Disney evil' that the good guys can easily vanquish.

Sigh.

The poor kid is going to have a reality check someday, and I'm dreading it. I hate the idea of what it might do to her. She can't stay the same forever, though. Gah. Is this how parents feel? They want their kids to stay adorable and innocent... or at least some do. No matter how old we get, Dad is going to see us as little kids, making messes and being cute. He probably adores how the Universe put the brakes on me at eighteen. Fate gave him a pause in having to cope with one of his kids becoming an adult. More time to get ready for when it's Sierra's turn.

If I'm Mom to Chloe, I've been given a cheat. She'll always be my cute little nugget with an adorably inappropriate mouth. What is it about small children and old people? Whenever they curse, it's cute. Like, tell me you can see a little old grandma give someone the finger and not find it hilarious and endearing.

Anyway... speaking of middle fingers, it seems the Universe is trying to give me one right now.

Specifically, Ashley and Chloe are *not* where I expect them to be. Tom's car is gone (which I expect). Ash and Chloe are also gone (which I do not expect).

After landing in the empty parking spot formerly occupied by Tom's Toyota, I look around at a pronounced lack of Ashley and Chloe. Commotion from the direction of the apartment buildings is growing louder, so I don't want to stick around here.

I sigh at the ground, raise and lower my toes once, then sigh again.

Of course, they're gone. This is my unlife, after all. It's become one of Dad's Eighties movies. Why should I expect my best friend and kinda-sorta daughter to still safely be where I left them? It's the first law of movie logic. As soon as the best friend and child are asked to wait somewhere off camera, *something* bizarre is going to happen. Surely, Ashley is furious right now. A significant part of her decision to ask Aurélie to turn her into a vampire was so she didn't get abducted again.

"Let go of me, fuckhead!" shouts a tiny voice in the distance.

Aha. That would be Chloe. Sweet and lovable as ever. She's making friends.

Crap.

Due to the high chance of people being near enough to see me thanks to the Leigh situation, I decide against flying and sprint out of the parking lot, running along the sidewalk toward where the shouting came from. Following the continued sounds of a scuffle, I keep going for about a minute before cutting south across the parking lot in front of a Big 5 Sporting Goods store. Behind the building is a fairly large empty lot that's mostly sparse dirt with a few hints of crab grass. There, Ash and Chloe appear to be engaged in a scrap of sorts with three vampires, two guys and a woman. One guy's holding Ashley in a bear hug from behind. Their dynamic doesn't look like a fight to the death—more like the way a guy might hold his randomly psychopathic girlfriend down to stop her from hurting someone. Not that Ashley is a psycho, but the guy with his arms around her appears to be focused on containing her rather than inflicting harm.

Ashley's trying to get away from him, her stare locked on the other dude who's got Chloe sort of the way an animal control officer might be struggling to get a hold of an enraged alley cat. Ever see those old Looney Tunes shows where someone's trying to get a grip on a small, furry, vicious animal and the critter turns into a blur of fangs and claws that shreds all the fur/clothing off some much larger character's leg? Chloe's kinda doing that. The guy is struggling to get a grip on her while she flails and shreds at him. It's very Looney Tunes because as furious as she looks and sounds, she isn't inflicting any serious damage to the guy.

The lady vampire is angling around the man as if she's looking for an opportunity to lunge in and grab Chloe, but thus far remains too afraid of being clawed to commit to anything more than making pained grimaces at the struggle unfolding in front of her.

Both guys look reasonably normal, thirtyish give or take five years, and kinda resemble a cross between aged-out skater boys and surfer dudes who never got day jobs. The one struggling to get a grip on

Chloe is wearing camo pants with a multicolored tie-dye Grateful Dead shirt. His dark blond hair is kinda shaggy and probably hasn't seen shampoo in a few weeks. Other dude's in khaki shorts and a black T-shirt with a graphic of an old man superimposed over a rainbow prism. It's captioned: 'Pink Freud: the dark side of your mom.'

The woman's totally rocking the slacker chic fashion. Baggy off-white top, baggy jeans, canvas sneakers. She kinda looks high, as though she'd recently polished off a whole bag of weed by herself. Obviously, she can't be high since she's a vampire. I *really* hate to say it, but she kinda resembles a possible future version of Sierra when she's closing in on forty. No, this is not me saying Sierra's going to become a weed fiend. The woman just physically resembles her aged forward: thin, long straight light brown hair, similar facial structure.

Anyway, camo pants guy is grabbing my kid, which warrants more immediate action than carefully contemplating the whys of the scene playing out before me.

I charge, jumping into the air. The guy isn't a titan, but he's also not small. In order for me to mount any sort of noticeable attack, I'm going to need speed and gravity on my side. A thirty-foot-high arc gives me enough momentum to crash down in a body check maneuver that would make an NHL player proud. Canadians, not so much. They're harder to impress.

Dude flies off his feet. Chloe springs out of his grip while he's sailing through the air. Her feet hit the ground about the same time his shoulder does. Guy flips legs-over-head and lands flat on his chest, sliding. Like any ordinary seven-year-old being picked on by an older kid, Chloe zooms over to hide behind me and cling while making 'ooh, you're gonna get it now' faces at the guy.

And ouch. Don't think I broke anything, but my left arm isn't happy with me.

"Whoa," mumbles the woman, staring at me. "Where'd you come from?"

"Washington. Just here on vacation." I rest a hand on the kid's shoulder and give her a comfort squeeze.

"Hey," yells Dark Side. "You stay out of this."

I step back, pivoting to keep both guys in front of me, Chloe behind me, and lock stares with the guy holding Ash. "Can't do that. She's my kid."

The woman snort-laughs at me.

"Bullshit," moans Camo Pants Man. "You're not old enough to have a kid."

Ashley snickers.

Ugh. I pinch the bridge of my nose. "Why is everyone always so literal? 'My kid' is much easier than saying the child I am responsible for."

"Bunch of dumbasses," mutters Chloe.

Camo Pants Man picks himself up to stand and points at her. "I'm going to slap some respect into you, you little shit."

Chloe gives him the finger.

"No, you're not." I glare at him. "She's only seven."

"Only *looks* seven." He walks up to us, inches short of arm's length.

"Not that it's any of your business, but she still is seven." I frown. "She's *really* new."

Chloe raises her other hand to give him a double middle finger. Then she waves them back and forth. I think they call that giving someone the 'New York bird.' Don't hold me to it, the rumor might have been wrong.

His face reddens.

Ugh. I sigh mentally. Ease back, kiddo. You're not making this any easier.

"Hold on." I hold my hands out at the local vampires like a crossing guard telling traffic to stop. "Start over. What the hell happened here? How did you guys go from waiting for me outside to being in a field a quarter mile away, being manhandled by two palookas?"

"What's a palooka?" asks the woman.

"A winter coat, I think?" Camo Pants Man scratches his head.

"That's a parka," deadpans Ashley. "Palooka's like a big dumb muscle-head from a really old movie."

The two guys exchange a glance of hesitation.

I'm not honestly sure why I called them 'palookas.' I don't think people used the term seriously since like, oh the 1940s or so. First word my brain seized on that wouldn't get Mom giving me 'the look.' Dunno why she's so sensitive to profanity. However, it looks like me letting an ancient word slip out might get these two morons mistaking me for being much older than I am. No need to clear that up just now. If it makes them less willing to resort to violence, great. This sort of quasi-lie, I have no problem with.

"Slow down and tell me what happened?" I ask to no one in particular.

Ashley gestures at Camo Pants Man. "Everything was all fine and dandy until dickless here shut off the containment grid."

I raise an eyebrow at her. "Is that true?"

"Yes," says Ashley. "This man has no—"

"Are you two seriously quoting *Ghostbusters*?" The woman rolls her eyes.

Ashley and I shrug at each other and say, "It just kinda happened" simultaneously.

The men exchange a stare.

"What containment grid?" asks Dark Side.

"The containment grid holding back the kid's mouth." Ashley snickers.

Chloe fake scoffs.

Ashley squirms. "Umm, you can stop squeezing the crap out of me now."

Dark Side lets go of her. She steps forward, smoothing out her shirt.

"Seriously, though." I rake a hand up through my hair in frustration. "How did you guys end up here? I go into a place for five minutes expecting to find you waiting for me, and…"

"Was a bit longer than five minutes." Ashley wanders over to stand next to me, smiling. "So, we were standing there just waiting for you and these two wandered by. They mistook us for mortals and figured they'd make an easy meal of us."

"Just you," mutters Camo Pants Man.

Ashley points at Dark Side. "He clearly referred to Chloe as 'dessert.'"

The child defiantly folds her arms. "I am not a nom-nom. I do the nomming."

I almost laugh. It's a serious challenge to keep a straight face. Okay, it seems I might've overreacted in my panic. Ash and Chloe weren't in serious trouble.

"So, these guys came over and I guess they realized we're like them, so…" Ashley puffs at a flop of hair over her right eye. "Yeah. They started giving me attitude for kidnapping Chloe and turning her into a vampire too young. That ballooned into an argument. Chloe's mouth got dickless angry enough to try slapping her."

"Stop calling me that!" barks Camo Pants Man.

She disdainfully gives him an up-and-down glance. "What else should I call a guy who thinks slugging a seven-year-old in the face for calling him a moron is an appropriate response?"

"I didn't slug her in the face," snaps the guy.

"Because I'm too fast!" yells Chloe. "You tried!"

"You could just call him Montague," says the woman.

Camo Pants Man facepalms. "That's not my name either."

"I said she could call you that. Didn't say it was your name." She examines her fingernails.

He stares at the sky.

"Guys…" I let out a long breath. "Everyone, just relax, okay? Neither I nor Ashley here turned Chloe. I've basically adopted her."

"Basically?" Chloe scrunches her face at me, a tiny hint of worry in her eyes.

Aww. I pat her on the head. "Only said basically because it's not like we filed any legal paperwork or anything."

"Oh." She grins. "Duh."

"I'm Todd," says Camo Pants guy. "That's Derek, and this is Lily."

"Todd, puncher of little girls." Ashley slides her hand across the air as if illustrating a marquee. "Has a nice ring to it."

Maybe he's Terry the Toucher's cousin.

He scowls. "I didn't hit her."

"Only because she ducked." Ashley leans at him.

"Hey, okay… we're trying to start this over here." I pull Ashley into a one-armed hug. "Not reignite a brawl."

Lily approaches and crouches to eye level with the kid. "She's adorable. Try not to worry too much about Todd. He's old and not very fun."

The guy isn't *that* old. At least, he doesn't feel like an elder to me— or even significantly powerful. So, he's less than a century as a vampire. Safe bet he's older than me, but that's not saying much. Compared to Ashley, I feel like an established vampire who knows what she's doing… but I'm still only on my second year of unlife. It's August now, which means I've been a vampire for one year, a month, and a week or two. Doesn't feel like that long ago my life flipped on its head.

Then again, being in a near constant state of paranormal freakout over crazy things going on does tend to make time blur.

Out here in this dirt lot behind a sporting goods store, we end up hanging out with these three and talking. After setting the misunderstanding aside, it seems they aren't really as butthead-ish as I assumed. They mistakenly believed Ashley—a vampire they didn't know—had abducted and turned a little kid into a vampire. Can't fault them for being upset at the concept. Seems like quite a few vampires aren't happy with the idea of a child receiving the Transference. Honestly, it bothers me, too… but given the circumstances, I've kinda set aside my feelings. Like… randomly grab some kid with a nice life and turn them into a vamp, yeah that's really bad. But Chloe was in my situation, basically murdered already and had seconds left to live.

We don't share those details with these vampires. It's sorta personal. Suffice to say, I explain that we found Chloe as is and objected to her being summarily destroyed for her age. Hearing that I volunteered to be responsible for her endears me to Lily. And yeah, she does seem high. Wonder if she was on drugs when the Transference occurred? Does the same mechanism that will keep me mentally eighteen forever and Chloe mentally a child forever work on *all* mental states? If someone's smoked themselves into another dimension at the moment of the Transference, are they stuck in that mode? Some people do just kinda seem high even when they're not. Could be, she's one of them.

Other than a few lingering resentful glowers from Todd, they seem like reasonably nice people. Todd comes off as one of those guys with an over-inflated sense of self-importance. Despite the Grateful Dead shirt and burned-out surfer appearance, he definitely does *not* like it when those he considers weaker than himself talk back to him. I'm still not sure exactly what Chloe said to him, but it's not difficult to imagine how she pushed his buttons. It's totally fine she stands up for herself, but knowing her, she sensed how much it bothered him to have a little kid talk back and laid it on extra thick, gleefully pushing things from 'standing up for herself' into wanton insolence and mockery.

Can't say he didn't deserve it.

And now we're just hanging out talking like nothing happened. Apparently, a small group of vampires reside in Crescent City. These three find it somewhere between cute and hilarious we're on vacation with a mortal family. Perhaps it's not the wisest thing in the world for me to mention having a mortal family, but I do so in hopes of encouraging the local vampires to avoid feeding on them if they should happen to stray out of the city into the woods. Though, as out of the way as it is, campgrounds would offer a ready source of out-of-towners to feed on who won't be back. It's a variant of the 'don't crap where you live' mentality that gets me going to Seattle downtown to feed instead of breaking into our neighbors' houses.

Dark Side—umm, I mean Derek—twitches. "Uhh, guys. You said you're from Washington? Like Seattle type Washington?"

"Duh," mutters Lily. "What other Washington is there?"

"Umm… D.C.?" Ashley tilts her head.

Lily waves dismissively. "Yeah, but that's like, all the way across the country and stuff. Too much work for a vamp to go on 'vacation' here."

Hmm. Kind of a decent point. I nod. "Basically Seattle, yeah."

Derek raises both eyebrows, arms out in a sorta welcoming gesture. "Portia would like to have a word with you, if you don't mind."

"Your car talks?" asks Chloe.

Todd and Lily crack up.

Derek struggles not to smile. "Not Porsche. Portia, as in Portia Ward."

Ashley and I exchange a glance.

"Oh." Chloe fidgets her toes at a tuft of grass. "Was a girl in my class named Mercedes. Why do people name kids after cars?"

"Good question." Lily laughs. "Though, our Portia was around before cars."

"You said her name like I'm supposed to know it. Should I?" I nibble on my lip. "Cause, I don't."

"Not unless you spent time around here as a vampire." Derek chuckles. "Portia's the oldest among our group. She's my sire, and more or less the one in charge here. Your man Wolent was supposed to send a diplomatic emissary. You're kinda late."

"Umm. What makes her think I'm the emissary?" I fidget.

"You're not?" asks Todd.

"Well… I am part of his circle, but I wasn't sent down here officially." I hold my hands up in a gesture of innocence. "Honestly, that stuff about family vacation is totally above board."

Ashley leans closer to me. "You think maybe Wolent counted on you being here anyway and just mentioned it?"

I smirk. It doesn't sound like something he'd do. At least, not without telling me first. However, I *am* affiliated with him and it's not too much of a stretch to see how this Portia Ward person might assume me to be the aforementioned emissary. There's a bigger chance Wolent simply forgot or perhaps intentionally snubbed contact with her than he told her to contact me without first letting me know I'd be 'on the clock' down here.

Still, my family is asleep for now and it's not like I've got anything pressing to do. Playing nice with the local elder is probably not on the list of worst possible activities to engage in while visiting Northern

California. Might even come in handy someday to have her on good terms. You know, that social networking stuff that always made me feel awkward and self-conscious.

I exhale. This is not good. If Portia is expecting an emissary and none showed up, there's a strong chance something unpleasant happened or is about to happen. Depending on how I handle myself tonight, the situation could smooth itself out or get much, much worse.

No pressure, right?

Ashley seems okay with the idea of going to talk to her. She's a weird kind of shy, won't initiate social activities, but if she gets pulled into one, she's comfortable enough to interact with new people. However, she still prefers staying at home with geeky media to any sort of gathering. Priorities, right?

"Okay." I raise my arms and let them flop against my sides. "Let's go meet her."

6

AMBASSADOR

Enast and a little south from downtown Crescent City, we turn onto a meandering road and follow it into the woods.

Neither Lily nor Todd can fly, so as a group, we're stuck on the ground like mortals. Cue Todd's enormous land boat. I'm not entirely sure what this thing is. Looks like it's from the late Seventies. It's as big as a pickup truck, but only as high off the ground as a car. In fact, it rides a little low. It's super boxy and, well, enormous. I think he called it a Pontiac, but I have no idea what that word even means. The interior smells like a rental bowling shoe, but given how old the car appears to be, it's in fairly decent shape. Something tells me there's a mental pathology going on here. Like, this is probably the guy's actual car from his mortal life that he *still* maintains.

I don't really mind being obliged to act normal (meaning no flying) except for the glaring reminder I'm not. That reminder is, of course, my willingness to get into a strange car with three strange people to meet some mysterious fourth person in some remote place. No way in hell would mortal me have ever done this. Yeah, they might have been nice people. They also might have been serial killers or weird cultists. I was not an adventurous teenager. Adventurous people have fun, sure... but adventurous people also end up having their short life stories narrated by Robert Stack while the country wonders where they disappeared to.

Now, things are different. It's not that I've become any more adventurous. The level of risk has gone down tremendously. Not to jinx myself, but the odds of vampires randomly wanting to kidnap and destroy other vampires for no reason is lower than that of mortals. For one thing, we're really hard to permanently kill. For another, it's just not worth the effort to do on a whim. Finally, fellow immortals often value immortality enough to where it is considered poor form to take that immortality away from someone else. As a general rule, vamps need to be *really* angry to want to go there. Or nuts.

Another thing I'm finding as reassuring as it is weird has to do with Chloe. Ashley is proof that even Innocent vampires have some differentiation in supernatural powers. Aurélie gave her the Transference, and her status as the mistress of all things charm related definitely shows in Ash's vampire self. So far, I haven't really noticed anything 'Daltonesque' manifesting in my powers. Wonder if it's because Aurélie is so much older than him that her powers shone through Ashley much faster? Anyway, point being… Chloe also will likely exhibit some talent of her own she inherited from the man who saved her from death. We know nothing about him. But… Chloe seems to have good instincts about people, an almost supernatural ability to sense danger. Ugh. Considering the horrible life she had with those sad excuses for parents, that ability might be hers and not from her maker. Either way, she seems at ease with Todd, Lily, and Derek. And no, she didn't react at all to Tom, even though he was pretty much a bad guy. A mortal like him posed no threat to Chloe's health.

So, Ash, Chloe, and I pile into the massive back seat of this 'Pontiac' land yacht. I think it's even bigger than Mom's Yukon, though it wouldn't get too far off road. The back seat is a single giant slab of cushion. And holy crap! It doesn't even have seat belts. Overwhelming brown reeks of early Seventies décor. The dashboard and console are so plain I can't help but stare at the nothingness. One little radio—okay, it's not *that* little, the car around it is huge—is the only functional item in the center console. No air conditioning. The dials are merely a speedometer and a fuel gauge, both with enormous needles. Despite the lack of seat belts, I kinda feel safe in this thing. It's a freakin' tank. If we hit anything, I pity the other car.

The behemoth of a vehicle trundles along the uneven dirt road, going farther and farther away from Crescent City. We're driving only a little faster than we could've run on foot. Another sign all is not quite normal here: the headlights are off. Makes sense to me since everyone in this car is a vampire capable of seeing perfectly well at night. If anyone happens to see us, though, it's going to stand out as weird—as if this ancient car wouldn't already be odd to see. Wonder if the locals around here recognize the car as sort of a celebrity? Note to self: if and when I'm ever a hundred years old or more, do *not* keep driving the same car. A... what is it... 2008 Nissan Sentra is going to stick out like a sore thumb in 2108. It's unlikely to be a problem, though. Modern cars aren't built to last like these old dinosaurs. Modern things are built to go for three-to-five years and then be replaced. Gotta keep people shopping, right?

Know what's really stupid? Dad just got a new car only a few months ago. The dealership is *already* sending him junk mail trying to tempt him to buy another new car. I mean, he hasn't had his new one for six months yet. What are they thinking? Ugh.

Ashley keeps opening and closing a small silver trapdoor on the armrest to her right. It's definitely weird. Never saw anything like that before. Tiny storage compartment with a lid. Chloe keeps staring at Todd, making no secret of her continued annoyance. I hadn't noticed before during the confrontation, but none of the local vamps are wearing shoes either. We've stumbled into something between burnout beach culture and hippie vampires. Ash and I left our sneakers at the camp purely out of laziness and not wanting to disturb anyone asleep in the trailer to get them.

We also didn't expect to be away from camp for more than about twenty minutes.

Ugh. Sophia was counting on us to 'stand watch' over them

during the night. I *really* hope it isn't a mistake on my part agreeing to meet Portia. Blix sounded pretty convinced any sasquatch which may or may not be in the area wouldn't have any interest in messing with people. Here's hoping 'the weird' gives us a break for at least tonight.

"Who keeps flicking the ash tray?" asks Todd. "Would you mind stopping? That sound is annoying."

Ashley pauses. She peers at the little hatch, then at Todd, then back to the hatch. "This is an ash tray? Why would anyone want to store ashes in their car?"

All three local vamps twist around to gawk at her.

"Yeah," says Todd in a hesitant tone, like he isn't sure if she's serious or playing with him.

"Who puts an ash tray in a door handle of a car?" I ask, confused.

The locals exchange glances, then start laughing.

"So, Ms. Palooka," asks Lily, "how old are you?"

Busted. I chuckle. "Umm, are you asking how old I was at the time I turned or how long I've been a vamp?"

She shrugs. "Why not both?"

"Eighteen… and not quite two years." I flash a cheesy smile at Lily.

"What's an ash tray?" asks Ashley.

"A tray for ashes, duh," says Chloe past a wiseass grin.

"Or a tray that belongs to her." I point my thumb at Ashley. Sorry. Can't help it. I blame Dad.

Ash groans.

Derek pantomimes holding a cigarette to his lips. "People years ago used to smoke in cars. The weirdos used the ash trays. Normal people just flicked ashes out the window."

"Smoking is bad," says Chloe in a serious tone. "You shouldn't do it, 'cause it can kill you."

Everyone is silent for a moment until the kid's expression gives away she is fully aware she just cautioned vampires on the dangers of smoking—then we laugh.

"Eww," whispers Ashley. "Who'd want to smoke in a car with the windows up? That would stink so bad."

I shrug, unable to explain that one. Some people do have disgusting habits.

After a few more minutes of relative quiet, a stark white house like a scene out of an old gothic horror movie comes into view out of the woods up ahead. Even though it appears to be in good repair and lived in, the place gives off a total haunted house mood. I feel like the girl in a movie who thinks she's approaching a normal house, but it's a hallucination. In reality, the place is collapsing and decrepit, home to a host of dark energies that will devour my soul sliver by sliver.

Relax Sarah, it's the home of an elder vampire, not a business college.

Something is not quite right with this giant three-story house out in the middle of the woods, and the exactitude of what that is doesn't strike me until after Todd pulls up and parks near the porch. At that point, I realize it feels weird because there isn't a horse-drawn carriage parked somewhere in sight. This isn't the time wonk like going into the Aurora Aurea lodge, which I swear really does exist in the 1800s in some bizarre dimensional pocket. It's more like going to one of those places where they re-enact the Civil War.

Todd's door emits a strained groan of metal when he opens it. I swear each individual door on this car weighs more than my Sentra. I open the door on my side, which gives off a similar metallic noise. To me, it doesn't feel burdensomely heavy since I'm online. During the day, this would be a struggle. Not only is it heavy, it's in dire need of some grease.

We're soon out of the land boat and filing up the steps onto a large porch.

Trees surround the small clearing serving as a 'front yard.' I pause at the top step to gaze around behind me at the forest. A brief moment of peacefulness settles over me where the scene feels as placid as it does eerie. This is totally a case where this property could be used to film a sweet family movie as easily as a horror film, depending on how they handled the lighting. So bizarre.

Lily stares into space for a few seconds, not apparently noticing the rest of us going in the front door until she's alone on the porch. As if snapping out of a haze, she hurries in behind us. Kinda looks like she's stoned out of her head, but the truth is almost certainly far stranger than her simply taking marijuana as her life's mission statement. Maybe she's seeing into the spirit world or having a telepathic conversation with her sire.

Thinking about how vampires today can get away with that and not be thought of as crazy—thanks to wireless cell phone earbuds—almost gets me laughing.

Dylan leads the way across the parlor and into a hall. The house seems empty of people. It's decorated in a style reminiscent of what I've seen in movies about the Old West. Unsurprisingly, there aren't any electrical fixtures. This house is out in the deep woods, quite well separated from the reach of the city's power grid. Going to guess there's no sewer service out this far, either. Thankfully, I'm a vampire and don't need to care if there is a septic tank and normal toilets or an external outhouse. Eww. History sounds romantic, right up until you find yourself stuck in it. The truth is far smellier than Hollywood would lead us to believe.

The hallway's loaded with dark wood and plum (the color, not the fruit). Padded chairs, purplish fuzzy fleur-de-lis on the wallpaper, purple glass on the oil lamps, and so on. Chloe floats up off her feet to touch the walls. It's one of the fundamental laws of childhood: anything that appears fuzzy must be touched to confirm it is, in fact, fuzzy.

At the end of the hallway, the wall on the left opens out into another parlor type room. Not sure what they really call a house with two living rooms. Is this a living room or a sitting room? What's the difference? Why do people make things so complicated? Anyway, this room is slightly larger than the one at the front of the house. It also contains a fireplace, two sofas, multiple enormous wingback chairs, a handful of small tables, and several tall cabinets against the walls.

This room, however, is not empty.

A young vampire woman sits in one of the wingback chairs, reading a fat, seemingly ancient book. An unlit oil lantern sits on the little table next to her, its presence likely out of habit, as she wouldn't need its light to read. It's beyond obvious she's one of us, as her presence is throwing off clear 'elder vibes.' She's in a super-frilly black gown with lace cuffs at the wrists and puffy black frill around the neck. The girl's got shortish black hair in a pixie cut. Her eyes seem slightly oversized for her delicate face, which is as pale as Mom's good dinnerware. She appears to be maybe fifteen or sixteen and somewhat vaguely resembles Winona Ryder's character in *Beetlejuice*—if the movie had been set in the 1800s. She's the only one in the room with shoes on... fancy boots that totally go with the extra-ness of her dress.

"If someone starts singing Day-O, I'm going to lose it," I mutter just loud enough for Ashley to hear.

Ashley clamps a hand over her mouth to hold in the laugh. Chloe peers up at me quizzically, not understanding what I said. Todd makes a noise like he's attempting to cover up a chuckle with a cough.

To my surprise, Portia—I assume—lowers the book she's reading and laughs while looking right at me. "Cute moving picture, that *Beetle Juice*."

The way she says it as two distinct words is as offbeat as her appearance. It's so weird for me to be looking at a girl who appears to be slightly younger than me talk about a movie the way an old person who doesn't understand pop culture might. Of course, where vampires are concerned, outward appearances mean little.

Chloe clings to my side and stares in awe at this goth princess. It's unusual for her to act shy. She doesn't seem frightened, per se. At a guess, she's likely sensing Portia's age and isn't sure what the feeling means. Yes, she's been around Aurélie before, but this woman isn't gushing with radiant charm. The instant Aurélie laid eyes on Chloe was like Ashley finding a sick kitten on the side of the road. The 'aww factor' was epic. Pretty sure the kid is trying to figure out how to react to this woman. If we get out of here without a stray f-bomb setting off an interstate crisis of vampiric diplomacy, I'll consider it a win.

"I appreciate you taking the time to come socialize." Portia stands, sets her book on the chair, then approaches us. She's surprisingly short, roughly about the same height as Sierra. It's rare I feel tall. Even more awkward being taller than someone ostensibly way more powerful than I am. Even Aurélie is at least the same height as me. No sooner do I have this thought than she gives me a bemused smirk. "Yes, yes. I'm little. People were shorter back in my time, you know. I also wasn't in the best health during most of my mortal years."

"Sorry." I bite my lip and fidget awkwardly. "Can't help thinking. Tact is a filter between brain and mouth... doesn't work inside the head."

She chuckles, batting a dismissive wave at me. "No bother. I don't take myself too seriously, or I wouldn't dress up like this. So, can you please tell me why you are late?"

"Late?" I blink. "Probably because I'm not the person Wolent sent. I'm here on vacation."

Portia tilts her head. "Vacation?"

"Yes, you know... annual family road trip?"

She stares. "Oh, this I simply must hear."

I rush a quick explanation of still living with my mortal family and trying to balance life with unlife. Portia nods sporadically as I talk, seeming curious and a little amused.

"Are there really sasquatches around here?" blurts Ashley out of the blue.

Portia shifts her gaze to my friend. "Every so often, yes. I do not believe they are native to this reality. The creatures occasionally traipse across holes in whatever fabric separates our worlds, linger briefly in our realm, then go back to where they belong."

"Whoa," whispers Ashley.

I stare at the ornate tinned ceiling. Just once, can I have a vacation that doesn't involve portal fantasy stuff? *One* troll is enough for an unlifetime. Swear, if we end up tripping into an alternate world populated by sasquatches and need to save the bigfoot princess from another monster, I'm going to scream. Hopefully, Sophia is not writing this episode of my story.

"Hmm." Portia rubs her chin. "So, you are not Wolent's emissary?"

"I'm not specifically the emissary he sent here, no... but I suppose it's fair to say I *am* an emissary of sorts since I'm part of his, umm... organization."

She purses her black-painted lips in thought. "Since you are wondering… 1848. I was turned near the beginning of the California Gold Rush. Lived not far from here back then. Spent half of my life sick with tuberculosis. It would've killed me if not for the vampire."

Ashley leans back.

"Do not worry." Portia flicks a smile her way. "I am not contagious."

"Yeah… vampirism is the ultimate antibiotic," I mumble. "Wow, another mercy case?"

She tilts her head at me, then glances at Chloe. "Not quite. The one who turned me made a habit of sneaking into the sanitorium and feeding on those too weak to escape him. It's difficult to sleep when terribly sick. By chance, I discovered his existence and observed him feeding. As soon as I realized what I beheld, I resolved to escape my fate by whatever means possible. I thought it quite unfair fate decided I should die at sixteen. To be honest with you, I still do not know from where I summoned the strength to get out of bed that night, but I did. Followed the old man out into the countryside and pestered him until he gave me the gift."

"Wow…" Ashley raises her eyebrows. "He didn't just kill you?"

"I suppose he could have." Portia shrugs. "I didn't have anything to lose. Another month and I would've been dead, anyway. What about you two?" She glances at me, then Ashley, before lowering her gaze to Chloe. "And this little one? You must tell me how it has come to be that someone so small has become like us."

One thing vampires, especially older vampires, love to do is talk. Anyone turned in the days before television or even radio has a fondness for sitting around talking the same way Sierra loves her PlayStation.

Talk, we do… it is, after all, a sitting room. No real reason to hide the details of my existence here. I explain the Scott/Dalton situation before Ashley goes over the story of being around me as a vampire and seeing me as the same person as before, only with superpowers… and not wanting me to go through the pain of watching her grow old and die. Portia appears to love the story of how we've known each other since we were little, and Ash just couldn't let that go.

"I had bad parents," says Chloe when Portia's attention shifts to her. "They were mean and hit me all the time. They hit me too hard once, and I wasn't gonna get back up, but a vampire fixed me."

Todd, Derek, and Lily all gasp and aww. Lily scoops her into a hug. Chloe, draped over the woman's shoulder, stares down at Ashley and me with the put-upon face of a housecat being squeezed against her will. It's painfully adorable. She tolerates the hug, though. The kid might only be seven, but she's aware her story is the sort of thing that can make some adults all weepy and clingy.

Portia shakes her head in disgust at what happened to Chloe. (Not the vampirism part, the abusive parent part.) When the emotion settles, I go into a brief summary of how the vampire community around Seattle is cautiously accepting her existence provided someone—that's me—watches over her.

When I get to the part of St. Ives trying to 'fix' Chloe, Portia bursts out laughing.

"Poor kid," says Todd.

Ashley quirks a glance at him. "Why 'poor kid'?"

"Stuck so small forever." He shakes his head.

"So?" Ashley ruffles Chloe's hair. "She'll never have to worry about responsibilities, day jobs, taxes, paying rent, high school drama, homework, stress, PMS, or any of that other crap. Gah… sometimes I wish I could've stayed seven forever, too."

I elbow-nudge her. "You basically did, Ms. Unicorn Princess."

She blows a raspberry at me. "Still… what's she missing out on? All the bad stuff?"

"Nonetheless," says Portia in a somber tone, "the girl is still a risk."

"I know." I exhale hard. "Doing everything I can."

Chloe folds her arms. "I'm not a risk. Why does everyone think I'm a dumbass because I'm little?"

Derek and Todd snicker.

"Sorry." I grimace-smile at Portia. "She's from New Jersey."

"Oh. Poor thing." Portia nods once. "Well, if Wolent and his people up north have seen fit to trust you to keep her from drawing too much attention to our kind, I shall do the same. If you aren't the one he sent here, what brings you to California?"

She obviously knows already since she is Derek's sire and can read his mind. However, her asking means she wants me to say it again... so I humor her and talk about my family vacation. Might as well explain everything about the feeding trip gone awry, in case any complications arise from my interference with the Leigh Bennett abduction. This sets off a sub-conversation among Todd, Lily, and Derek, who discuss how they'd have handled the situation. Derek would've compelled Nick to turn himself in. Todd would've killed all three guys, then dialed 911 and let the cops find/save Leigh in the back bedroom. Lily says she'd also have killed all three guys, but wouldn't have left the woman hogtied until the cops found her.

Portia doesn't seem to care that I involved myself in 'mortal affairs' like that. She also doesn't add any commentary about how she might've handled discovering such a thought in a potential meal's mind. I suspect she probably would've mind controlled Tom to go kill his two friends before they hurt Leigh, or just go to the police. Old vampires tend to do things subtly, after all, rarely getting hands-on.

"So, umm, what was Wolent sending an emissary here for?" I ask when the topic of playing vampire super hero wanes to silence.

"Nothing of any great consequence." Portia smiles. "Merely routine communication."

"Fuck off!" blurts Chloe.

I want to crawl into a tiny dark space and disappear.

Lily gasps. Todd cracks up. Derek coughs. Portia starts to look genuinely offended—until she stares at Chloe long enough to see into her thoughts. Evidently, the expletive was not directed at Portia, so she calms down.

"Chloe?" I ask, hesitantly. "Be nice."

The child shivers. "Sorry. Some butthead just tried to steal me."

I blink. "What? Steal you?"

"Yeah." Chloe shrugs. "Like take over my body and stuff."

Ashley turns her head to glance at me... only she doesn't look like herself. Her expression is way too serious and entirely devoid of cheer. "Sarah, is it? Follow me. There's something I need to show you."

Portia raises an eyebrow.

I stare at Ashley, who is probably not Ashley right now. "Oh, shit..."

7

SO MUCH FOR VACATION

Not-Ashley turns on her heel and walks out.

Know what's weird? I mean, besides *everything* about my life. The way she's walking is totally different. People have 'walks.' It's not the sort of thing many people notice. But, if you pay attention to your friends and family, you'll eventually recognize the manner in which they move. Granted, there's only so much variation possible in the mechanics of human locomotion, but it's enough to perceive.

For example, Sophia is a creeper. I don't mean that like 'internet creeper.' She creeps along, half-tiptoeing like she's a video game character stuck in stealth mode. Her usual run is more of a flounce unless she's seriously scared, then she sprints in a more normal sort of way. Sierra and Sam have similar walks. Sam is slightly more plodding in his gait, letting more weight thud into the ground with each step. Sierra's walking is a statement of 'I have somewhere to be and I'm not patient about getting there' while Sam's is basically an 'I'm going this way now.'

Anyway, my point is Ashley has a gait most people would consider 'girly.' She tends to step in-line, placing her feet in front of each other like she's on a balance beam. Add a pinch of bubbly, a little bit of butt wiggle, and you get her stride. At the moment, she's walking like a man. Her feet are tracking two separate 'rails', so to speak, and there's little if any grace involved.

Chloe starts to follow her, not seeming particularly concerned with this new development.

I glance at Portia. "I think my friend is possessed."

"Yes, it does seem that way." Portia leans to one side, glancing at the rapidly distancing Ashley with concern. "Perhaps you should go with her. Do let me know if you require any assistance." She glances at her people. "Derek, would you be so kind as to go with them?"

"Sure, no problem." He gets up from his chair.

"Thanks." I smile at Portia, then Derek. "I'll try to return as soon as I get Ashley back to normal. If we don't show up again tonight, that means it took longer than the sun allows."

She nods. "I feel this is related to the matter of Wolent's emissary."

Huh. That's weird. As far as I know, we don't have any mystics. Still, Ashley's not slowing down, so I don't exactly have the time to worry about minor details right now. I hastily mutter a 'thanks' to Portia, then dart off down the hallway after my friend.

Derek jogs along as well.

Ashley pauses on the porch long enough to look back at me like Lassie making sure Timmy is right behind her. Seemingly satisfied I'm following her, she flings herself into the air.

I skid to a stop at the end of the porch stare-gawking at her. Ashley's takeoff isn't 'vampire graceful'. She looks as if she's been shot out of a catapult, tumbling head over heels and flailing her arms. Dad made me watch—okay, 'made' is a bit of a strong word. He 'strongly encouraged' us to watch his recordings of an old TV show: *Greatest American Hero*. I don't remember too much of it other than it being about a bumbling superhero who could fly but kinda sucked at it.

What Ashley is doing right now reminds me of that poor guy on the show. She's part drunken Supergirl, part Cirque du Soleil performer experiencing a nasty wire malfunction.

"Sorry," I say to Derek. "Gotta go after her."

"No problem." He scratches his head. "Guess I'll stay here and watch the kid."

I fly after Ash.

Chloe zooms into the air behind me.

"Or not," mutters Derek.

Hmm. Do I allow Chloe to follow me into a potentially dangerous situation or leave her in the care of four total strangers, one of whom is an elder who didn't seem entirely on board with a child vampire's existence? Portia's concern is reasonable. A kid who doesn't grow up can easily attract unwanted attention to our kind even if they don't do anything wrong. They absolutely couldn't be left on their own, both because she's still mentally a child—and will always be. But, she needs backup, more pairs of eyes to make sure any mortal who takes notice of her has their memories altered.

Without me being willing to take her in, she'd be dead. Same could be said for any infant. Yanno, if there is any sort of intelligence behind the design of living beings, they really screwed humans over big time. Like... with some animals, the babies can kinda-sorta fend for themselves a little bit. Human babies are totally helpless. That the only reason Chloe's been given the chance to continue existing is me agreeing to keep her really does kinda make me into Mom.

Though, not to be overly melodramatic here... I'm sure Aurélie would've taken her in, too. As it is, we're kind of sharing responsibility. Aurélie is like my older sister who couldn't have a kid of her own so now that I have one, she's appointed herself Mom2. Or something like that. As long as Aurélie doesn't dress Chloe up in a fancy doll gown and plop her on the shelf with the other dolls, we're good.

Yes, that's a joke. She wouldn't treat the kid like a doll. It's merely funny to think of. Oh, she'd absolutely dress her like one... she just wouldn't put the child on a shelf.

Know what's creepy? I mean, besides Ashley being possessed and tumbling off into the sky. Chloe adores the collection of creeptastic dolls at Aurélie's place. Little girls often enjoy playing with dolls and talking to them. However, most little girls tend to freak the hell out if the dolls talk back. It's honestly difficult for me to say if she would've been as calm as she is around them if she remained a mortal kid. I'm not sure how much of her ease with the concept of possessed dolls comes from her normal personality or the vampirism part.

On some level, she does understand she is no longer alive in the traditional sense, perhaps even more than I do. I try to pretend everything is normal, though fate and the Universe are conspiring to constantly remind me my life has gone to plaid. Ashley and I joked awhile back about picking a town somewhere far away from Washington sometime in the future after the 'rents are gone and the Littles are all grown and moved out where we'd fake being high school students for a while just to have the chance to play with our vampire powers in ways we would've loved when we were actually in high school.

Both of us could easily fake being fifteen. And it really wouldn't be like we were grown adults pretending to be high school students. Mentally, we would be the same as we are now, legit teenagers. However, there's a big problem with the idea, fun as it sounds. Neither one of us could wake up in time to go to school. The earliest I can make my eyes open is right about the time school's over. So, yeah. Our daydreams of messing with teachers (strictly in funny, non-mean ways) will have to remain theoretical. Maybe the sheer impossibility of it makes it all the more hilarious to talk about all the stuff we could get away with.

Right, so Ashley…

She flips over and over in a clockwise manner while careening dangerously fast among the trees. After six rotations to the right, she inverts and spins the other way, flailing her arms like she's attempting to grab the air to stop herself from spinning.

I'm tempted to yell and ask what the hell is wrong with her, but we're not very high off the ground. Shouting could attract the attention of mortals… if there happen to be any out here in the middle of the woods near a creepy house. Odds are pretty low there's anyone down there, but my luck can be seriously bad sometimes.

Ash bumps a tree, bounces off, and flips over twice more. She barely let out an 'oof' on impact. Unfazed by sideswiping a tree, she windmills her arms for balance and manages to stabilize herself in the usual orientation for vampire flight. Most of us who can fly just kinda let our arms go wherever. Mine typically trail along at my sides unless I'm fiddling with my phone, carrying something, or in an extreme hurry. When I want to go as fast as possible, I clamp them against myself to reduce drag—no idea if it really helps. I don't generally do the superhero thing and stretch my arms out in front of me.

At the moment, Ashley's kinda waving her arms as if she's 'swimming' in the air.

This is so bizarre. I think the entity who possessed her has no idea how to fly, but realized Ashley is capable of it, so decided to try. It's kind of like that time Grandma Sheridan tried to borrow Uncle Ricky's Corvette to go to the store. Ricky had an old jet-black 1979 C3 Corvette he'd been working on restoring. Grandma was used to driving things like big pickup trucks or that behemoth of a Lincoln Town Car they had for a while. She got into the Corvette, 'pushed gently' on the gas pedal, and laid rubber for two and a half blocks before getting the car under control. Poor Grandma was so rattled, she parked it right where it stopped, got out, and walked home to get Ricky to retrieve his car.

Ashley is flying like she's the Corvette with Grandma Sheridan behind the wheel.

I'd almost laugh but... it's Ashley and I don't know if she's in trouble or not.

Chloe doesn't seem worried. Should I take this as a good omen, or merely that she's too innocent to understand what could possibly happen? Meh. No time to ponder that now. I pour on speed and catch up to Ashley—not difficult since she isn't pushing herself anywhere near full speed.

"You okay?" I ask once we're only about ten feet apart.

"Never did this before. It's really kind of amazing, but terrifying." She stares down. "I am in the air, not on the ground."

I open my mouth to ask who I'm talking to, but before I can get a word out, Ashley dives. Rather than speaking, I go after her. Like a little shadow, Chloe quietly follows me without making a sound. One might say it's bizarre for a seven-year-old to be so well behaved. It kinda is. It's simultaneously reassuring as it is depressing, though. She's totally attached herself to me since I'm like the first person she's had in her life who acted like they cared about her. The other part of why she's so conscientious is knowing what might happen to her if we screw up. I hate that she comprehends the risk of final death she's facing all the time. Maybe Eleanor was right... reversing the Transference might have been the kinder thing to do, if only because a little kid shouldn't live in constant fear of being killed if she messes up.

Sigh. No wonder she's handling it. This isn't too much different than her short mortal life.

Ooh. I want to resurrect her father so I can kill him again.

Bad Sarah. Dark thoughts. Sunshine and bunny rabbits. C'mon. Breathe.

Ashley manages a relatively decent landing. By decent, I mean she didn't eat dirt. She falls out of the air like a doll thrown to the rug by an angry child. Somehow, she manages to land upright for a few strides before falling over.

I glide down beside her.

She stands, dusts herself off, then looks around. Seeming satisfied, she faces me and smiles.

We're in the middle of absolute nowhere. Trees as far as I can see in all directions. A distance to my left and behind us, the burble of a stream provides the only sound louder than silence... at least until Chloe's feet disturb the forest floor with a faint crackle of long-dead leaves.

Ashley's eyes flutter. "So, umm, what are we supposed to see?"

"How should I know?" I mutter. "You brought us here."

She peers at me.

I look at her. "Ash?"

"Yeah. It's me again."

Her posture confirms she's back to herself, so I relax a little. "Ugh, what happened?"

"A ghost asked for help. Said he needed to show you something." She rubs her hip where she hit the tree. "Ugh. Dude has no idea how to fly."

I blink. "A ghost asked you for help and then possessed you?"

She waves me off. "It's cool. I let him in."

Shaking my head, I sigh. "You shouldn't just let any strange guy inside you just because he asks nicely."

Ashley cackles.

Oh, dammit. I spoke too fast, not realizing what I just said. The fire of a wicked blush creeps up my face.

A transparent blue-tinged apparition of a man fades into being in front of us. He looks roughly about Dad's age, maybe a few years younger. Grey suit, short black hair, very business... very Arthur Wolent employee. Hmm. Blue-tinged ghosts. Okay, either George Lucas has seen real ghosts or my brain is processing them this way. Hey, could be, right? I mean... blood tastes different depending on what my brain wants to do with it. Why shouldn't ghosts appear differently to people depending on how they think ghosts should look? Not like I had vast experience seeing ghosts before as a mortal. My only frame of reference for ghosts is *Star Wars*.

Still, it's kinda weird they look so similar. I'd like to think real ghosts have a better special effects budget than whatever was available in the mid-1970s.

"Hang on a sec." I raise an eyebrow at the ghost. "Are you Wolent's guy? You kinda dress like them."

"Indeed." He offers a hand. "Jesse Stroud. You are Sarah Wright, yes?"

Without even thinking about how dumb it is, I attempt to shake hands with the spirit. It's no different from me waving my hand up and down through a patch of freezing air. "Yeah. And wow..."

"Wow?" He chuckles. "I'm not that impressive nor famous."

"No, I mean..." I gesture at him. "You were a vampire, right? Or... just a thrall?"

"Vamp." He grumbles. "Not that I got to enjoy it for too long. Figured immortality would last longer than seventeen years."

I furrow my brow. "What's that supposed to mean?"

"Huh?" He peers at me.

Ashley leans closer to me. "I don't think he's mistaking you for seventeen."

"No." Jesse smiles. "I meant I had a seventeen-year-run as a vampire before this happened." He scowls at the ground. "When one thinks 'immortality,' it usually means several centuries, at least."

"Oh." I rub my temples. "Sorry. Yeah, not thinking right. You got me worried about Ashley."

"Aww." She squeezes me.

Chloe sticks her hand through the ghost's leg.

He peers down at her. "Why, hello there."

"Hi," says Chloe before again sticking her hand through him. "You're a ghost."

"Yes. I am... unfortunately."

Chloe twists around to stare up at me. She's gone from calm to visibly scared, which can mean only one thing: she's afraid of her parents.

"Shh." I pull her into a hug. "Don't worry about them. If they turned into ghosts and come anywhere near the house, Max will eat them."

"Phew." Chloe relaxes.

"So..." I glance at Jesse. "What did you want me to see here?"

The spirit walks a few steps to his left and points at the ground. "Here. I was on my way to visit Portia Ward, bringing a scroll."

"Yeah... elders and their scrolls." I roll my eyes.

Ashley starts giggling.

I look at her. "What?"

"Elder scrolls."

Ugh. Leave it to her to come up with a video game reference about anything. Though, she's not wrong. Vampires of a certain age seem to have an instinctual aversion to email. I wonder if it's basically the undead version of those people who dress up and keep reenacting the Civil War. Great. Old vampires are basically the original LARP-ers, trying to stay in character.

Chloe crouches and begins rummaging at the ground where the ghost pointed.

Jesse faces me and clasps his hands. "I was rather hoping you'd be able to recover the scroll from the ones responsible for destroying me... and possibly exact some revenge."

Sigh. I hold my arms out to either side. "Do I look like an assassin?"

"No. The revenge part is strictly optional. Ideally, you should get the scroll away from them before they alter it and cause trouble."

Ashley grabs my right butt cheek in a clawing sort of manner. This is her saying 'this will bite you in the ass' without using words.

I give her side eye, projecting a 'yeah, I know but ugh...' mood. She shrugs back as if to say 'whatever, let's do it.'

"Who is 'them'?" I ask.

Jesse paces. "A small group of anarchists. Nothing to worry about."

Ashley points at him. "They destroyed you, didn't they?"

He shakes his head. "No. *They* didn't. Their pet did. Well, I suppose technically they did. Their pet savaged me quite horribly and the damn anarchists must have done something after. I suspect fire. Wasn't exactly awake for it. One moment the damn thing is twisting me into a Pablo Picasso piece, the next thing I know, I'm a spirit."

"A pet?" Ashley raises both eyebrows. "What kind of pet are we talking about here?"

Chloe peers up from her digging. "I bet it's not a hamster."

"Hah." Jesse chuckles. "No, it most certainly is not a hamster. They keep it well away from civilization out in the woods. The anarchist with the green hair seems to have control of it."

I shift my weight onto one leg, my right eyebrow slightly raised. "What is 'it'?"

"No damn idea." Jesse rakes a hand over his head, messing his hair —which instantly snaps back into a perfectly styled hair helmet. "Kind of looked like a vampire, but acted like an animal. Likely a Scrap, but it would have to be at least five or six decades old to be as strong as it was. Now that I think of it, it's best if you swipe the scroll back unnoticed. Forget the revenge part. Just try not to be seen."

Ashley and I exchange a look. She has charm powers that could allow her to basically turn invisible as long as she doesn't do anything aggressive or loud. So far, I haven't really manifested anything weird like that, but it stands to reason I probably do have something inherited from Dalton... who is a thief. Perhaps not the best thief, but he's a sneaky sort. Lost Ones tend to be all about stealth and such. Wonder if I tried really hard to concentrate on being sneaky if it would do anything paranormal? I can't help but think of that time I tried to break into the old church and nearly broke my neck climbing a fence.

To be fair, it was daylight at the time, and I had no powers.

I also epically failed to sneak into Club Abaddon. Of course, I was *super* new then. I'm not really 'experienced' as a vampire now, either, but my confidence has definitely gotten stronger. Sneaking into a place without being noticed is the sort of activity that plays to our strengths. Getting into fights is never what I *want* to do, anyway. Going to a place intending to start a fight and kick someone's ass is so not me, especially when the target is a complete stranger who hurt another complete stranger. Now, if someone tried to hurt my family, I'd make a change to my violence policy.

But, this guy? Nah. Sneaking is fine. I would also much prefer not to end up like him—a ghost. If whatever this 'pet' is managed to destroy a guy who'd been a vampire for seventeen years, it's going to eat me, too.

"Okay, Jesse..." I raise a hand at him. "You know Ash and I aren't very old yet. Neither one of us are Furies. I'm willing to go check it out... but if it looks dodgy, we're going to back off and call in the big guns."

"Dodgy?" asks Ashley with a bit of laughter in her voice. "Where'd that come from?"

I smirk. "What? It means suspicious, risky... not quite right."

"You've been watching too many Guy Ritchie movies," mutters Ashley.

"Oh." I chuckle. "It's gotta be having Dalton around."

Jesse nods. "That's fine. You two are so young, I don't want you to get hurt. But, you are here right now and time is short. If you can get the scroll away from them before they can alter it and send it to Portia, please do so."

"Umm." I tilt my head. "Wouldn't Portia be able to tell the scroll's been changed? I mean, she knows you're late. I could tell her you got killed and the letter from Wolent was stolen."

"Oh, yes." He nods. "It wouldn't much matter what she thinks about the thing if she reads it after those vampires get done with it. They're occultists, and they intend to weave something of a curse into the scroll. If she reads it, she'll fall victim to whatever it is they're doing."

Ashley fidgets. "This is starting to sound scary."

"Skull!" chimes Chloe.

I blink at Jesse, then turn my head to stare at the child.

Like a triumphant treasure hunter, she holds a charred, fanged skull up over her head in both hands, still squatting by the hole she's dug. A writhing earthworm falls from the skull's nose opening and lands on her left knee. She doesn't appear to care.

Ashley grimaces and takes a step back.

"That's what I was intending to show you," says Jesse. "Would you terribly mind cremating it the rest of the way so the mortals don't start asking questions they shouldn't?"

Chloe stands—sending the worm sliding off her leg to the ground —and begins shaking the dirt out of the skull… or at least out of the eye sockets. I'm not sure what's disturbing Ashley more, the sight of a dead vampire skull or watching the kid touch it without any hint of hesitation or disgust. I mean, Sierra wouldn't have much problem with a skull like that, but I bet she'd want gloves on before handling it. I almost tell Chloe to put it down, but catch myself. She's not exactly going to get sick from any bacteria that might be on it. Do vampire skulls even carry bacteria? Hmm. Probably not. For us, permanent death is something of a fiery affair. All the wet and squishy bits rapidly combust, leaving only charred bones.

I don't understand what about vampirism turns us into walking magnesium flares, but… magic isn't bound to follow any sort of logical scientific principles. Vampires spontaneously combust for the same reason some people end up inexplicably famous despite having no particular talents or importance to society. Ashley made a 'full superhero' joke earlier. I wonder if I could refer to the fiery final death of vampires as going 'full Kardashian?'

Meh, that's a little clunky. I'd have to explain it every time I used it, which totally negates the purpose.

"Sure. We can make sure no one finds your skull," I say.

"Where's the scroll?" Ashley starts to reach for Chloe, but chickens out, not wanting to touch the poor guy's remains. It's a strong statement when a girl who has no trouble picking up dog poo in her hands—with latex gloves on—doesn't want to touch something.

Can't say I'm all too interested in doing so either. Is it bad of me to let the kid hold it for now?

"Not terribly far from here. They've holed up in a smallish house east of Del Norte County Fairgrounds. There's an algae-covered pond just to the south of the place. Can't miss it thanks to the smell."

"Lovely," I mutter. And ugh... even when I'm on vacation, I'm forced to deal with political crap. That's at least one nice thing about vampires. Yeah, there's politics, but at least we don't have to go door to door begging for campaign donations. Our 'politics' are a bit more like high school drama than mortal politics. Well, part high school drama, part medieval society type politics. I might as well help the guy out since, well, we're going to be up all night anyway and scoring some points with Wolent is never a bad idea. "You know we're not from around here? I have no idea what a Del Norte even is."

Chloe bonks the skull against a tree to encourage more dirt to fall out of it.

Jesse winces, almost as if he can feel it. "I can show you where it is."

"You're not going to possess Ashley again, are you?"

"I could... or perhaps you could follow me from the air. I can move quite fast in this form." Jesse blurs off to the right.

"Guess we're not having a discussion about it." Ashley snickers, then leaps into the air—much more gracefully than she did at Portia's house.

"C'mon, kiddo," I say to Chloe.

She stops bonking the skull against the tree and looks up at me. "Okay."

We zoom upward, chasing after Ashley who's pursuing the ghost like a cat desperately attempting to kill the laser pointer dot. Jesse's blurred into a bluish smear of light that's weaving among the trees. It's anyone's guess why a ghost is going around them rather than through them. Maybe because trees are alive? Or maybe he's intentionally slaloming as a means to slow down enough for us to keep up. It *is* a bit taxing to keep his pace. I don't break my neck, figuratively or literally, since my eyes are quite capable of picking up his unnatural light for a good distance. As long as I can see the blue glow, it doesn't matter if I'm a couple hundred feet behind him.

Chloe's got the skull held between her hands, just under her chin. She is once again personifying the word Ashley made up to describe her: creepdorable. Jesse couldn't have been destroyed more than a month ago at most, yet his bones look like he'd been buried there for years. This skull being so close to me is making me keenly aware of my own immortality. It's the same thing that plagues me during the daylight hours when my vampire abilities are offline. Having the capability to live forever makes me even more nervous about getting hurt. There's more at stake. I'm potentially losing thousands of years of time versus a mere sixty-to-eighty.

No point dwelling on it, though. As vampires go, I'm rather tame. I don't go looking for trouble and I don't crave power or fortune. Problem is, trouble keeps hunting me down. Here's hoping this particular episode of craziness is manageable.

The chase lasts only a few minutes before the spirit comes to a stop. Ashley and I land on either side of the cloud of blue light as it coalesces back into a recognizable image of Jesse Stroud. Chloe sets down behind me and presses herself into my back. She seems uncharacteristically frightened all of a sudden.

"A bit farther that way." Jesse points ahead into the woods.

Faint music—some manner of heavy metal—emanates from a point in the distance. There are too many trees in the way to see anything more than forest; however, it does appear they have at least one light on. Strange for vampires to use lights. There are only a few reasons I can think of why we would: trying to seem normal to mortals around us, cutting down on the glare of a television screen, or they have mortals with them. We are seriously out in the weeds here, so it's super unlikely they're worried about what neighbors think. I'd doubt they have a television or working electricity out this far, but… the light appears electrical, not like a lantern. Weird. Guess they have solar panels or something.

"Do be careful," says Jesse. "They aren't the nicest people."

8

THE FIRST IMMUTABLE LAW OF VAMPIRE LIFE

I t seems that all too often in my life I don't ask questions when I clearly ought to.

Like, why is Jesse hesitant about going any closer to this house? Why am I bringing Chloe into a dangerous situation? Why was *Firefly* cancelled? Why haven't any of us gone back to the campsite to grab our shoes? At least the last question, I can answer. If we went back to camp, the temptation to stay there would've been too strong.

The three of us make our way forward like a pack of kids playing soldier in the woods at night. By this, I mean none of us are professionally trained in being sneaky. We're not even amateurly trained at being sneaky. Prior to becoming vampires, the sneakiest thing we ever did was slip into an empty classroom and 'vandalize' a whiteboard with dry-erase marker. Yeah, I know, horrible of us, right? We were such delinquents.

Chloe keeps herself a few paces behind us. She's following, but doesn't seem thrilled about it. The kid's giving off an air of anxiety like the slightest unexpected sound is going to result in her zooming into the air and noping the hell out of here as fast as she can fly. What does it say that she appears this scared, yet is still sticking with me? Does that make me an idiot? Maybe I shouldn't do this… how much time could it take to fly her back to the campsite? She ought to be able to babysit herself for an hour, right? Though, she doesn't like to be alone. Poor kid already spent most of her life alone, hiding in her bedroom, terrified 'the monster' would burst in at any time.

Sigh.

As we sneak through the woods, my mind wanders in circles around Chloe. How much of her is vampire now and how much is innocent child? I didn't know her before she turned, so have nothing to compare her personality to. Ashley's easy. No, not like that. Gawd. I mean, she's easy to evaluate from a personality standpoint. The only noticeable change to her personality post-vampirism is how easily she gave up on wanting to go to college to become a veterinarian. She had been pretty driven to that goal, as well as eventually having kids and a family of her own—but she's not given off the least bit of hint she regrets her decision. It seemed rash to me in the moment, but she probably had been considering it ever since I told her the truth about what I'd become. Ashley is totally like 'okay, we're staying teenagers forever, party on' without a backward glance at the future she gave the finger to.

In every other way, she's the same person… except maybe for a slight increase in confidence. Can't blame her for that. Being *really* hard to kill does wonders for one's bravery. So, maybe Chloe's personality is pretty much the same as she used to be in life. But she's still a child. Parents usually have to worry about their kid getting into poisonous cleaning stuff under the sink if left unattended, not undead brawls, black magic, demons, or crazy vampire scientists zapping them with various forms of electromagnetic waves.

I don't need to worry about the usual things responsible adults think about when leaving seven-year-olds alone. In Chloe's case, it's not what might happen *to* her, but what she might do to someone else. As little kids go, she's extremely sedate and mature, but she's still only seven. She has a button to push in there somewhere, and a temper tantrum remains a possibility. Worse, she's a traumatized seven-year-old who had a life no child should ever be subject to. If something reminds her of her parents in a sufficiently scary way, who knows what she might do. It could be as simple as seeing some random stranger who bears a striking physical resemblance to them and she might freak out thinking he's come back to life to kill her again.

Ugh. Bad thoughts. Out of my brain.

I'm trying to criticize myself for being a horrible mom here, not dwell on tragedy. What kind of self-respecting parent brings their seven-year-old on a burglary job? Or an assassination job? Granted, we're not going here intending to get into a fight. Suppose I could go full *Leon* and train Chloe how to use a sniper rifle. Nah. Too over the top. She gets to stay normal. Ordinary little girls walk around carrying a real vampire skull like a doll, right? Totally normal.

Hmm. If it wasn't after three in the morning, I'd ask the 'rents to watch her. My lazy side wins out. We're already here. Besides, even if I did fly the kid back to our campsite, I'd get lost trying to find this place on my own.

Duh. Stop being a dumbass.

I pull my phone out and check a navigation app. Drat. No signal. We are in the middle of nowhere. Dammit. Why do vampires constantly choose such out-of-the-way places to do their violent nonsense? The jerks who kidnapped Ashley also picked a spot in the deep woods where no one bothered to build cellular towers. So much for figuring out where we are via the magic of technology. How the heck did vampires hundreds of years ago know where they were going without GPS?

"Who are you going to call?" asks Ashley.

"Ghostbusters," I whisper.

She blinks, then snickers.

"Just trying to figure out where we are in case we have to find it again."

Ashley bites her lower lip. "Umm, why would we have to find it again?"

"You know my luck. Something's going pear-shaped."

Chloe emits a nervous giggle.

"Pear shaped?" Ashley scrunches her nose. "Are you doing it again?"

"Doing what again?"

"Dalton-ing."

I pause. "Oh, yeah, maybe. I'm pretty sure pear-shaped means messed up."

She tilts her head. "What does the shape of a pear have to do with things going wrong?"

"I don't know. It doesn't make any sense. It's British. It makes sense to them." I shrug.

"But you said it." Ashley pokes me.

"It just kinda slipped out." I scratch my head. "I think when Dalton uploaded sword skill into my brain, some of his mannerisms went with it."

"Right-o, bloody hell," says Ashley in a horrible attempt at a British accent.

I smirk.

Chloe stares at us in a 'you are both dorks' sort of way.

We continue to sneak along for a few minutes more until it becomes obvious we are getting close to a house. At that point, we try to be even sneakier, crouching lower in the weeds. Soon, we find ourselves hiding in a thick swath of bushes bordering a clearing in which sits a run-down one-story building. It looks like the sort of home you always see on episodes of COPS filmed in the deep south where the police end up dragging drug addicts out the window. The only thing missing here is a couple of broken-down pickup trucks parked outside. Chloe squeezes in between us on all fours, her head raised just enough to see over the foliage in front of us.

The light's coming from the front room, shining out a pair of windows on either side of the door. Like extremely lazy medieval castle guards, two thirtysomething guys occupy cheap folding chairs on the porch, also on either side of the door. The man on the left is big, both muscular and overweight. Bald on top with a reddish-tinged beard. He's dressed in a black T-shirt bearing a giant red pentagram, dirty jeans, and construction worker boots. His left forearm is covered by a leather bracer—also black—studded with bright silver spikes. Dude's also got a bunch of amulets on, pentagrams, goat heads, and some symbol I don't recognize, though it looks kind of occult and dark.

His friend is rail thin. Guy's maybe got four teeth left. His eyes are sunken into their sockets, tinged dark, and he's so damn skinny a pair of faint bumps appear in his face where his retracted fangs are. Never really thought about it before, but vampire fangs are like four times as long as ordinary canine teeth. Guess it makes sense they'd take up more space inside the head. Just... if a person is at a normal weight—or heavier—the bumps aren't visible. He's covered in tattoos on his arms and neck, lots of which appear to depict satanic type imagery. Goat heads, runic marks, daggers, naked succubus figures, and so on. He's also taken the body modification thing a bit to the extreme with horns. They're not real horns—at least I don't think so—more like horn-shaped objects surgically implanted between his skin and skull. Purely decorative. Creepy and icky if you ask me.

Oh, did I mention the skinny guy has the word 'satan' tattooed across his forehead?

Yeah, real class act, this guy.

Guess he's not too worried about getting a day job.

The absolute craziest thing, though, is the super weird vibe I'm getting from them. It's way beyond their outlandish attire. Not being metaphorical here at all; these two genuinely feel like they have some serious dark energy going on.

Ashley mouths 'wow' at me.

I keep studying the two vamps for another minute, certain they're more than simple idiot vampires. "Pretty sure these guys are legit into demons."

"Ya think?" whispers Chloe. "Look at them."

"Kid's got a point." Ashley rolls her eyes. "They totally look like those goofy demonic cultists from that one movie your dad let us watch when we were like twelve."

I stifle a snicker. "Right? We've found Beelzebubba and *Methe*stopheles."

Ashley covers her mouth in both hands, shaking, glaring at me for making her want to laugh when we're trying to be quiet and sneaky.

A long, slow exhale slips past my teeth. "Ugh. Why are they sitting there? Like guarding the front door."

"They have nothing else to do but sit on the porch and chug beer," whispers Ashley once she conquers the need to laugh. "But they're vampires, so no beer."

My mind races for a way to handle this situation that isn't saying screw it and leaving. Not sure why I'm all of a sudden insisting on being part of this. Wolent wouldn't mind if I walked away. At least, I think he wouldn't. I *do* know he'd be quite happy if I handled the situation. Am I that desperate for validation? Meh. It probably boils down to it being a case of the happier I make Wolent, the safer my family is in vampire society. I do this for them.

I grumble.

Chloe looks at me.

"Hmm. I could try to distract those two so you could take advantage of your inconspicuousness to sneak inside, grab the scroll, and get out?" I fidget, already not liking the sound of my idea.

Chloe looks at Ashley.

"Okay. What am I looking for?"

Chloe looks at me.

"A scroll."

Chloe looks at Ashley.

"Like, a legit scroll?"

Chloe looks at me.

"Yeah. Old vampires are allergic to progress." I fold my arms. "Convincing an elder to send an email that takes a thousandth of a second to get where it needs to go instead of a hand-carried letter is as difficult as trying to get Uncle Hank to use a television remote. He still thinks remotes are a liberal conspiracy."

Ashley facepalms.

Chloe makes a face of confusion, then looks at Ashley.

"Okay. Legit scroll. Got it. Be right back."

"Wait." I rest a hand on her shoulder. "Let me distract them first."

Chloe glances at me, then back to Ashley. Poor kid looks like a spectator at Wimbledon, her head constantly turning back and forth.

Ashley waves me off. "Nah. It works better if there's calm. If you get their attention, they'll be more alert for crap going on and might see me... unless you keep their attention on you. But, then their attention will be on you and we'll have to figure out some way for you to get out of there. Better they don't know we were even here."

Chloe points at Ashley. "I like her idea."

"Okay, fine." I sigh. "If anything goes wrong, I'm charging in there."

She smiles at me in an 'I know you will' way, then stares at Beelzebubba and Methestopheles. After a moment of intense glaring, she stands up straight and fly-floats over the bushes to land in the clearing. Amazingly, neither guy reacts to her. They ought to be able to see her quite easily, but don't show any signs of having noticed a random red-haired girl show up on their proverbial doorstep.

Silent as a drifting phantom, Ashley pads toward the house. The occasional twig or bit of forest debris crunches under her feet, though the guys remain oblivious to her presence as far as I can tell. Beelzebubba is reading a magazine of some kind. The skinny guy is staring into nowhere. I called him 'Methestopheles' because he's a demon-obsessed vampire who totally looks like someone in the advanced stages of meth addiction. The way he's vacantly gazing into nothingness only makes him seem even more like he's high out of his mind.

Chloe clings to me. I put an arm around her and mentally cross my fingers. I know something's going to go wrong here. Nothing about my unlife ever happens quick and easy. The idea of Ashley walking into that house unnoticed, plucking some scroll off their coffee table, then coming back outside so we can take it to Portia, and us calmly going back to the campsite before sunrise is as laughable as it is improbable. This is us we're talking about. I'm probably going to spend the remainder of the night running for my life. Ashley had a good point. If these guys *do* dabble in genuine demonic magic, it's better they don't see me. In the unlikely event she's successfully able to get out of there with the scroll, these guys won't have the first clue who to be angry with. If they see me, that will give them a starting point we're better off not letting them have.

I can't help but hold my breath as Ashley nears the porch. Still, neither man reacts to her presence. Step by step, she ascends the three stairs, her arms slightly out to either side, palms facing down as if it somehow makes her lighter on her feet. Even as she passes between the guys to the door, they don't pay her any mind.

Wow. That is a seriously neat trick. Guess having an almost-400-year-old sire has its perks. I'm sure it works in a manner similar to being around sleeping vampires. The instant she means to do harm, it'll stop working. As long as she remains a non-threat, she may as well not exist as far as their brains are concerned.

C'mon Ashley. Concentrate. Be careful.

She goes through the doorway into the house.

So far, so good. I really don't like that 'the bad guys' have her surrounded. I'm sure there are more inside. Jesse said the 'green haired' one controls the pet that killed him. Neither Beelzebubba nor Methelstopheles have green hair, so that means there is at least one more vampire here. Guessing possibly two additional vamps at most since we are kinda rare. Wouldn't make sense for this to be a large group.

Ashley screams.

Craaaaaaap. Figures. It's like a law or something. Anything I—or by extension everyone around me—tries to do *will* be as complicated and messy as possible.

Chloe peers up at me. "She forgot to put on a headband."

9

THE NON-DIPLOMATIC
APPROACH

I warned myself. Sorta. The whole walk here, the undeniable sense of it being a mistake nagged at me, but I didn't stop. I feel like the girl who knows it's a seriously stupid idea to get in the car driven by her drunk boyfriend, but for reasons unknown, caves in and does it, anyway. Nothing quite like bleeding out on the side of the road to make regret hit home. Fortunately, in life, I was *way* too skittish to dare take chances like that. I totally would've been the uncool girlfriend who stormed off rather than get in that car. Uncool, but alive.

Course, that ship sailed. I'm not alive anymore, despite being careful as hell.

Maybe I wasn't as smart and careful as I tell myself. What kind of idiot takes an arrogant jerk of a boyfriend off somewhere alone to break up with him? That was a case of me psychoanalyzing things the wrong way. Figured if he didn't have an audience watching him be dumped, he'd take it better than if I made him look like a loser in front of everyone. Whoops. Maybe he still would've stabbed me in front of witnesses. Not like he acted with a great amount of thinking there. I guess in some weird sort of way, my decision did save my life —sorta. If he'd killed me inside the house in the middle of the party,

I'd be *dead* dead. Dalton wouldn't have been there to help, and even if he had been following me already at that point, there's no way he would've barged into a crowded room to give me the Transference in front of seventy some odd teenagers.

Weird how luck works sometimes.

Anyway…

Ashley is in trouble. The only thing keeping me remotely in control at the moment is the tone of her scream. It wasn't horror movie victim sheer terror, more like she walked into the kitchen and saw a bear halfway in the sliding glass door.

"Go help," says Chloe. "I'll wait here."

I bite my lip. Ashley screams again. This time, it's even less fearful sounding and more of a 'holy shit' type sound.

"I'm not a freakin' stupid head." Chloe nudges me. "Go. Ash is in trouble. I'll stay right here. Not like you gotta worry I'm gonna get kidnapped."

I hate it, but she's right. Not only is there no one around for miles, if anyone does try to abduct her, they deserve everything she does to them. No time to argue, so I do the second most dumbass thing of the night and leave the seven-year-old by herself.

Beelzebubba and Methestopheles rush into the house, no doubt in response to the screaming. I have no damn idea what I'm getting into or what I'm going to do once inside, but immediate violence is not off the table. Hopefully, I have a clear line of sight on Ashley and can fly-tackle her out a convenient window so we can fly the hell away from here.

I Supergirl it across the clearing and swoop in the front door, only to encounter a giant, bald, bearded roadblock barely two steps inside. Rather than smash into him, I slam on the proverbial brakes and hang in a hover, my toes a couple of feet above the floor. Beelzebubba is even bigger up close. Damn, this guy is massive. Methestopheles has charged into the middle of a dingy living room, paused halfway between us and a brawl going on in the back left corner. Ashley's tangling with two more vampires: a dude with lime green hair and another guy dressed up as a member of a poser satanic rock band.

Nothing about him stands out as particularly unusual or noteworthy, so he's probably the bass player. Well, he does have really bushy, long black hair. Wonder if he's going for the Slash look. All he needs is the old timey top hat. His face is like totally hidden behind a wall of hair. How the hell does he see?

'Slash' is as accurate a sarcastic nickname for him as it gets, since he's presently trying to chop Ashley up with a sword. She's fast—panic is a super effective motivational force—dodging around the lime-haired guy who's trying to grab her. It's like they're playing life or death Twister while frantically evading a clumsily wielded broadsword.

Methestopheles seems hesitant to get anywhere near Slash and his inebriated attempt to impersonate Conan the Barbarian. Unfortunately, there is no window anywhere near Ashley. I can't fly into her and drag her out of here. We'd be stuck in a corner. Dammit. This is going to require violence. Since they're trying to hurt Ashley, I have no qualms about going there.

I extend my claws. No point starting off soft and trying to de-escalate. Time for 'first day in prison' rules. Drop the biggest beat down on the biggest, scariest vampire here and the others might be afraid of me. Beelzebubba is obviously the largest, and he looks like he'd be the biggest threat. Methestopheles, however, makes up for what he lacks in brawn with visible crazy. It's the sort of crazy that says he doesn't care what happens to him, which makes him scarier. He probably wouldn't care what I did to any of his friends. Logic says it makes the most sense to take him down, since everyone else watching me shred that guy with painful claw wounds *might* hesitate. He definitely won't.

However, Slash has a sword, and it's getting entirely too close to Ashley. This shifts him up the target priority list. Amazing the sort of threat analysis my brain is capable of in four-tenths of a second.

I start scooting around Beelzebubba in preparation for a flying claw buzz at Slash, but a flash of silver catches my attention. The big dude is pulling an enormous handgun out from under his biker vest. Vampires love shooting other vampires in the head. It's instant naptime. Only, this gun is so damned big it raises other questions. Like, how would vampire anatomy react to the head exploding into a cloud of chunks and red mist? I'm not a 'gun person,' but I recognize the thing as a Desert Eagle. Also, not being a gun person, I have only what movies say about them to go by. As far as I'm concerned, that thing is a massively overpowered hand cannon capable of instantly destroying any vampire it touches.

So, nope.

Target change.

Beelzebubba doesn't see me coming—since I'm right behind him and barely a quarter of his size. I grab the wrist of his gun arm and shred my claws the whole length up the underside of his forearm, destroying all the muscles and tendons responsible for manipulating his fingers. The giant gun goes flying out of his now-limp grasp as he tries to swing his arm out to aim at Ashley. A heavy *thud* near the doorway tells me the weapon is safely out of reach from anyone in the room. Before the giant can fully commit to screaming in pain, I've ripped my left hand claws across the front of his throat.

I'm not an expert in combat, far from it. Probably why he doesn't instantly lose consciousness, but falls to the floor, flopping around and scream-gurgling. Not every huge guy has a high pain threshold. Some big dudes are real teddy bears. Also, the supernatural pain involved with vampire claws is serious. If the guy never got sliced up by a vampire before, it's understandable why he's down for the count so fast. As they say, the first time hurts the worst.

Methestopehles spins around at the scream bubbling past the blood pouring down the big guy's throat. He stares at me... smiling. I do not like this smile. It's a darker version of the smile my little brother would give a chocolate cupcake before biting it, only... more evil. Like, this guy would take delight in whatever pain he inflicted on the cupcake as he devoured it. Sam just loves chocolate.

He launches himself at me, yanking a pair of knives off his belt. I have no choice but to go on the defensive right away due to this guy being stupid fast. Beelzebubba didn't move with vampire speed at all, probably because I didn't give him time to boost himself. But, whoa, this guy got the supernatural agility boost for both of them. Gah! I take a few superficial cuts to my arms before managing to backpedal enough to where my attempted dodges spare me any further slicing.

Like a little kid attempting to avoid a spanking, I run around and around the sofa. This guy is too fast for me to get any openings for a counterattack. My only option is to wait for him to commit to a stabbing attack that won't hit me in the head or heart. I'll have to let him hit me in order to get my claws on him. Gotta make sure it's in a spot that won't disable me. He seems to know this, too, so keeps on trying to jab me in the head.

I'm so occupied trying to dodge this bastard, I've lost track of what's going on with Ashley. A little help comes in the form of another vampire trying to grab me from behind. His stomping run thudding across the floor up behind me is ample warning for me to dive to the side. The timing couldn't be better. The oncoming guy commits to a diving tackle at the exact perfect second for Methestopheles to stab him in the face instead of me as I drop straight down out of the way. New guy hammers the skinny, horned freak into the rug like something straight out of WWE pay-per-view. Dude might be fast, but I'd be shocked if he weighed more than ninety pounds.

This gives me about a second and a half to check on Ash. She's still sorta-wrestling with the lime-haired guy. Don't see much blood sprayed around there. Good chance the broadsword hasn't landed a hit yet.

I pivot to leap at Slash, but new guy rolls over and grabs my right ankle. Reflexively, I shift to fly-hovering and stomp my left heel at his face in a rapid-fire barrage. The fourth (or maybe sixth) time my foot makes contact, his nose breaks with a satisfying crunch. This, predictably, encourages him to let go of my leg. I'm free—for all of half a second. Methestopheles comes flying (not literally, he's merely jumping) over the sofa and grabs me in a tackle grip. My flight ability prevents him from dragging me to the ground. He does, however, pull me down so my feet are on the disgusting carpet again. Carpet should not be sticky. I do not want to know why this particular carpet is.

New guy shrugs off the stomp to the face, leaps to his feet, and grabs my left arm. Like a pair of amateur animal control officers dealing with king cobras for the first time, the two guys focus on holding my wrists and keeping my claws away from their tender bits. It's an improvement over the guy trying to stab me, but not a big one. We're all about on par for strength, so this is moderately less terrifying than a couple normal dudes grabbing mortal me. That means I'm in serious trouble. Grunting, I struggle to pull my arms away from them. Each guy has both hands clamped around one of my wrists, holding on with as much desperation as if to let go of me would mean their immediate destruction.

Yes, Beelzebubba is shrieking in agony.

No, I don't regret it.

However, his reaction has apparently scared these guys. They don't really know what to do next, now that they have me under control. Me kicking them repeatedly in the legs, groin, and gut isn't doing much but making my foot sore. I'm pretty well trapped at the moment and I really don't like feeling this vulnerable.

A heavy *thud* comes from the left. I drag my brawl around to the side enough to see what's going on with Ashley. The green-haired guy springs back to his feet, recovering from performing a legit *Karate Kid* style foot sweep that's put Ashley flat on her back. Slash is already swinging his sword down at her as if to take her head off. Ashley screams, having no time to move. I start screaming, too.

Boom!

Time seems to stop. On some subconscious level, I am aware that a gun just went off. The noise is *so* damned loud, the walls of the room seem to wobble, or maybe that's merely a trick of the light from the muzzle flash. My brain undulates under the sonic shock wave. I feel like a mouse inside a steel drum someone just walloped with a sledgehammer.

However, my headache pales in comparison to Slash's headache.

I somewhat overestimated the Desert Eagle. Go figure that Hollywood isn't the most scientifically accurate representation of guns. Who'd have guessed? The man's head does not completely explode into a shower of gore... he's still got a flap of skin where his face used to be. Pretty much everything behind his face plate is now dripping down the wall. Brain, eyeballs, muscles are everywhere. Lime haired guy stands there stunned, painted with blood.

The two guys holding me also stop fighting, caught off guard by the sudden loud blast. Everyone—except Slash for obvious reasons—looks toward the doorway.

Chloe's in mid pratfall, legs splayed up in the air. The enormous Desert Eagle is still somehow firmly in the grip of her tiny hands. It knocked her on her ass so hard she's almost did a backward somersault right out the front door. She catches her momentum, swings her legs down, and sits up, head spinning. "Holy shit, this bastard kicks. Wow... real guns are *way* different than the light blaster."

Methestopheles and the new guy gawk at the child. Yeah, she has that effect on people.

I take advantage of their bewilderment and thrust my hands upward through their grip on my wrists—impaling my claws into their throats. It feels so disgusting to squeeze everything inside their necks together in my fists... but it's effective. They attempt to pummel me off, but I refuse to let go. In seconds, their attacks lose strength. I keep squeezing until the welcome *crack* of neck vertebrae giving way jolts my hands. Both guys go limp on their feet. Having been on the receiving end of a broken neck before, I'm aware they are not unconscious. But... they also can't move. It will be at least twenty minutes to half an hour before they can stumble around groggily and probably a few hours before they're back to full coordination.

Works for me.

I flick my fingers open and let both guys flop to the ground.

Lime haired guy seems to lose his desire to grab Ashley. He runs across the room to the opposite corner, ducking behind a large, battered recliner. The poor chair looks like it either served four tours of duty in WWII or got on the bad side of a neurotic large dog. Wow. I've never had anyone run in terror from me before and hide. It's a weird feeling being scary, and not one I really like. But... I won't feel guilty about terrifying some jackass who tried to kill Ash.

I zoom over and help her up. "Ash, you okay?"

"Yeah, just a bit tired." She brushes her hands down her front, neatening her shirt.

"What hap—?"

Ashley's eyes go huge. I haven't seen such an expression of total fear on her face since the first time Ms. Bell hit us with a surprise pop quiz in Algebra II class.

I whirl.

Lime-haired-guy has stood up from behind the reclining chair, right arm cocked with a legit hand grenade in his fist. Seems a bit larger than I imagined a hand grenade would be, but its shape is unmistakable.

"Are you effing serious?" I blurt.

He flicks his thumb. With a metallic *ping*, a small metal bar goes flying off the side of the grenade he's about to fastball at us. I think that's the part that arms the bomb inside. Like, as soon as the metal bar springs away, the grenade is gonna explode. No take-backsies. Oh, shit.

Boom!

A loud bang is not the thing you want to hear a split second after your brain registers the presence of a hand grenade. If my biology had been capable of it, I absolutely would've messed my pants. Thankfully, the grenade has not detonated—yet. At the edge of my peripheral vision, Chloe flies backward from a four-foot-long dragon breath of muzzle fire. An explosion of blood splatters on the wall behind the dude. She hit him almost dead center chest. Damn. Nice shot, kid. Her little body slaps into the floor and bounces over once. An almost one-inch hole has appeared in the guy, giving me a clear view of the gory wall behind him. The heart shot saps all the strength from him. His arm flops down, grenade tumbling from his paralyzed fingers to land on the floor between his feet.

He looks down at it, his expression the most pure 'oh, shit' I've ever seen. He's only upright for another eighth of a second before he crumples to the floor in a heap behind the beat-up recliner that's about to get a whole lot more shredded.

Speaking of 'oh shit,' I grab Ashley and dive to the floor.

Whud!

I no longer think the Desert Eagle is loud. Well, it was, but it's got nothing on being across the room from a damned hand grenade exploding. A swarm of enraged, mentally disturbed hornets descends on me. Not really. Just feels like it. Tiny bits of shrapnel embed themselves all over my body, though thankfully, none are more than annoying. Such a rapid barrage of painful zings stab into me so fast it's like I posted a comment on the internet asking people to be nice to each other.

Not quite sure how to process what just happened, I lay there for a moment on top of Ashley. Her face is probably mushed into my chest, but she's too shocked to make an embarrassing joke about it. About the time I start feeling my heartbeat pulse inside a metric crapload of minor wounds, I decide it's probably time to get the hell out of here.

I push myself up.

Ashley's sprawled out on the floor, hair fanned out above and behind her. She's also peppered with little bleeding wounds, but she's grinning. It's an unsettling 'wow, what a ride, let's do that again' type grin like the first time we went on a rollercoaster.

She raises her arm.

I grab her hand, and pull her up to her feet for the second time in two minutes.

Both of us are covered in gore… but it's not ours. Judging from the condition of the back corner of the room, I think we are wearing Mr. Lime Hair's inside bits. His mangled remains lay draped over the coffee table about ten feet from where he'd been. A red, smeared imprint on the ceiling shows where he hit and bounced away. What's left of him looks like a bloody skeleton with a few bits of gloopy stuff still trapped inside the ribcage. One of his eyeballs dangles from a length of optic nerve, swinging down by his teeth. The other eyeball is… anyone's guess where it landed. Hmm. This amount of destruction to a body seems excessive for a hand grenade. But what do I know? I'm hardly a demolitions expert. Maybe vampires react in weird ways to point blank explosions. Still, near-liquefication of an entire body does stretch the limits of believability for all things here being perfectly normal. Either that grenade was weird (in an occult sort of way) or vampires plus explosives equals oddity. However, he didn't catch fire. The gloopy bits are still gloopy, so he's not permanently dead. On the positive side, he probably didn't feel it.

The more I stare at the mess, the more I'm sure something had to be unusual about that grenade. Maybe the same sort of thing Wolent's guy did to the bomb I used on the nest of Anselme's people. Some glittery anti-vampire agent added to the plastic explosive.

Ashley reaches both hands up and wipes gore away from her eyes. "Wow… is he gonna recover from that?"

"Possibly… in a few months," I deadpan.

COMPLICATED

C hloe wanders over to us, grumbling, "Son of a bitch, piece of shit, cocksucker."

Ashley gasps.

I stare at the child, refusing to accept she knows what those words mean. She heard her parents say them when they were angry and merely repeats them.

Sensing us staring at her, Chloe looks up, then raises her arm. Her hand seems to be draped at an odd, limp angle. "I think the stupid gun broke my wrist."

It's more than a little unnerving to see a kid her age having such a non-reaction to a broken arm. Ugh. This can't be the first time it's happened to her. Overcome by emotion, I drop to a knee and go to wrap my arms around her—but stop myself. I'm a bloody mess and she's not. Chloe makes a cringing sort of face like she isn't too thrilled about me smearing blood all over her, but she'd tolerate the mess in exchange for the hug. Poor kid is totally a love sponge.

"Oops. Promise a hug later. Let me clean up first?" I ask.

She nods once.

Since she's already right in front of me, I check her over for grenade shrapnel. Her clothing appears undamaged, though she's picked up a ton of small, clingy bits of debris from the rug. Some is plant matter tracked in from outside, the rest is lint, yarn bits, and the sort of detritus that gathers on the floor of a house occupied by squatters who don't give a damn about the condition of the place. A quick glance at the room behind her explains her remarkable lack of injury. At the instant the grenade went off, she'd still been on the floor thanks to the giant handgun. The sofa absorbed most of the shrapnel headed her way. I gently grasp her hand and—ack. Yeah, her wrist is definitely broken. All things considered, she got super lucky. Then again, so did Ashley and I.

Lime Hair Guy took most of the blast, having collapsed to the floor on top of the grenade right before it went off. Guess that old thing about soldiers heroically throwing themselves on top of grenades to save their squad mates might really work. Though, the way this guy blew apart into gloopy bones is definitely not normal. I could spend all night wondering how a simple (okay, really big) hand grenade could strip almost all the muscles off a skeleton without pulverizing the bones—but I'm not going to. I have much less interesting and far more depressing things for my brain to get stuck contemplating. No, I'm not talking about watching my family get older. I mean... like... why the hell did they cancel *Firefly!?*

"Ash?" I whisper.

"Yeah?" She walks around to stand in front of me. "Why are you whispering?"

"No idea." I pluck a tiny bit of metal out of my left arm and fling it aside. "What happened? How'd you get noticed?"

She points at the spot where she'd been fighting for her unlife, then walks over beside Slash's inert body. After a second or two to look around, she sticks her foot under his side and kick-flips him away, revealing a moderately large scroll on the floor, which she picks up. "Here it is. I guess they really cared about this thing. As soon as I touched it, they both jumped like I appeared straight out of invisibility. Already had the scroll in my hand so I couldn't really play innocent."

"Ugh." I go to pinch the bridge of my nose, but there's blood all over my hand, so I don't.

The scroll unfurls in her hand, dangling like a window shade, twisting slightly side to side. On one face, neat (but super gothic) handwriting looks like a fairly ordinary type of diplomatic letter that powerful leaders might send each other—in 1498. However, the back of the scroll is about halfway covered with a mixture of strange characters and some writing *not* using normal letters. It kinda looks like written Russian if the Cyrillic character set took massive amounts of LSD. It's sloppy like an amateur making their first attempt at brushing Japanese writing onto paper. Clearly the work of someone in a rush or who doesn't care for perfection. Kinda looks almost childish. I only say this because I'm used to seeing 'magical rituals' done by Sophia and she tends to use crayons a lot. Quill pens dipped in her own blood are a wee bit too dark for my sister. Yes, that's a joke. Her type of magic doesn't even really need ritual stuff. She does it anyway because she thinks it's cool and it helps her concentrate.

So... it does look like these vamps were in the process of tampering with the scroll.

"What do you think this means?" Ashley studies the bizarre scribblings.

"I think it's like that Anime where writing stuff down summons demons." I gesture at the scroll. "If they finished it, anyone looking at that writing would've invoked the spell it contained. Kinda like demonic time bombs."

Ashley frowns at the scroll. "You're sure they didn't finish it?"

I gaze around at the relative calm. "Considering we're not screaming, on fire, or running for our unlives from a demon at the moment, yeah."

Chloe gives a thumbs-up with her intact hand. "We're good. I don't feel scared."

"Hmm." Ashley rolls it back up. "Whatever this is, these guys had enough of an emotional investment in it that me touching it broke whatever hold my power had on their minds."

I start to nod, then glance at her. "Why did you scream like that? I thought you saw a five-headed nopeasaurus."

Chloe blinks. "What the heck is a five-headed nopeasaurus?"

"Exactly what it sounds like." I grimace. "A big monster with five heads."

"Did you see the size of that gun?" asks Ashley. "It scared me."

I gesture at the big guy. "Beelzebubba didn't even go inside until *after* you screamed."

Ashley points at another Desert Eagle on the floor near the fireplace, this one black. "This guy"—she means Slash, who's on the ground right by us—"had one, too."

"Oh. And it's almost funny." I shake my head.

"Funny?" Ashley puts a sticky, bloody hand on my forehead. "Are you feeling okay?"

"Yeah, fine. I mean funny in like how the bad guys almost always have Desert Eagles. Ugh. We really are in an Eighties movie. The only thing missing is Stephen Segal or Jean Claude VanDamme."

Ashley snickers, then points at Beezlebubba, who's still laying where he fell when I attacked him, only he's apparently out cold. "You could call him John Clawed Van Dammit." She pauses, staring at him. "Oh, wow. I've never seen a vampire faint before."

"He didn't faint," says Chloe in a matter-of-fact tone. "I knocked him ta sleep."

I gasp. "You did *what?*"

"Chill out." She rolls her eyes. "He was about to shoot you in the back."

My brain doesn't like the information being fed to it. I peer over at the large form of the guy lying on the rug a few feet inside the front door. Nothing looks weird at first, but after I take a few steps closer and get a look at him from a slightly different angle, I notice a bizarre wooden club stuck to his head, jutting off to the side like a crazy Pablo Picasso version of a bent unicorn's horn. There's some sort of huge screw sticking out of the top end at a ninety-degree angle impaled in his skull. Oh, wait… it's not a club. It's a detachable leg to a fancy dining room table. The other three legs are leaning against the wall right next to the door. And sure enough, he's got a second—much smaller—gun in his left hand. Looks like the kid saw him pointing a gun at me and clobbered him with whatever random junk happened to be in easy reach when she needed a 'bonking stick'.

Talk about unsettling. Guess Chloe does have superhuman strength... or at least more strength than a kid her size should have. We can't tell Mom about this. *I* don't even want to think about her participating in a fight. Mom could not handle it. Chloe's unlife is supposed to be all about dolls, Disney cartoons, and happiness. Not bashing bad guys' brains in with table legs.

Sigh.

What bothers me more is her blasé reaction to everything. She's not crying or even acting upset. Her response to having a broken wrist is moderate annoyance. Like I said, everything about my unlife is completely crazy. Nothing ever goes normal.

Chloe abruptly turns in place, casting a quick glance around the room before staring up at me. "Something is watching us."

Ashley sucks in a bit of air. "Maybe the scroll magic *was* finished?"

I spin, claws out, ready for another idiot. No one here but us and the four downed vampires. "Where?"

"It's hiding out in the woods where it's dark," says Chloe in an unintentionally eerie tone. "Watching us."

"Nothing is dark anymore." Ashley nudges her.

The kid smiles. "I know. It just sounded scarier to say that."

Okay, maybe her eerie tone wasn't unintentional. "Are you messing with us?"

She shakes her head, making her long, black hair dance back and forth. "Nope. I feel a bad monster watching us."

"Maybe it's a sasquatch," I deadpan.

Ashley quirks an eyebrow at me. "Are you being serious?"

"Umm." I shrug. "Yes, and no. All this talk about sasquatches, you know we're going to run into one. It's like a law or something. Talk about it enough and it's *gotta* be part of the story."

She puffs air upward in a futile attempt to chase her hair away from her eyes. "I'm covered in blood. I do not want to remain covered in blood."

Chloe fusses at her hand, tugging it back into place. "Can we go? I'm kinda scared now. The thing is gonna hurt us if we stay here."

I gaze around at the carnage. Wow. Normally, a pair of teenage girls and a little kid don't leave this much blood in their wake outside of Japanese anime movies... or overcrowded Justin Bieber concerts. Thank the Universe I never got into his brand of music.

We hurry across the room and slip out the door. The forest is not dark to my eyes, but it *is* ominous. Can't say for sure if it's because Chloe said something's watching us or there's a definite mood in the air, but it really does feel like eyes are on us.

"Umm," whispers Ashley. "We can't go back to camp like this. We're covered in blood."

"Speak for yourselves," says Chloe.

Ashley boops her on the nose.

A soft *snap* comes from the bones in her wrist as they knit. She swooshes her hand around in an over dramatic mimicry of a high-society debutante. "I'm too fast to get messy."

"What do you suggest?" I ask, glancing at Ashley.

"The usual. Home invasion, borrow someone's shower and washing machinery." She shrugs.

I put a hand on her forehead. "Where is Ashley, and who are you?"

She laughs. "I'm still me. Just being practical. I figure we either do that and wash our bloody clothes... or we strip naked, burn the clothing in a fire pit so no one finds it and calls the cops, then come up with an explanation for why we're not wearing anything if anyone catches us streaking back into the campsite. Oh, and we will need to be quiet so the 'rents or Littles don't see us before we can get dressed."

Squirm. "Home invasion it is."

BY SOME MIRACLE, NO MONSTER CAME RUNNING OUT OF THE WOODS before we took off.

Huh. Maybe it was a sasquatch checking us out. We fly to a residential area of Crescent City, pick a house that doesn't show any obvious signs of having children or a large family living inside, and go in via the back door. Crazy how many people leave their doors unlocked.

To prevent any sort of complications, I decide to go to the master bedroom and charm the homeowner right away, rather than trying to use the shower and laundry machines and simply hoping they don't wake up. Last thing I need is some suburban Rambo-wannabe coming after us with a gun.

Turns out there's a not-quite-elderly couple here. It's really easy to invade the minds of mortals who are sleeping. Doesn't take much effort for me to give them both a compulsion to ignore any strange sounds they become aware of and just stay asleep until morning. Making things even easier is us having zero interest in harming anyone here. No need to overpower any primordial need for self-preservation. That done, we retreat toward the bathroom.

Conveniently enough, there's a small alcove in the hall containing a mini washer and dryer. This place doesn't seem to have a basement, so the appliances are on the ground floor. It's impractical for us to wash our clothes in separate cycles—we don't have enough time before sunrise—so, Ashley and I strip and stuff everything in the washer. We got blasted with so much gore even our underwear is bloody. Since we're both in our birthday suits already, we decide to shower together. Not the first time we've done that, and the reasons are almost the same: we both got covered with something unpleasant. As kids, it was skunk spray once, dog poo another time, automotive grease once, mud a few times... So, yeah, we're basically used to it. No awkwardness whatsoever.

Chloe sets Jesse Stroud's skull atop the washing machine to stand guard, then follows us into the bathroom, opining on how 'dumb' showering is compared to taking a bath. Her logic is sound: it's much more difficult to play with toy ducks in a shower. I don't remember how old I was when I made the transition to mostly showering instead of taking baths—at least when my goal is cleaning. I still take plenty of baths, but they're for relaxation. And right now, relaxation couldn't be farther from my mind.

Trying to be fast and quiet, Ashley and I rinse bone fragments and brain matter out of our hair, then proceed to pluck bits of shrapnel out of each other's backs where we can't reach them ourselves. Foreign objects like that do eventually work their own way out of a vampire's body, but it's significantly faster to pluck stuff out manually. It also itches *much* less. Chloe eventually gets bored of watching us and wanders out, saying something about it being time to move the clothes to the dryer.

I was wrong. The number of little fragments we absorbed is way more than 'a few dozen.' The wounds are relatively minor and close as soon as the invading metal is removed. We gather the fragments into a pile to take with us when we leave. To say the two of us 'hustle' is putting it mildly. We have to make ourselves look presentable and get out of here as fast as possible while doing everything we can not to leave evidence behind. As potentially unlikely as it is the authorities will even investigate this house, there's no reason to be slapdash. Also, the 'forces of evil' might follow us here via paranormal means. Everything we can do in order to distance the people who live here from our mess, we have to do.

Once we are free from shrapnel and gore, I cut the water. To avoid leaving wet towel evidence, we decide to just stand around in the hallway by the laundry machines air-drying. Chloe sits cross-legged on the floor by the dryer, holding the skull like she's playing with one of those magic eight-ball things. Hanging out naked in a stranger's house would be embarrassing except for my full confidence anyone who sees us will not remember doing so. When the dryer is three-quarters done, my patience runs out. I interrupt it by yanking the door open. Ash and I hurry into our still-sorta-damp-and-hot clothing.

"The man woke up," says Chloe. "He heard you guys in the bathroom, but I made him forget seeing me."

I pause, shirt halfway on, peering at her through a shrapnel hole in the fabric. "What? He woke up? How? I zapped him to stay sleeping."

"Not him." Chloe points down the hall. "Another man in a different room. He's gonna forget."

"Oh…" I finish pulling my shirt into place. "Good."

"You wanna check my homework?" She grins.

"Should I?" I tilt my head and run my hands down my wet hair, squeezing out a few more drops.

"It's probably okay, but better to be sure." She grins at me.

Heh. She's not afraid she messed up. She's proud and wants to show off what she did. Okay. I can work with that. I pat her on the head and follow her to a smaller bedroom I completely missed noticing before due to my rush. If I had to guess, I'd say the couple's young twenty-something son still lives with them. Both he and the room look pretty normal. I head over to the bed, peel one of his eyes open, and dive in.

I don't find any trace of his waking up or seeing any of us left in his memory, though I do pick up on a faint, almost dreamlike hint of hearing girls talk. He probably heard us in the shower and came to investigate. The guy would've come out of his doorway to find Chloe sitting by the washer and dryer. It's pretty impressive there's no trace of that memory left in his head. Spotting a strange little girl talking to a fanged human skull in the middle of your house at four in the morning isn't the sort of sight many people would react well to. Chloe's so pale that in the dim bluish moonlight his mortal eyes would've registered, she'd totally have looked like a spectral phantom.

Yet… this guy doesn't even remember waking up.

Nice work, kiddo.

I lift my thumb, allowing his eyelid to snap shut, then give her a big smile. "Perfectly done."

She beams.

I'm simultaneously proud of her and a little creeped out. Wonder if this is why Stefano has it in for me? Looking innocent and harmless really can be a weapon. Chloe could do so much damage if she wanted to… and didn't have the mind of a child. Honestly, it's a good thing child vampires remain mentally the same age. She will always be sweet and innocent with the directness and honesty of a little kid. The idea of someone like her remaining outwardly small while developing into a mental adult is truly horrifying. Not only would they suffer the frustrations of having desires and urges their body couldn't cope with... a devious adult could use a childlike appearance to get away with all sorts of bad things.

Ugh. I don't want to think about it.

The Universe likes simple. It makes sense. Looks like a child, *is* a child. If something has the outward appearance of a child but the mind of a grown adult, it's a demon. They do crap like that. Though, from what I've heard, if a demon pretends to be a kid to mess with mortals, it's all ghosty and hard to see. Just voices and random sounds.

Right. Creepy thoughts need to stop. We're in someone else's house and the sun's going to be up soon.

"Final re-check," I whisper.

While Ashley does a sweep of the bathroom to make sure we didn't leave evidence, I stick my head into the washer and dryer. Nope. No one forgot anything. Not like we had socks on to lose. Oops. There are a few bits of shrapnel in the dryer. I grab them and add them to the stash we collected from the bathtub. These, we can toss randomly somewhere in the woods on the way back to camp.

Once we're satisfied this house is in exactly the same state as it was when we arrived—less a small amount of soap and a slightly higher reading on the water meter—we leave. As fast as we're able to fly, we race back to our temporary 'home'. Okay, we get lost a bit... but not for too long. And hey, the extra minute or four of flying near top speed helps dry our hair. Eventually, Ashley spots a familiar tree and we use it to locate the campsite. My internal clock is screaming at me. We have mere minutes left before sunrise.

What a night. Ugh.

The three of us hurry into the trailer, attempting to be as quiet as possible. Nothing looks out of place. Parents and littles are all asleep in their beds. Blix is awake, sitting on the little table in the middle of the trailer playing the PSP. He waves at us.

I open the cushioned 'bench' atop our sleeping box.

Ashley steps in. We don't have time to change, nor do we really care. Once we're out, we're *out*. Damp clothing won't be uncomfortable. "So… just a quick trip to get a bite, huh?"

I lower myself to sit. "Something like that, yeah."

Chloe floats into the air, drifts over the wall of the box, then glides down to land, snuggling between us—after setting Jesse's skull at the foot end of our little chamber. Uh oh. Please tell me she isn't going to want to keep that as a friend. We need to burn it before the authorities discover it. Vampire skulls have some rather unexplainable bits of anatomy. I'm sure most people casually looking at it will think it's fake. The problem is if the authorities get it and start doing tests.

"Something like that." Ashley chuckles.

I lie flat and pull the lid down. "Stuff sure loves to get complicated."

11

DIMENSIONAL DOORWAYS FOR DUMMIES

A s beautiful as the forest is, there are only so many possible activities while camping in it.

Guess what one of the most common ones is? Yeah. Hiking. It's currently about twenty after three in the afternoon. Ashley and I are begrudgingly awake and stumbling along the Grove of Titans hiking trail with the family as part of a guided tour group of about twenty tourists and three guides. It's not like a museum, though. Our guides aren't stopping every two minutes to talk about the significance of what we're seeing. They're here mostly to keep people safe and from getting lost. Chloe's got it easy. Dad's carrying her. She's still out. Her pink hooded sweatshirt is more or less enough to keep anyone from noticing she doesn't look quite right.

A keen observer might mistake her for a dead body.

However, as anyone with a brain knows, dead people don't move. All Dad needs to do is jostle her awake, and she'd look normal again. The girl is pale as heck normally, so we can blame any perceived ghastliness on a trick of the light. Maybe it's taking needless risks, but it's not like we will see any of these people again.

Due to our grogginess, Ashley and I are more or less at the end of the procession. The tour guides think we are sluggish and trailing behind because we stayed up too late thanks to trouble falling asleep. I am somewhat more alert than Ash, mostly due to being older as a vampire. Her determination to 'hurry up and tolerate the daytime' is stronger than mine was at the same 'age'. I didn't know what my body was capable of back then, meaning: I thought a bright day would forever keep me trapped inside. Never imagined an Innocent could develop their powers enough to function pretty much normally in the day. Since she has me to use as a reference, she's working on it. If things keep on going for me the way they have so far, I'll eventually be able to laugh off the sun except for the mandatory sleep time.

It isn't exactly an epic vampire superpower, like turning into wolves or ravens, charming a whole room of people, or using magic—but hey, it's perfect for me. I'm happy.

So, yeah. We do the nature thing. We walk. The tourists around me are all like 'Hey, there's trees and wow are they big'.

"Did you know that park rangers can get in trouble if escaped convicts hide in their forests?" asks Dad in a voice low enough that only our family (mostly) can hear him.

Sam smiles, knowing what's coming. Sierra tenses up like a pilot preparing to do a high-G turn.

Sophia, all innocence, looks up at him. "Really? Why?"

"Because it's 'arboring a fugitive,'" says Dad.

Sierra lets out a cry of 'auugh!' worthy of Charlie Brown.

Mom groans.

Sam keeps smiling.

Blix facepalms, then shakes his head.

"Wow," whispers Ashley. "That was bad, even for him."

Sophia blinks at us, confused for another eight seconds, before she realizes Dad was telling a joke. As soon as she gets it, she rolls her eyes, huffs, then starts giggling. Her laughter is all the reward Dad needs to flash a broad smile of punny triumph.

Pardon my lack of enthusiasm—either for the puns or the theoretical magnificence of nature all around us. I'm not awake all the way. And, well, trees are trees no matter how huge they happen to be. I can only summon so much excitement for being out in the woods.

For me, this trip is entirely about spending time with the family. Maybe it's got something to do with my recent supernatural experiences, too. After all, a hike through the woods doesn't exactly get the blood pumping in comparison to having a swarm of angry vampires trying to tear my head off. Don't get me wrong. I'm not complaining. I'd much rather be hiking in some boring-ass woods than fighting desperately for my unlife. Just… I don't understand how Dad can get literally excited about it. Then again, he works from home as a computer programmer and doesn't go out too often. His reaction to a camping trip in the woods is on par with those videos where like cows that have spent their whole lives inside barns finally see grass for the first time. Guess it does make sense in a way.

Conversation going on in front of me mostly consists of people ooh-ing and ahh-ing at the sheer size of the redwood trees, except for the Littles. Leave it to my family to be the weird ones. Sophia's on the hunt for faeries while Sam and Sierra keep talking about sasquatch sightings. No matter how often Sam pauses to stare into the woods 'thinking he just saw bigfoot,' Sophia gets freaked out each and every time.

Eventually, Sierra seems to feel guilty about making Soph whine and beg them to stop scaring her, so she switches gears. "We're more likely to see faeries out here than a bigfoot."

This elicits a squeal of glee from Sophia. Sam takes the hint as well. Like any good little brother, he enjoys teasing his sisters to a point, but he won't push it too far. Sophia has clearly had enough about sasquatch.

"Blix thinks there could be faeries around," says Sam after a minute or so of walking without saying a word.

The imp, perched on his back, tilts his head, ears flopping in an 'I most certainly said no such thing' sort of manner.

"Ooh," chirps Sophia.

At her immediate shift from fearful to happy, Blix makes an 'oh, okay' face, then whisper-babbles at Sam. I don't understand demonic —and I'm still not sure how the hell Sam does—but I'm guessing he's telling my little brother that there aren't any faeries around here.

I'm not really sure what about Bigfoot scares Sophia so much. It's not like the folklore makes him-slash-them out to be dangerous monsters who bludgeon unsuspecting tourists to death all the time. The most credible accounts of sasquatch sightings are pretty much all the same: a fleeting glimpse of a furry man-shaped thing hauling ass away from the humans. Okay, I think there might have been one story about a couple guys who hid inside a cabin or some such thing while 'unknown large creatures' outside made a whole bunch of noise and hit the walls of the structure. Who's to say if those creatures were actual sasquatches, something else, or the story is entirely made up. The two guys who claim to have been trapped in the cabin for hours by these things never got a direct look at them. It could easily have been some manner of angry spirits rather than a physical creature—or even an elaborate hoax.

Anyway, my point is, little about the sasquatch folklore suggests they would pose an immediate threat to a large group of people walking through the woods.

"Maybe it's the fuzziness," I say out loud without intending to. I blame being half-asleep.

"What about fuzziness?" asks Mom.

Everyone (meaning my family) peers back at me expectantly. That statement is likely the first words I've spoken today since waking up, so it got attention. I'm suddenly on the spot and lack the mental faculties to construct a believable diversion, so my traitorous brain simply continues blurting truth.

"Why Sophia is weirdly afraid of Bigfoot."

"Staaaahp!" wails Sophia. "I don't wanna think about them."

"Sarah..." Mom gestures at the kitten perched on Soph's shoulder. "Your sister isn't afraid of things because they're fuzzy. Look at Klepto."

"She likes bunnies, too," adds Sam.

Sierra whips a small rock off into the woods, bouncing it off a distant tree trunk with an echoing 'thok' noise. "It's size."

A nearby guide gives her an annoyed look but decides against scolding her. Guess every kid gets one free thrown rock before they are in trouble.

"Size?" asks Mom.

"Yeah." Sierra stuffs her hands in her pockets. "Anything fuzzy over thirty pounds scares her."

Sam tilts his head, his expression contemplative.

"What's on your mind, kiddo?" asks Dad.

"Something I don't want to say out loud because it will scare Sophia." Sam continues pondering.

Sophia looks down and sighs. "Go ahead. Say it. Thanks for the warning."

Sam shrugs in a 'well, okay, you asked me to' sort of way, then looks at dad. "I'm evaluating Sierra's theory about weight. How much does Fuzzydoom weigh? What's the mass of a large sphere consisting mostly of hair and extreme contempt for life?"

"George The Animal Steele weighed 275 pounds," says Dad.

The Littles all ask 'who?' at the same time. The name sounds kinda familiar but I still can't place it.

Dad chuckles. "Teasing. He was a wrestler back when they still called it the WWF."

"Ugh." Sophia rolls her eyes.

"Hair can get kinda heavy." I ponder stupid things... like exactly how much of Fuzzydoom is hair. Does he have a little nugget of meat somewhere inside? Or is he all fuzz?

Sierra swipes her hair away from her eyes, tucking it behind one ear. "Maybe it isn't entirely based on weight. A giant ball has the appearance of being heavy, so it counts as scary."

"C'mon, guys," says Sophia in a whispery whine. "Please stop talking about me like you're narrating a documentary about the kid who's afraid of everything. I'm right here."

Sam turns to walk backward so he can face her. "Are you afraid of being the subject of a documentary?"

She smirks. "No."

He smiles. "Then you aren't afraid of *everything.*"

Sophia starts to sigh but ends up sorta laughing. Sam spins a 180 again to walk like a normal person.

The 'rents hug her. Sam gives her a shoulder squeeze. Sierra lightly punches her on the arm (that's basically a hug).

Okay, feeling a bit more awake now. I take a deep breath and look up and around. "Wow... these giant trees really are huge. Feels like something straight out of a fantasy movie. Where are the elves?"

"Seriously," says Dad.

"Right here." Sierra gestures both hands at Sophia like a game show hostess displaying the prize.

Mom sighs. "Don't give her any ideas. If any of you kids sprout pointy ears, it better be temporary."

"Relax, mom." Sierra pokes herself in the belly. "I'm just teasing Dad about giving us all skinny genes."

Sophia squirms, almost guiltily at Mom basically telling her not to enchant anyone to appear more elven than we already do.

Her reaction gets me thinking once again of the strange ritual Sophia did not too long ago and wondering what the heck she did to herself.

"Sure does look like there ought to be elves living up there." Dad shields his eyes and gazes into the treetops. "I can just picture all the walkways and such."

"They're elves, not Ewoks," mutters Sierra. "And they're probably hiding from the bigfoot."

Sophia gives off a strangled 'meep' sound. The noise started as a wail of fear mixed with exasperation and cut off in a resigned huff of annoyance. It seems she's realized what Sierra is trying to do. The constant bringing up of sasquatch isn't meant to torment her but to oversaturate the topic and maybe get her to stop being scared. At least, this is me guessing. It's not like Sierra to be mean on purpose.

"Yeah, yeah," mutters Sophia.

Dad starts rambling about certain tribes of wood elves who live in elevated villages, compared to the more traditional high elves who construct cities like the one shown in the *Lord of the Rings* movie.

Leave it to him to interrupt our relaxing vacation with a nerdcore discussion on the differentiations between various elven subgroups.

"They're more afraid of us than you are of them." Sam smiles.

"Elves are afraid of people?" Ashley scratches her head.

"No, I mean bigfoot." Sam picks up a tennis-ball-sized rock.

"I really doubt that." Sophia emits a nervous laugh.

The guide near us starts giving Sam 'the look.' My brother's oblivious to the man watching him. However, he simply gives the stone a light toss, as if his goal was simply to remove the obstruction from the hiking trail. Seeming surprised, the guide raises both eyebrows at him. What boy his age would *not* throw such a prize rock as hard as he could into a tree? Yeah, my family's a bit offbeat.

"These trees are making me feel like I got shrunk again." Sierra nearly falls over backward while trying to stare up at the treetops.

Dad chuckles. "Sure does."

"Don't sound so excited," mutters Mom. "That was dangerous, not an adventure."

"It was a dangerous adventure." Dad holds up a finger.

The guide watching my siblings in case any of them throws another rock probably thinks we're crazy… or talking about a game.

We keep walking the trail. Over the next like twenty minutes or so, the chatter going on between the Littles and the 'rents veers back to the normal sorts of topics a family hiking around here might discuss. The nearby tour guide fills in some answers when Dad starts guessing wildly—specifically in response to Sierra wondering *how* these trees got so big. They're legit like something from an alien planet. According to the guide, the giant sequoia trees aren't aliens. They are so big because they live for an extremely long time and also grow fast. The guide tells us all about how the Sierra snowpack accumulates over the winter months, then melts into the earth, supplying these trees with water.

Ugh. This is supposed to be vacation, not school. Feels like I'm on a field trip. Sam and Sophia listen intently, both of them—plus Dad—absorbing the sciency stuff eagerly. Sophia's got a disgruntled expression, but she's still paying attention.

A few minutes after the science lesson, Sophia stops short, staring off to her left. Her mannerisms are pretty much the same as a small plains rabbit catching a fleeting glimpse of a leopard too close for comfort. It's the same sort of reaction most prey animals have upon sensing the approach of a higher order predator... or most people have upon sensing the approach of children looking for donations for their sports team.

I expect her to either resume walking—albeit faster—or panic. Surprisingly, after three seconds, Sophia darts off the trail into the woods. Sam and Sierra chase her, no doubt curious to find out what got her attention. I zoom after the Littles as well, but my intention is more 'capture and contain' than exploration.

"Don't go too far off the trail, guys," calls Dad.

Mom adds, "And don't tear open any dimensional gateways."

A few nearby tourists and the guides laugh. That's cute. They think Mom's being funny and making a joke. I agree with her. We really don't need to visit alternate worlds every time we take a vacation.

Kids going off the approved trail is enough cause for the entire hiking party to come to a stop and wait. About thirty feet from the path, Sophia stops and turns in place, scanning the area.

Sam and Sierra skid to a halt beside her. It's daytime, thus I am merely mortal, and lag behind a few steps.

"What's up?" asks Sam.

"Soph? You okay?" Sierra edges closer to her, ready to jump between her and whatever might be out there.

I jog up behind them, half tempted to grab the three of them in one big armful to carry back to the trail. Alas, I am not presently strong enough to do that. "What the heck are you running off for?"

"She saw a faerie," says Ashley from behind me.

"No..." Sophia continues turning around, staring at the air. "There was something here... like a doorway. I saw it for a second and it flashed away."

Crap. I hang my head. "What kind of doorway?"

"I dunno." She shrugs. "A patch of glowing light like a door. I'm not gonna try to open it again, but... I'm sure an entity crossed over here."

"Which way?" asks Sierra. "Entering or leaving?"

Sophia scrunches her nose, looks around in a full circle one more time, then shrugs again. "Can't tell. If it entered our world, it's either really fast or invisible. I don't see anything."

"Is it a problem?" I ask.

"Umm." Sophia digs the toe of her sneaker into the ground. "I'd say 'no idea,' but this is us we're talking about, so… probably."

I put an arm around her. "C'mon, let's get back to the trail before the tour guides have apoplexy."

"What's apoplexy?" asks Sierra.

"It's a fancy word for getting angry," says Sam in a blank tone. "I assume you don't mean they'd suffer a sudden loss of control over their bodies due to a blood vessel rupturing."

Sierra gives him side eye. "What… do you read the dictionary for fun?"

"Sometimes," deadpans Sam.

It's impossible to tell if he's serious or messing with us. But, honestly, how many ten-year-olds know what apoplexy is? Hell, I didn't even know it had anything to do with aneurysms… just thought it meant having a fit of anger so bad you forgot how to speak for a few seconds.

Anyway…

I usher the Littles back to the trail. We go with the cover story of her thinking she saw a faerie. Of course, no one—except possibly the 'rents—takes it literally. If their expressions are any indication, the other tourists and the guides think she's being an adorable kid with an overactive imagination.

After the nearby guide cautions her on the dangers of running off alone, the hike resumes.

"Probably bigfoot," says Sam like ten minutes later.

"What?" asks Sophia and Sierra at the same time.

"Crossing over." Sam goes out of his way to step on a small boulder sitting beside the trail, then veers back. "Maybe the reason they're so hard to find is they live in an alternate dimension where humans didn't evolve the same way and they stray across into our world every now and then."

"Eep," whispers Sophia.

"There's a thought. They're probably so bewildered by ending up here, they're too scared to do anything but run home." I pat Sophia on the shoulder, trying to reassure her.

"Or..." Sierra spins to walk backward so she can smile at all of us. "What if the bigfoot are really super intelligent and they are coming back here to study us?"

Well, she's successfully shifted the idea of sasquatch from scary to humorous. At least for now.

I glance back over my shoulder in the general direction of where Sophia spotted a 'portal.' No idea if she really saw something or experienced an anxiety-induced hallucination. Maybe sunlight reflected off a tree and looked like a portal. I suppose it's possible she really might've observed a magical effect. The portals could be like ghosts... only certain people can see them. My ability to see spirits goes away while I'm offline, so I can't tell for sure what went on there.

Grr. I really hope it's nothing to worry about.

Somehow, I have a feeling we won't have too long to wait to know for sure.

12

FUZZY NOT QUITE DOOM

O ther than the portal sighting—which may or may not have even been a portal sighting—the hike was relaxing.

Even while offline, physical activity doesn't tire me out. Same goes for Ashley and Chloe. Well, hiking generally doesn't tire out ordinary seven-year-olds either. The Littles, being between ten and twelve, tolerated it fine. Mom and Dad, not so much. A most-of-the-afternoon hike sounds great on paper, but to people who spend the majority of their time working desk jobs, it's a bit of a shock.

This leads into the second purpose for choosing camping as a vacation: relaxation.

Mom and Dad stretch out in their folding chairs, recovering from all the walking while Ashley and I deal with the chore of cooking dinner and feeding everyone. Thanks to the nonzero chance of random strangers seeing us, Ashley, Chloe, and I also eat. This camping trip isn't exactly going to win any awards for health food. Hot dogs, burgers, and trail mix are the staples.

So yeah. Dinner and sitting around the campsite staring at the sky, trees, each other, and my no-signal-having iPhone fills the rest of the day. At least it's dark. I feel better being online. Honestly, I've kinda been on edge ever since Sophia ran after the portal she thought she saw. It's so unlike her to charge *toward* something unknown. I still haven't figured out what to make of her doing that.

As wonderful as this time with my family is, the part of me which remains very much a teenager gets a tiny bit grumbly over this trip. I miss Hunter and hanging out with Michelle and Tilloa. Ashley's kinda migrated from best friend to legit sister now. What we lacked in a genuine blood connection (not being related to each other) we've made up for with immortality. Her essentially moving in with us is the final step toward our assimilating her into the Wright clan.

I kinda feel a little bad for her mom. Maybe we'll do the Old World thing and have Mrs. Carter also move in with us. Dad said something last month about how connected families back in Medieval times would often live together. If anyone doubts our commitment, just know that I'm also now going to their house and helping Ashley clean it... as well as mine. The two of us can do an entire week's worth of cleaning in one night. Mrs. Carter is certainly happy to be free from that chore.

Yeah, bleh. Teenage selfishness. One week away from my friends and boyfriend is hardly anything to be upset over. This is family time. Almost as soon as I realize I'm being grumbly, I set those emotions aside. A bit of guilt seeps in to replace it, reminding me how little time we have left together. Little compared to immortality, anyway. As a family unit, we have maybe five years left. Sierra will turn eighteen and possibly go to college. Not sure if she'll go out of state or not. Perhaps she would have before the supernatural monkey wrench fell into the Wright Family Gearworks. I'm pretty sure she's committed to sticking close to home now to help protect Sophia as well as the parents from whatever tries to eat me.

Either way, it won't be all that long before the Littles are adults. The older they get, the more independence they'll probably want. I am the weird one, of course. What eighteen-year-old in her right mind wants to stay living at home? What kid my age thinks of it as 'home' instead of 'the parents' house'? Hmm. I guess it doesn't technically become 'the parents' house' until one moves out to their own place. Since I've never had my own place, it's still 'home' to me.

And yeah, I'm lame. I don't wanna leave.

Now I'm wondering again about the weird stuff as it relates to my family being a family. Sophia's magic did something to Sierra. Somehow, she ended up with boosted strength, speed, and toughness like she'd recently taken a hit of vampire blood… without the blood. Good thing, that. She'd started to develop an addiction, not to the blood itself but to being boosted. Perhaps giving her a 'permanent high' isn't the best way to cure an addiction, but at least she won't suffer withdrawal, or worse—not be boosted when the Forces of Evil™ try to tear her head off.

Sophia's pretty sure the enchantment had an effect on Sierra's lifespan since she used vampires as a focal point for the magic. She's not certain if Sierra is going to age gradually over some extended timeframe, freeze at age twelve, or become whatever the universe considers to be an 'adult' and then stop seeming older. It could be any of those options or even none of them.

Ugh. My life.

A sudden mental image forms where we're all standing around at some future event—like Sam's wedding—where everyone's older except for Sierra who's still twelve and standing in the midst of the family picture with this little black cloud over her head. It's cartoony and momentarily hilarious until it isn't. She would totally resent being stuck as a kid for an extended time. Though, even if that is how the magic worked on her, it's not like she's in Chloe's situation. She *will* grow up… eventually. However, if she's growing up super slow, we're going to have to deal with it. Fortunately, some kids go through high school and stay small. She's not *so* little that she'd stand out as paranormally weird if she's the same size when she graduates high school. We had a kid in my class who looked like he was legit ten years old despite being eighteen. Poor guy. Everyone picked on him. Sure, they laugh now. But when they're all fifty and Joey Marshall still looks like he's twenty-five, he'll be the one laughing.

So, not quite as delicate a situation as hiding Chloe from the world.

Still, it's weird. And I know Sierra's going to be pissed. Like most kids, she *can't wait* to grow up and be an adult. Doesn't matter how often Dad cautions us to enjoy it while we can before we end up over forty and wishing we were teenagers again. It's totally like her, though, to bristle at being told she can't do something. Like, Sophia's magic telling her she can't grow up fast is the same as Mom telling Sierra she can't stay up until midnight yet.

Yes, we're weird now.

I mean, we were kinda weird before, but this is legitimately weird, not merely offbeat.

"What's the point of camping if we can't pee on trees?" asks Sam.

"The boy's a philosopher." Dad chuckles.

"Eww, gross!" whisper-shouts Chloe.

I look up from my phone screen. Thankfully, the conversation is a merely theoretical discussion of the concept of tree-peeing and not anything happening. Sam is still sitting on a cooler box near the campfire, in no danger of watering any local foliage.

"He's only teasing Mom." I grin at Chloe.

Sam fidgets a stick at the edge of the campfire. "I'm not teasing her as much as questioning the nature of what people consider civilized. Do you think sasquatches have bathrooms?"

Mom stares at him. It's rare to see her stumped for a response.

The question gets Ashley giggling. She is no doubt imagining a secret network of concealed forest outhouses used by large furry beings that has thus far escaped the notice of humanity.

Chloe jumps to her feet, staring into the woods. "Something's coming."

Everyone gets quiet.

I listen for a moment, tuning out a dozen different voices from other campsites. Nothing stands out as a suspicious or dangerous to my ears. "I don't hear anything."

"I don't either." Chloe peers up at me, her expression genuinely worried. "I feel it. It wants to hurt us."

"Oh, no," says Sophia in a brittle voice that wavers in time with her body shaking. "It knows I saw it. I found the portal, so it's gonna come after me."

Dad stands with a grunt, leaning a bit to one side on his sore legs. He faces the direction Chloe stared at, as if to intercept whatever might come running out of the trees toward us. He's not only exhausted, he's mortal. I can't let him be the first thing an angry monster gets to, so I glide out of my seat, flying over the campfire to land beside and a bit in front of him. Ashley zooms up on his other side.

"Uh oh," says Sam.

"What?" rasps Mom. "Do you feel something evil coming, too?"

"Yeah." He looks at her. "I gotta poop."

Mom groans. Sierra starts laughing. Sophia whimpers.

Boys. Why does everything end up being either a fart or poop joke? I swear.

We stand there in tense silence for almost a minute. Finally, a crackling noise comes from the woods like a huge, heavy beast moving around. Sophia draws in a gasp, clutching her hands at her chin. Poor kid. She's shaking so hard she could churn milk to butter right in the bottle by holding it.

Motion catches my eye.

A bear, up on its hind legs, ambles out of the trees.

"Bigfoot!" shouts Sophia right before she sprints away, screaming like she's got Jason Voorhees on her heels.

Oh, for crying out loud…

I look back and forth between her and the bear, unable to decide between staying to shoo the animal away or chasing after her.

"Sophia! Stop!" yells Mom. "It's only a bear."

"This supports your theory of weight and size exacerbating the scariness of fuzzy for Sophia," says Sam in a clinical tone.

Dad yanks his folding chair off the ground, snapping it closed, then raising it like a weapon.

Ugh. Really? That's a large bear. It's not gonna notice an aluminum chair. "No, Dad. That'll only make it angry."

"Soph. It's Not Bigfoot," shouts Sam, hands cupped around his mouth. "Bear."

"Umm, that's not better." Sierra backs up, her voice quiet and heavy with nerves. "Actually, it's worse. A bigfoot would run away from us."

"I got this." Ashley steps toward the bear. "Hey, buddy. What's up?"

Head tilted, the bear seems curious about the (comparatively) tiny red-haired human approaching it. A few seconds later, it drops to stand on all fours, sniffing at her almost like a dog.

The rest of us—except Sophia, who's still running off screaming—stand there silently watching this exchange.

"Sorry we invaded your home." Ashley brushes a hand across the bear's cheek. "We won't be here long. You should try to avoid people. They're stupid and can hurt you if they get scared."

Mom swallows, then advances toward the bear, stopping about halfway between Dad and Ashley. She definitely seems like she wants to chase after Sophia, but is perhaps afraid the bear will go after her if she runs. She's doing the thing some animals do, putting herself in front of the dangerous predator in hopes of distracting it away from her babies.

"Can I pet him?" asks Chloe.

"No, he bites," I whisper.

"So do I." Chloe folds her arms.

"Aww, that's okay, buddy." Ashley pets the bear, getting all sorts of friendly with him like he's an ordinary pet someone brought to the vet clinic. Somehow, the bear tolerates this without mauling her.

I'm nervous, but not too much so. A light-to-moderate mauling from a bear is not too big a deal for us. Worst part would be having to replace the clothing destroyed... and likely being blood-hungry.

It takes Ashley only a few more minutes to essentially smoothtalk the bear into wandering off and leaving us alone. Once it's disappeared back into the forest, she turns to face us, hands on her hips, and grins.

"Simply amazing," says Dad. "Looks like you got a critical roll on your animal handling check."

Sierra sighs. "Dad, she's a vampire, not a D&D character."

"Pooping..." Sam stiff-legs it to the trailer and goes inside.

"Aww." Chloe pouts. "I wanted to pet the bear."

"So, uhh... how the heck did you *talk* a bear into leaving us alone?" Sierra scrunches her nose. "Since when are you Dr. Doolittle?"

Ashley snickers. "I dunno. Guess my charm stuff works on animals, too. Maybe it's 'cause I was so into animals before?"

"Or you're just so adorable even bears can't bring themselves to hurt you." I wag my eyebrows at her.

Ash looks around for a pinecone or something harmless to throw at me, but ends up laughing, too.

Mom backs away from the spot where the bear appeared, not fully trusting it won't pull an abrupt about-face and come right back. "Sarah, would you please go collect Sophia before she gets hurt?"

I glance in the direction she ran off. The sounds of her continuing to run tell me she's not hurt, merely terrified. "Yeah. On it. Be right back."

THE WEIRDEST TRUTH BOMB

Some people might judge my parents for not freaking out and running after Sophia themselves.

I can see why they'd react that way. However, they don't know the truth about our family dynamic. Mom knows I can find Sophia super easily. Not only can I fly much faster than a normal person can run, all my vampiric traits like night vision, heightened senses, and so on make finding someone in the dark easy. Mom or Dad wouldn't be able to run effectively at all without smashing into trees over and over. The forest around the campsite is seriously dark to mortal eyes. Vampires are pros at hunting people. It's especially easy to find them when our quarry is alone in the woods and making a lot of noise.

After all, vampires are predatory in nature. Even if we're not primarily focused on *killing* our prey, hunting is pretty high up in our skill set.

It's surprising how much distance Sophia has put between herself and the campsite. She set a new world record for fastest mile barefoot through the woods in the dark. Hmm, from the sound of it, she's not sprinting anymore. Terror has given way to fear. When she comes into view up ahead, she's standing more or less still while staring around at the woods making an 'oh crap, I messed up and got myself lost' face.

My sister is surprisingly free of 'damage.' By that, I mean she has none of the cuts, scrapes, dirt smudges, and so on one would expect from a blind panic flight into the forest at night. It's obvious from the way she's looking around that she can't see much of anything. I'm at a loss to explain how she managed to run so far without crashing into a tree or wiping out after tripping over a root or some such thing. She's breathing super hard, practically doubled over. Yeah, she seriously panicked. Her hauling ass away from the campsite was not a conscious decision.

She doesn't even react to me gliding closer. To avoid scaring the hell out of her by a sudden appearance right in her face, I call her name while I'm still like twenty feet away.

"Sare?" asks Sophia in a whisper. "I'm here."

"I know. I can see you."

Sophia takes a huge breath, then sighs it out. "Duh. Of course you can. Where are you?"

"About to land next to you. Don't freak."

"Too late." She frowns. "Been there, done that already."

I land beside her and put an arm around her. Naturally, she startles, but having expected me to be there, doesn't scream.

"Sorry," she whispers.

"It's okay. You got yourself all worked up over Bigfoot. I figured either something like this or a nightmare was going to happen."

"I feel like a derp," she mutters.

"Don't." I give her a squeeze. "The bear did kinda look like Fuzzydoom. This big, sorta-round ball of fur. It's poking you in a primal fear you've had ever since you were little."

She slouches. "Doesn't make me feel any less dumb. I shouldn't be afraid of bears. I can magic them to be nice."

"If you can stay calm enough. Your magic doesn't work if you're freaking out."

Sophia bites her lip. "True. I still feel like a derp. Am I in trouble?"

"No. Mom's just worried about you."

"Whew." Sophia looks at me—or at least points her face in my general direction. It's pitch black here to her. "The bear's gone?"

"Yep."

"Good. Can we go back to camp now? It's scary out here."

"Yeah."

"Umm." Sophia fidgets. "It's not really the fuzzy that scared me. I felt bad energy, too."

"Too?"

"Yeah." She nods. "Like Chloe. Before the bear showed up, like... *evil* was in the woods watching us. It got stronger and stronger, like an invisible demon creeping up on us waiting to attack. It felt like it wanted to destroy us and cause as much pain as possible."

"Sam did have to go to the bathroom," I deadpan.

"Ugh." She gags, then shoves at me. "No, I'm being serious. I was super scared of that feeling. When the bear popped out of the trees, I panicked. So scared I didn't even see it as a bear, just a big furry monster."

"Right..." I scoop her up to carry.

"My legs still work, you know."

"Yes, I know. But it's dark and you don't have shoes on."

She wiggles her toes. "True."

I can't help but notice the lack of scratches on her legs. "Okay, spill."

"Spill? I'm not holding any liquid."

"Ha. Ha." I smirk. "I mean... that ritual you asked me to help with. You did something to yourself. You should be a mess of cuts and scrapes right now. What did you do?"

She nibbles on her lip again. "Umm... you mean you don't really know?"

I shake my head and start walking back toward camp—in no great hurry. Got a feeling she won't want to talk about this when the 'rents can overhear. "Nope. I kept my promise. Didn't read your mind."

"C'mon, Sare. How can you not know?" She timidly rolls her eyes. "What else could I possibly need soul goop for?"

"I have no idea."

"What kinda magic usually requires sacrificing people?"

"Black magic and you don't do that."

She exhales. "No, I don't. But I found a way to do it nice. Raw soul goop. Remember, I purified the evil out of it. The spell's the same. Sacrifice spells aren't really interested in the killing part. They just need the soul energy."

I stop walking and stare at her, draped across my arms like the damsel being carried off into the night by Dracula. "What did you do?"

Sophia squirms. "Umm… tried for immortality."

Oh, is that all? It's so extreme, yet sounds so normal. "Tried?"

"Uhh, yeah. Remember how you said I think of the world as a nice place because I'm still innocent and when I grow up, I'm gonna realize it's really scary and the world sucks and I'm gonna be all sad and stuff and crawl under my bed and never come out?"

Ugh. Crap. "Umm, not exactly what I said, but yeah…"

"Well…" She swishes her feet around, hemming and hawing. "I, kinda… was gonna freeze myself so I don't have to grow up and the world is always nice to me."

My jaw drops open. I can't help but gawk at her… my permanently elven-year-old little sister. "Mom is gonna lose her damn mind."

"No…" Sophia fidgets. "Relax. I didn't do that."

"You're not permanently eleven?"

"No. Well, not physically." She makes a goofy face. "Maybe mentally."

I chuckle.

"Or as far as Dad thinks."

"Oof. Yeah. He's always gonna think of us as kids. But that's what dads do."

"Seriously, though, I didn't freeze my age." Sophia kneads her hands together.

"So, what did you do?"

"Turned myself into a high elf."

I can't help but look at her ears. Nope, still round and normal. "What do you mean?"

Sophia fills her lungs all the way and lets the air out her nose, real slow. Not sure if she's trying to calm herself down or stalling. "Assuming I did it correctly, I'm going to stop looking older when I'm like eighteen or so, and I probably won't ever die just from time passing."

The urge to facepalm is strong, but my arms are full. This is my fault. My whole family is not just bending the rules of reality, but tearing the entire book in half, peeing on it like a spiteful dog, and lighting the shredded remains on fire.

"Don't make that face. You should be happy." Sophia reaches up, feels around at my face until she finds my mouth, then forces my lips into a smile shape with two fingers. "You won't have to watch me get old and die."

"Yeah, but..."

"But what?"

"You were still normal."

"Pff." She scoffs. "Hardly. Hello? Weird magic? Teleporting kitten? Contagious happiness and optimism that defies the depressing reality around us? That's not normal."

"Heh. True."

"So, umm... how much 'if' is involved?"

"Well, I used some of the magic to protect myself from vampire mind control." She keeps kneading her hands together. "Remember how when you took Sierra to Canada, she got mind controlled? I didn't want that to happen to me."

"I'm not going to bring you on any jobs for Wolent."

"I know, but the bad guys aren't gonna care. What if they come after us?" She twirls a lock of hair around her finger. "Anyway, I tried to shield myself from that. It's really bad they got control of Sierra, but if they got me... magic could do really baaaaad things."

"True."

"I dunno if I'm truly immortal since I used some of the spell's power on mind shield stuff." She taps her big toes together. "Won't really know for a while if I'll live forever or just a few thousand years... assuming nothing kills me."

The vulnerability in her voice right there is too much for me. I'm already holding her, so it takes little additional effort to squeeze-cling. She lets out an 'oomf' noise. Oops. I squeezed too hard.

"Sorry," I mutter.

"It's okay," she rasps. "I still need air, though. Sorry to make you sad."

"The 'rents are gonna flip." I exhale, and resume walking.

She shakes her head. "They won't. I didn't do anything crazy. I'm not gonna stay little forever, just not gonna get old and die. You can't say Mom and Dad will be upset over that."

I sigh. "No... pretty sure 'not dying' is at the top of their list of stuff they want us to do."

"Sorry." She bows her head.

"Now what?"

"For worrying you. I didn't wanna be left out."

"Left out?" I raise an eyebrow—not that she can see it.

"Whoops." Sophia grimaces. "That just kinda slipped."

"Speak, child." I stop walking again.

She fidgets.

"Utter the words." I jostle her.

Sophia laughs. "Okay, okay, fine." She takes another stalling deep breath. "Well, Sierra is already kinda immortal. Sam, too. I didn't wanna be the only one you guys lose."

I can't facepalm while carrying her, so I smack my forehead into her belly a few times.

"What?" she asks in between giggles.

"What about Sam? No one said anything about him being weird, too."

"Oh, that." She wobbles her head side to side.

"What did you do to him?"

She raises her hands. "Not me. The demons. Coralie said Sam's gonna stop growing up at like twenty-two. Wait... I'm wrong."

"How so?"

"Boys never grow up," she deadpans.

I'd laugh, but I'm too freaked out. Okay, I do manage a weak chuckle. "Seriously, though. What? Sam's immortal, too?"

"He didn't ask for it." Sophia shrugs. "They just kinda like him or something. As long as he keeps being nice to the demons, he's gonna stay young and live a really long time."

Oh, this couldn't possibly go wrong in any conceivable way, could it? Demons never give away stuff like immortality or eternal youth for free. There's going to be some nasty fine print in the contract somewhere. But, maybe not. If Sam didn't ask for it, perhaps my need to worry is overstated. My unlife is, after all, rapidly turning into one of Dad's dark comedy movies. Maybe the Littles' future won't be that bad. I mean, whoever imagined a modest succubus embarrassed to be stuck outside naked or even Blix—an imp who's helpful, nice, and into video games?

Still, I'm not going to let my guard down. I just can't. My—our—lives just got a whole lot weirder.

Exponentially so.

14

A TEENY BIT WORSE THAN BEARS

Sierra would be embarrassed if anyone saw me carrying her like a firefighter hauling a kid out of a burning house. Sophia doesn't mind. She owns her vulnerability and wears it proudly. Any excuse to hug or be hugged, she takes no matter how childish or 'helpless' it makes her look. Sometimes, I wonder if there's a Faustian kind of thing going on here where she outwardly conveys a sense of being weak and defenseless, but she's really using the projection of apparent vulnerability to get what she wants.

At least all she wants is love and attention… and feeling safe.

Pretty sure she'd take a pony, too, if offered. But, we don't have the land for it. And they are kinda expensive.

Soph's kind of like an overly needy housecat who keeps pawing at your leg until you pick them up and let them sleep in your lap. Sierra's the cat who might sit two inches outside arms reach beside you on the sofa and will totally scratch you if anyone sees you patting her on the head. Sam's the big ol' tomcat who flops wherever he pleases and doesn't care who notices him or ignores him. Not that my brother is big. He's scrawny like the rest of us.

One advantage of my family being so thin: it's easy to carry Sophia. Even easier at night when I'm online. She barely even registers as a weight in my arms. And yes, she is completely content to be carried all the way back to our campsite.

Another thing I notice is she didn't answer my question about how her legs aren't all scratched up. The most experienced survivalist in the world would be hard-pressed to walk cautiously through the forest barefoot in shorts and not get at least a few scratches. An extremely inexperienced hiker like Sophia, at night, sprinting in a blind panic, should have dozens of cuts and scrapes. I'm certain it's a side effect of the spell she put on herself. That in and of itself doesn't worry me nearly as much as her not talking about it. I have three theories. One, the spell made her magically tough so the weeds *couldn't* break her skin. Two, she did suffer all sorts of cuts, but they healed fast. Three, magical 'luck' kept all the sharp things out of her way, so she never hit them.

Hmm. If she got cut and healed, there would be blood smears on her legs. I do not smell strawberry (or some other variation of sweet) wafting from her, so... she either avoided or resisted harm.

An effect that protects my sister shouldn't worry me. Not sure why it does. Probably because Sophia and magic thus far haven't exactly been predictable. Case in point, she tried to fix some boy's clothing and nearly destroyed her school.

"Star light, star bright," whispers Sophia, while raising her hands like a wizard. "Show me what hides beneath the night."

Weak but noticeable energy radiates from her all of a sudden. My face and chest tingle as though I'm standing too close to a microwave oven. No, spells don't have specific words. She just made that up. Her magic also doesn't need words at all, but she finds it fun to come up with stuff to say.

"Oh, wow," says Sophia, while looking around at the forest as if she can now see in the dark. "I went far."

"Yeah, you did. I'm still wondering how you covered so much ground so fast."

Sophia rests her head on my shoulder. "Behold the power of panic."

"Really? You didn't amp yourself? Or teleport? Or do something weird?"

"Umm." She looks down at herself, fidgeting some hair between her hands. "I didn't try to make myself stronger or anything. Just wanted to have more time. I don't think it's the enchantment... maybe I unconsciously did magic to run away faster. Mr. Anderson said the kind of magic I use can sometimes just happen if I'm really emotional. Like when Mom almost made me get rid of Klepto?"

"That was 'really emotional'?" I raise an eyebrow. "Compared to a giant bear coming after us?"

"Umm, yeah." She gawks at me. "Kittens were at stake!"

"Mew," says Klepto while simultaneously appearing in a flash of purple light. The little furball drops into Sophia's arms, curls up, and begins to purr.

"Relax. They're almost back," says Ashley in the distance. "I can hear them."

Mom's voice filters through the trees, conveying her typical blend of worry and annoyance. She's not angry with Sophia or me, rather herself for being ordinary and stuck dealing with all this paranormal stuff.

Even though she can see now, Sophia remains content to let me carry her the rest of the way back. As soon as we enter the small clearing around the campsite, Mom stops pacing and bee-lines toward us. She must really have let her guard down, because she's not trying to hide how relieved she is to see Sophia unhurt. There's no way she'll be able to act angry and pretend to scold her for running off like that.

Mom doesn't take two full steps before Chloe springs to her feet and yells, "It's here."

The 'rents freeze in place. Ashley turns toward the kid. A tangible sense of darkness washes over me from the woods on the opposite side of our campsite. For no reason I understand, I can't peel my gaze away from a particular gap between two trees, even though there's nothing there.

"What's here?" I whisper.

Chloe sprint-flies over to hide behind me, clinging to my side. "The bad thing that was watchin' us last night. It's gonna—"

Mom screams.

Sophia, still in my arms, screams.

Oh, come on, Universe. We already had a bear. What now?

As if in answer to my mental question, a man blurs out of the forest, heading right for Mom, seemingly for no reason other than she happens to be the closest person to where he came from. Ashley, much closer to her than I am, leaps sideways as fast as she can accelerate herself over such a short distance, body-blocking Mom out of the way.

My mother hits the ground in a logroll at the same instant this guy grabs Ashley by the throat in a one-handed chokehold. Time does that thing again, where it seems to stop, allowing me to take in the situation. No, actual time hasn't changed. My brain is just on a thousand right now. The guy looks like one of those crazy people who live alone in the woods like hermits, only he's not that old. Maybe mid-twenties. His blue long-sleeved shirt is all torn up and muddy. His jeans are in slightly better shape. Rather than rips and tears, they're covered in bloodstains. They also look like he's been wearing them for months. Dude is barefoot, but evidently not by choice. Scrap remains of a sneaker flop around his left ankle like the entire lower half of the shoe got torn off some time ago. This guy has some serious toenail issues on the order of three inches, dark yellow, and pointy. Wait, no, those are claws. Eww. Okay, that's just nasty.

And kinda weird.

I mean... why are claws on vampire hands cool, but toe claws just... disgusting?

Mom slides to a halt, sprawled on all fours, disheveled but not apparently hurt. Dad slo-mo rises out of his chair, like he's going to get into a fistfight with this guy—who's obviously a vampire. He's only moving slowly due to my perception of time. Sophia is still screaming. Sierra dives off the cooler she'd been using as a seat close to the fire into a sprint for the trailer. The 'oh hell no' expression on her face is completely subconscious. She'd never willingly let anyone see her looking terrified.

Ashley tries to yell, producing a mere strangled gurgle noise. The guy holding her by the neck pulls her closer as if he's going to kiss her. Dark violet-blue vapor begins to coalesce within Ashley's mouth, seeping past her lips and out from her nostrils on its way into his mouth. Her eyes start to roll back into her head and her struggling wanes.

I feel like a monster dropping Sophia, but there is something seriously wrong going on with Ashley. Can't help but feel like he's in the process of killing her permanently. Gotta be the 'soul sucking' special effects. Sophia will understand. I'm sure she'd prefer I put her down *before* getting close to an angry vampire. Nice thing about supernatural reflexes and boosted speed: I put her down on her feet and charge at the bad guy before she can even try to grab me and hold on.

My attempt to ram-tackle the guy off Ashley fails in a pretty spectacular manner. It's like I've charged into a stone statue. Yeah, the man is not a literal statue and my impact maybe shifted him a couple of inches, but he doesn't move, nor does he go flying. Ouch. I've just about mentally processed the oddity of stopping cold on impact when he backhand slaps me across the face, knocking me on my ass and sending me sliding away.

Fortunately, the collision interrupts whatever he's doing to her. The weird vapor recoils back into Ashley, racing down her throat so fast she snaps out of her daze in the midst of a choking fit. By the time I recover out of my tumble and flip over into a crouch, Dad's taken a hit and is struggling to drag himself back to his feet. I can't see from this angle what happened other than my father cradling his face and swaying side to side on his knees, trying to figure out which way gravity is pulling.

Grr.

Enraged, I extend my claws and charge in again.

"Klepto!" shouts Sierra. "Get my sword!"

The kitten hisses.

"She said no," yells Sophia. "You'll just get yourself killed!"

"What?" barks Sierra.

"I'm her father and I approve that message," says Dad in a partially delirious tone.

"Dad!" shouts Sierra.

Ashley grabs the wrist of the arm choking her, wrenching it around in a twist that snaps bones. He loses his grip on her neck. Her victory grin lasts only a half second before he blurry-fast grabs her by the throat with his left hand.

I rip my claws in the general direction of his face—and hit air. Crap, this guy's *fast*. I just about have the time to think 'oh shit' before he whomps me in the back and sends me flying into a tree. Fortunately, my reflexes are good enough I'm able to turn my head and prevent smashed teeth. Trees are not soft.

Sierra, hiding under the trailer, continues demanding someone get her a sword. Mom crawls toward her. Chloe's wrapped herself around Sophia from behind like a human backpack. The child appears to be trying to fly-lift Sophia into a nearby tree. They are floating upward successfully, but too slow to get away if this bastard goes after them soon.

Ashley gurgles again.

I'm too angry and scared (for my family) to think. Shoving myself off the tree I just French kissed, I spin around in midair and Supergirl at the bad vampire. My attack is about as effective as one of the nameless bad guys in a Stephen Segal movie. Only, I didn't intentionally walk in at my appointed turn to be neatly lined up for a cinematically pleasing martial arts move. Ever notice that? The guy never gets mobbed. All the bad guys wait their turn and go in one after the next.

Anyway...

Dude grabs me by the neck. His fingers clamp around my throat with the force of a hydraulic vice. He's got both Ashley and I off our feet like a pair of otters about to be tossed into a pond. Only, whatever he's going to do to us isn't going to make for an adorable YouTube video. Head slightly tilted as though he's not sure what exactly he's looking at, the guy pulls me closer. We're not quite nose to nose, but the proximity is super uncomfortable. His breath smells like dead body. Of all the vampires I've ever seen who were *not* daysleeping, this guy is the most corpselike. His face is grey. Purplish venous lines trace Lichtenberg patterns over his cheeks and forehead.

Oh, did I mention his eyes are completely black? Like solid onyx orbs.

There's definitely something not right here. He's not acting like he's human smart. He doesn't feel old enough to throw me around like a helpless child, yet he's as strong and fast as a young elder. That, and he's got this whole 'radiating serious evil dread' thing going on. Just looking at this guy is making me understand how Sophia can be afraid of Fuzzydoom. If he hadn't tried to kill my mother, hit Dad, and choke Ashley, I'd be running away. Dude is seriously behaving like Frankenstein's monster, as if barely in possession of a mind. Oh, crap. Could this be the critter that killed Jesse Stroud? Nah, can't be. This is a vampire of some kind. No way he's a scrap, despite looking and acting like one. Scraps are not this powerful.

Pain wells up inside my chest. It's like being naked and mummified in duct tape, then having someone rip it all off in an instant—only the tape is stuck to my insides, not my skin. My face and throat turn cold. Purplish glowing vapor drifts out of my mouth. It's as if I've chugged a cup of liquid nitrogen. Gradual, creeping paralysis spreads down my limbs. The primal part of my vampire self lashes out. My eyes light up red, fangs involuntarily snap out to full length. I'm a cornered animal that knows it's about to die.

Mom! I scream in my head like a stupid child. As if she's going to be able to help me. Maybe I'm crying out for Aurélie rather than mortal Mom. Seconds from now, I'm going to cease to exist. This thing is eating my soul—and I'm not being metaphorical here. I've not been this absolutely terrified since I was five years old and had a wicked nightmare. If I could speak right now, I'd totally be crying for mommy.

Ashley's fist mashes into the open mouth that's inhaling the essence of everything I am. A faint *snap* barely reaches my awareness through the fog of panic and pain. The next sensation is almost worse. His power loses its hold on the vaporous essence of all things me, which abruptly races back down my throat into my inner core.

Imagine having a stomach full of really sticky, gooey mucous... and you start vomiting it up. About four feet of it is hanging out of your mouth and it all of a sudden congeals back into your gut like a snapping rubber band.

Yeah. Eww is right.

My senses fade back to normal as the numbness retreats. I lose control to a complete panic attack, clawing, slashing, and kicking in a blind frenzy—right up until a reassuring familiar voice shouts in my mind.

Cripes, yells Dalton. *Get the feck out of there right now!*

I scrabble at the hand gripping my throat, too weak to pry this guy's fingers open. 'Get out of there' is much easier said than done. And yeah, I kinda got the feeling this guy's a problem.

That's a sefil! Look at the eyes.

Oh, the solid black thing.

Yes, the solid black thing. I'm serious, lass. Get out of there.

Sefil. Holy shit. The boogie man of vampires. The thing that every vampire from anarchistic punk to prigs like Stefano and Paolo despise and fear in equal parts. Oh... crap. Now I understand what the big deal is about them. These freakin' things can devour a vampire's soul. No one bothered to tell me about that part. They're walking final death.

It's worse than that, luv.

I blink, still scratching at the hand around my neck. *Worse? What the heck is worse than being utterly destroyed and consumed?*

A sense of him cringing comes across our mind link. *Each time they feed, they grow stronger. One sefil, given enough dead vampires making it stronger, could wipe us out entirely.*

Well, shit. That's a serious problem.

Hey, no fair. I'm a vampire with supernatural powers and immortality. This should not be the most terrifying moment of my entire life. This thing's got me by the throat in a grip I'm unable to break… and he's easily able to utterly destroy me.

The sefil, apparently enraged at Ashley for interrupting his feeding on me, starts to draw her soul essence out—while entirely ignoring Dad walloping him over the back of the head with a folding chair. Apparently, his George 'The Animal' Steele reference before put him in a WWE mood. And here comes Dad with the steel chair… Only, my father is not a professional wrestler, and the chair's made out of cheap aluminum.

Somewhere behind me, Sierra is demanding a sword. Mom and Sophia yell 'no' at her repeatedly. Blix screeches, frantically trying to shout words over the chaos. Sam's voice, muffled by his being inside the trailer, yells back something about 'I can't, I'm on the toilet.'

Blix screeches even louder.

Well, it worked for her. I punch the sefil in the face as hard as I can, breaking his nose—and one of my fingers. The hit rocks his head backward a few inches. Doesn't seem to do much serious damage, but it is enough to interrupt his soul draining nonsense. Ashley sputters into a gagging, coughing fit.

It's understandable that Dalton wants me to save myself. He is my sire, after all. However, there's no chance in hell I'm going to take off and leave my family to face this thing by themselves. If *I* have no chance to kill this monster, there's no way they'll survive it. Best thing I can do is try to lure it away and give them time to hop in the Yukon and haul ass. Hopefully, they decide to do that. Of course, right now, I have a bigger problem to solve first. I can't run away and lure him after me if he's holding me off my feet in a one-handed chokehold.

What I'm about to do is very likely going to be the end for Sarah Wright, but it's better than allowing this abomination to kill everyone I love.

Growling, I rake a claw over the thumb joint of the hand clamped onto my neck. His body might've been stone-like when I rammed it, but the flesh cuts fine. The instant his thumb separates from the rest of his hand, I'm free. I drop to my feet and take a hasty step back. With any luck, the pain of losing a finger to a vampire claw will keep his attention focused on me. I can run and lead him away.

The sefil glares at me, then shifts his gaze to Ashley, his expression conveying a sense of 'I'll deal with you later.'

Crack.

Ashley's head jerks to the side at an unnatural angle. As soon as he lets go of her neck, she slumps to the ground in a paralyzed heap.

"Ow," deadpans Ashley.

Sophia and Mom scream in horror.

Dad wallops the guy over the head with the folding chair again. This time, the vampire fiend grabs my father by the face and shoves him away. Dad flips over twice in midair, lands on his chest, and bounce-slides even farther. I'm simultaneously furious, terrified, and taking things in analytically. This monster could easily have killed him, but didn't. The 'go away, peasant' treatment means something... but what? Hey, not going to complain. Dad is alive, if hurt.

The sefil lunges at me. He's too damn fast to avoid. Next thing I know, he grabs me by a fistful of my shirt and flings me across the clearing. My face misses the trailer by less than a foot as I careen past it and smash sideways into a tree, bending backward around it for a few tenths of a second thanks to inertia keeping me pinned. Oof. This is almost like when I fought the troll. Thankfully, the sefil isn't anywhere near as strong. My spine doesn't break this time. I do, however, lose a rib or three.

Pain jabs me in the back and left side an instant before gravity peels me off the tree and I collapse on the dirt.

"Wow," says Ashley, sounding calm. "This is uncomfortable."

My neck hurts, too. Probably came close to snapping thanks to whiplash. I'm glad it didn't. "It hurts less the more it happens."

"Oh, that's reassuring." Ashley rolls her eyes.

Mom stares at Ashley—who's neck is obviously broken—and screams again.

Dad makes it back to his feet. No sooner do I look at him than I notice he's pulling a red headband out of his pants pocket and tying it around his head. Ugh, Dad. No. Don't. Get away from that thing.

"Jonathan, don't you even think about it!" shouts Mom.

I sink my claws into the tree for help to pull myself upright. "Dad, why do you have a headband in your pocket?"

"Never know when you might need one," he wheezes.

The trailer door flies open revealing Sam, who's got one hand on his jeans, barely keeping them up. Guess Blix managed to interrupt him on the toilet. The imp pokes his head out the doorway by Sam's left shin, stares at the sefil for an instant, then babbles rapidly, wide-eyed.

Sam steps down the trailer stairs in that stiff-legged manner someone usually employs while venturing out of the bathroom in search of more toilet paper. The boy glares at the demonic vampire. He's hardly the picture of intimidation: ten, scrawny, one mostly bare butt cheek exposed to the world. "Go away."

"*Nil kura vas kor,*" rasps the sefil, lip curling in a hint of a grin. "*Dho oovas nura?*"

Okay, whoa. I guess it *is* smart after all. Just acting like a damned zombie.

Blix shakes his little head so rapidly his huge ears thwap against his face.

"It's not what *I'm* going to do you should be concerned about," says Sam in an eerily calm tone. "Mel?"

His succubus friend appears beside him. Except for being drop dead gorgeous, nothing about her appearance is the least bit demonic. She looks like an ordinary human supermodel of Middle Eastern descent—and she's currently wearing a turquoise bikini, huge sun hat, incredibly oversized sunglasses, and holding a mai tai in her left hand.

"Sorry to bother you," says Sam. "Can you please help? This dork is trying to kill my family."

Mel glances down at my brother, taking note of how he's clumsily holding his pants not quite all the way up. "Seems this one's rudeness has interrupted us both at an inconvenient time."

The sefil tilts his head at Mel. Two seconds later, his eyes widen in fear.

She stares at him—and he promptly explodes in a spontaneous

combustion fireball. Chunks of meat and bone fragments spray everywhere, all burning away into clouds of grey ash before they can reach the ground. In the span of half a breath, the biggest piece left of him is a burning severed head. The skin rapidly dries out, stretches tight against the skull, then splits down the middle with a crackling like someone's breaking an entire box of dry spaghetti noodles in half as the meaty bits are consumed by the flames into ash. A mere five seconds after the fatal glare, all that's left of the sefil is a char-blackened skull and a light haze of ashes in the wind.

"Thanks," says Sam.

"You're welcome." Mel takes a sip of her mai tai.

The 'rents stare at her. Mom's expression is about the same look she'd give someone showing up in a courtroom wearing a bikini. Dad's expression is... well... uncomfortable. Not his fault. She *is* a succubus, after all. She kinda does something similar to Aurélie's radiant charm power. Dad would never willingly cheat on Mom. At the moment, he's dazedly gawking at her like one of the nerds from *Weird Science*.

"Not what you were expecting to see?" Mel smiles at Mom. "I was on vacation in Jamaica."

And with that, she disappears.

Chloe and Sophia gaze down at the scene from a tree branch thirty feet off the ground, neither girl seeming too interested in coming down just yet. Mom aborts her effort to crawl under the trailer. She dusts herself off while Sierra crawls out to stand next to her.

Dad rushes over to Mom. It's difficult to tell which one of them is more worried about the other. Apparently satisfied neither one of them suffered serious injury, they hug. While they're checking each other over for bruises, I rush to help Ashley.

"Back soon. Gotta finish pooping." Sam hurries back into the trailer.

Mom sorta-storms over to me as I'm pulling Ashley to her feet. "Young lady, you have some explaining to do."

Ugh. This is not my fault. Or... maybe it is? I dunno. I resist the urge to let off an epic teenage sigh and simply hold Ashley so Mom can see her head flopping around. "Can it wait a few minutes?"

"Yanno, this surprisingly doesn't hurt." Ashley shifts her eyes back and forth. "Just feels *weird*."

Mom can't bear the sight and whirls away from us, hurrying back over toward Dad. As if she needed the distraction, she veers away from him to the tree the girls are hiding in. "Girls! Get down from there before you fall and break your—" She stops short with a strangled groan, unable to say 'break your neck' after looking at Ash.

"Sare!" whisper-shouts Sophia. "Help."

"What are you, a treed cat?" I ask.

"Umm. Basically. I'm scared." She grimaces.

"Don't be a chicken." Chloe grabs her from behind. "I can get us down."

"You barely got us up here," whimpers Sophia. "Without the immediate threat of a super scary demon-vampire, I can wait."

Chloe pushes them off the branch.

Sophia starts to shriek, but upon realizing they are calmly 'parachuting' to the ground, she quiets.

"See?" Gasps Chloe as if lifting a great weight. "Down is easy."

Mom rushes forward, arms up to catch the girls. It's not like they need it, but Sophia's never one to turn down help—especially if it's help disguised as a hug. Besides, Mom could really use a teddy bear to squeeze right now. Sophia's happy to play the part of plushie, and Chloe doesn't mind either.

"Whew." Dad walks over to me and Ashley. He's not quite limping, but he's obviously in pain. "You two okay?"

"Little banged around but I'm fine," I mutter, rubbing my broken finger.

"Not sure. Never had my neck snapped before. How bad is it?" asks Ashley.

"Twenty minutes from now, you won't notice anything happened. Just try to keep your head in a natural position as much as possible. Heals faster that way."

"Okay," says Ashley. Holding her head upright in both hands, she meanders toward the trailer in a semi-drunken stagger. "Good sign I can kinda move again."

Mom closes her eyes.

Maybe I should delete the memory from her head? "Dad?"

"Hmm?" He glances from Ashley to me. Unlike Mom, he's fascinated by the oddity of her walking around with mush for a neck. He knows it's not a threat to her life, so he's not upset or worried. Mom can't separate emotion from logic when it comes to watching us get hurt.

I lean closer and whisper, "Should I take that memory out of Mom's head?"

Dad purses his lips. "The neck thing?"

"Yeah."

He purses his lips, sucks air between his teeth, then nods once. "Just a little tweak."

I know what he's thinking without legit reading his mind. All I'm going to do is erase the memory of Ashley having an *obviously* broken neck. Crazy as it seems, I'm sure that's the only thing about what just happened that really pushed Mom over the edge. I approach the three-way-hug going on between Mom, Sophia, and Chloe, and add myself to it.

Five minutes from now, Mom will think Ashley just got the crap knocked out of her and fell over, stunned. This is mostly accurate to what really happened. I'm only removing the visual memory of the floppy head. Honestly, once we're back home, I might ask Aurélie to do the same to me.

15

TOO MANY THEORIES, TOO FEW FACTS

It's about fifteen minutes later.

We're all sitting around the campfire on a mixture of folding chairs and coolers. Chloe's put both Jesse's skull as well as the sefil's skull in the fire. So far, they're tolerating the flames rather well. Does an ordinary open wood fire like this get hot enough to reduce bones to ash? Crematory ovens are—as far as I am guessing—much hotter than a fire like this.

The family's been pretty much stone-faced silent for the past ten minutes.

Chloe jabs a long stick at the sefil's skull, repeatedly poking it. Her expression is fairly blank, with a hint of concentration.

"That's kinda disturbing to watch," I mutter.

Mom exhales out her nose. "Sweetie, would you please stop bothering the burning vampire skull? It's not a toy."

"I'm not playing with it." Chloe peers up at Mom. "I'm trying to break it so it doesn't look like a skull and get us in trouble."

"Oh," says Mom. She pauses, evidently clueless what to say in response.

I'm drawing a blank, too. Jesse Stroud did ask us to cremate his skull. Nothing mystical or ritualistic about that. The condition of his bones won't have any effect on him. He's merely concerned with the possibility the mortal authorities could find a skull with fangs. Hard evidence that vampires exist shouldn't be allowed to go mainstream. It would do more damage to the fabric of society than reality TV.

Wonder what would happen. Figure it would be one of two things. Either humanity would lose its collective mind and start a war to destroy us all—or capitalism would explode with all sorts of new vampire-centric products. Imagine Coca Cola releasing canned blood in various flavors. Then you'd have the vegan marketers trying to come up with a passable 'never human' synthetic option. Heh. Honestly? It would likely be a combination of the two. Religious wingnuts would be out there trying to kill us all while the corporations saw the undead as an opportunity for new profit channels.

Whatever might happen, I do *not* want to be the one responsible for setting it off.

Also, speaking of Jesse Stroud, I have questions. After nearly having my soul ripped out of my body, I'm not so sure any vampire killed by a sefil—in that manner—would be able to exist as a ghost. The ghost is, after all, made of the exact same stuff the stupid demonic vampire was eating. Hmm. Only thing that makes sense is it *didn't* do that to him. Easy to see how the fiend could have broken his neck or whatever to leave him helpless so the green-haired vampire and his buddies could do whatever. If the guy really did have control over the sefil, he probably forced it not to eat him. Those creeps are legit occultists, so they probably wanted souls. Black magic sounds so much like a thing from a video game where you have to run around picking up power crystals that are consumed by the spells you cast. Only, in this case, the 'power crystals' are souls. Sophia found a way to avoid the most evil part of it. She didn't consume any actual ghosts, merely scraped a whole bunch of scrap soul energy up off the floor of Hell. (I say 'hell' but I'm just using it as a generic term for wherever the heck it is demons live. It also sounds funnier.) So basically, my kid sister scavenged a bunch of fabric scraps off the floor of a garment factory and stitched them together rather than steal an entire dress. Amazing. Sophia is so darn nice she can effectively use black magic without hurting anyone and even turn it into light magic.

I sit there watching the Littles, all of whom *look* perfectly normal, wondering what they'll be in ten years. My brain fills in Sam looking about twenty, Sophia only slightly older, and Sierra still the same as she is now with a giant black cloud over her head. Or... for all I know, they might all grow up at a normal pace and just kinda 'freeze' around eighteen. It's equally possible Sophia's going to evolve into a flippin' Pikachu in four years.

I should probably stop playing the what-if game, sit back, and watch.

Easier said than done.

Sigh.

The attack hangs over us like a lead weight in the air. From expressions alone, it's clear we all want to talk about it. Mom has questions. Dad has questions. Sierra has questions—and a serious amount of resentment at being denied a sword in a moment of need. It didn't help matters I agreed with Dad. That damn monster was too fast. Now I know how mortals feel when vampires are kicking their ass. *I* couldn't keep up with him. Okay, to be fair, I already knew the feeling. Malcolm was even faster. But, hey, elder. I expect elders to be crazy powerful.

That sefil would have killed Sierra in an instant if it saw her as a threat. She knows it, too, which is most of the reason she's so furious. It's not Dad or Klepto she's angry with. It's... more the Universe. At least watching the thing kick my ass softened the blow. She's not feeling personally weak and helpless. We all kind of are. Except for Sam. The proverbial elephant at the campfire. My brother's taken the whole thing as a non-issue. Of all of us, he's the least fazed. The only reaction he showed thus far is being mildly annoyed at having to stop mid-poop to deal with the problem.

Very few things in the world are as uncomfortable and awkward as it is to trundle about unwiped during an emergency. It's right up there with putting a still-wet bathing suit back on and freezing your nether regions or having someone walk in on you while channel flipping and think you were intentionally watching Dr. Phil.

Dad's been atta-boying him since the attack, even though Sam didn't really do anything. I mean, the boy does have some weird ability to affect demons. Something happened at his friend's house a couple months ago. He is apparently able to injure demons with a nerf gun. Like, the exact form of the attack doesn't matter. Shooting them with a toy gun or a real one would have about the same effect. It's his intention weaponized, magic in a sense. Sam actually prefers the nerf gun because any stray shots can't possibly hurt people. That, and the police would have some teensy issues with a kid his age carrying a real gun. So would Mom.

Any minute now, someone's going to ask a question—either about where the sefil came from or how Sam managed to vaporize such a dangerous monster with seeming ease. The second question I can answer: he didn't. Mel did. She's at least a thousand years old, probably much more than that. Hell, a vampire her age would've been able to tear that sefil to pieces. Pretty sure Aurélie or Wolent would've smacked it around, no problem. So, I'm not *that* disturbed his friend basically destroyed a vampire with a glare.

Yes, I am aware this means Mel could do the same to me, or Ashley, or any number of vampires. Part of me wonders if the Universe has a certain set of laws that govern this sort of thing. Like, could Mel just randomly kill any vampire she wanted to or does she *require* someone like Sam asking her to act? Figure if demons could just pop into our world and go crazy, they'd probably do so all the time, creating chaos, discord, and suffering. Hmm. Maybe they do. I mean... the Oscars are a thing. Also, *Firefly* got canceled but *Duck Dynasty* went on and on and on. That's gotta be the work of demons.

The only thing preserving silence is the awkwardness of the subject, plus our inherent shyness. Mom's the boldest of us, the most prone to be the first person to talk. The quiet introversion comes from Dad's side. Weird how it flipped over when they made kids. Sam —the boy—is the unshy one, a trait he undoubtedly got from Mom. All the girls, myself included, are varying degrees of 'walk six blocks out of our way to avoid talking to someone who makes us uncomfortable' shy. In fairness, undeath has made me less shy.

Screw it. I might as well get this ball of poop rolling. It's going to happen eventually and this waiting is driving me nuts. "Okay, so I'm sure you're all—"

Two strange men run into our campsite.

They're not strange in the sense of being dressed like clowns, seeming supernatural, or even openly admitting to liking Creed songs. I mean strange as in we don't know who they are. Both guys seem to be in their thirties. The aromas of beer and grilled hamburger meat clings to them. They're also a bit out of breath and look worried. The short guy's wearing a Buffalo Bills T-shirt with jeans. Second guy's doing the designer polo shirt with khaki's thing. And ugh, he's wearing socks and sandals. Maybe we haven't quite finished killing demons tonight.

"You folks okay?" asks the taller man.

"Heard a bunch of screaming." The Bills fan looks around at us, then the woods.

Chloe freezes in mid poke, eyes wide as if she'd been caught reaching into the cookie jar right before dinnertime. I think she's overacting to draw attention to her frightened face rather than the two skulls sitting in the fire.

"Thank you, but we're all right," says Mom in a surprisingly smooth tone, considering how frazzled she was a moment ago. "Just a ghost story that got somewhat out of hand."

Wow. Totally straight face. Never knew she could lie so easily. Mom usually *hates* fibbing… but I suppose this is protecting the family. Some lies are kinda necessary, after all. Like telling a dying person everything will be fine, covering up the existence of crazy supernatural things people can't handle, or telling the economically disadvantaged that all it takes to succeed in life is hard work. We wouldn't want to be responsible for pointless suffering, the exposure of the supernatural world to societal awareness, or the collapse of industrialized capitalism. Well, maybe capitalism could use a few tweaks, but I digress.

The men exchange a bewildered glance.

"You sure?" asks Buffalo Bills Guy. "That screaming sounded real loud. Thought someone was about to do something horrible to some kids."

"Sorry," whispers Sophia. "I'm a big chicken. I scare easy."

"Ghost stories…" Tall guy scratches at his right eyebrow. "Huh."

With a loud *crack*, the sefil skull abruptly breaks in half, releasing a glowing neon-green apparition. The vaporous, vaguely person-shaped, thing stretches eight feet up from the flames while emitting a keening, ghostly wail of soul-tearing anguish. I haven't heard a scream that tormented since the power cut out when Sierra was playing *Dark Souls*. She was on her 300th or so attempt at the final boss and was finally about to kill it for the first time when the electricity decided to say nope.

Our entire campsite glows emerald for a few seconds as the apparition expands, then bursts apart into scattered bits of glowing ghost-plasm, which settle like a snowstorm of dead fireflies to the ground, then wink out one by one.

Sophia's making the most hilarious face I've ever seen on her before. It's part 'ooh, pretty' and part wanting to run screaming into the trailer and not come out until we're home.

"Yeah, just a ghost story," deadpans Sierra, her expression so *done* it's difficult for me not to laugh. "The special effects were *really* good."

The men stare gobsmacked at the fire, which has gone back to being normal.

"I didn't do it," whispers Chloe.

"Sarah…?" says Mom, flicking her gaze at the men.

"On it." I stand and zoom over to the guys, too fast for them to react.

They jump as if I'm someone else (who hadn't been sitting in front of them) coming up behind them unnoticed. It's nice the normal human reaction to being startled is to stare at the source of said startlement for a few seconds. There's gotta be some kind of subprocess running in the brain that's responsible for deciding between laughing off a prank, screaming at danger, or going into attack mode whenever a person is surprised. The tiny pause between shock stimulus and reaction is enough for me to derp slap them both.

"Ash? Hungry?" I ask.

"Not yet, but you're right." She stands, still bracing her head with one hand. "I'm going to be…"

"Do make sure those men get back to where they belong in one piece," says Mom. "Try not to make a mess."

I know she's just saying that to make what's about to happen sound like an ordinary mundane problem she can deal with.

"Okay, Mom."

I lead my guy a few steps away to put some trees between us and the family. Hey, having my butt kicked by a sefil made me a little snackish. Might as well take advantage of the situation instead of going back to Crescent City and finding some other catastrophe that gets me to go 'full superhero' again. There's something to be said for convenience. Thankfully, I don't need *too* much to drink. Once I'm done, this guy gets a mind wipe. He won't remember the green ghostly wailing whatever. I also tone down the screaming in his memory. Poor Sophia really cut loose. This guy thought some little girl was about to be axe-murdered. Aww. He dropped everything and came running, weaponless, in hopes of helping her. Not that he knew who Sophia was, merely thought he heard some little girl in trouble. He made assumptions. Boys don't scream the same way if they are facing mortal danger. Sophia has a distinctly girly glass-shattering shriek when she's legit terrified.

Ashley, in full view of the 'rents and Littles, feeds off the shorter guy. As much as I tell myself vampire feeding is not a sexually charged act, I still can't bring myself to do it in front of my parents. Watching Ashley do so and watching my parents watch her do it is squirmy as hell. The look Dad's giving her makes me imagine him doing a David Attenborough impression as if narrating a nature documentary about vampire teenagers. Mom's got a 'what am I watching' sort of horrified expression, as if she walked in on me making out with a guy old enough to be my dad.

Sierra's like Dad, observing with clinical interest. Sam doesn't even look. No big deal to him. Sophia cringes away. Vampire feeding to her is as 'eww' as kissing. That will change in a few years. I hope. I *really* hope. If her magic backfired and she's stuck at eleven forever, Mom is going to lose her effing mind. Soph seemed pretty confident she didn't do that, so I'll keep my fingers crossed.

At least, if she *did* pause herself at this age, Sierra will be happy. She's probably going to grow up at an inhumanly gradual pace. This means that in a few years, Sophia will be 'bigger' than her. Magic eight ball tells me our miniature Red Sonja will not be happy about this turn of events.

Anyway, Ashley and I rearrange these guys' memories to hearing less desperate screams and no signs of fighting. They rushed all the way to our campsite to investigate, discovered an innocent ghost story that got the better of an easily frightened tween, and went back to their families.

Problem solved. At least one of them.

We reconvene around the fire as the two men automaton-walk into the woods.

Ashley is no longer using a hand to keep her head upright. Good sign.

"So... what happened?" Mom asks.

"Lots of stuff." Chloe resumes poking the skull fragments.

Mom grumbles.

"She isn't wrong." Dad winks at Chloe, making her grin.

"Why did that vampire come after us?" Mom glares at me like I'm the one who let the stray dog into the house.

I release a long, slow sigh. "No idea. I can make some assumptions, but who knows if they're correct."

"Make some theoretical assumptions." Mom folds her arms.

"Well, Ash and I headed to Crescent City for a bite last night, and..." I relay the story of meeting the local vampires. Mom and Dad do not need to hear about the kidnapping. They get enough depressing stuff like that from the TV news. "... and apparently, an emissary Wolent sent to make contact with Portia got killed by some 'pet.' We got the scroll back from the vampires responsible, but didn't see their pet."

"I think we just did," says Dad.

"A vampire?" Ashley blinks. "We're not pets."

"That one did seem kinda stupid." Sierra scrunches her nose. "Didn't act normal."

I rub the bridge of my nose. "It wasn't really a vampire. Just looked like one."

The 'rents stare at me.

"What was it then?" Mom tilts her head.

"A sefil." I lower my hand from my face. "Before you ask what that means, it's what happens if a vampire waits too long between killing someone and doing the Transference. Instead of the person's soul who owned the body, a demon slips in and takes it over. Physically, it's a vampire, but spiritually, it's a demon."

Ashley shivers. "That's why it felt new, but kicked our ass like an elder."

Sam, having wandered a bit away from the campfire, stoops to pick something up off the ground. He examines it closely while the imp, perched on his shoulder, chatters away. "Blix says the vampire who made the sefil summoned the demon on purpose."

I facepalm. "Ugh. Didn't his sire tell him how *bad* those things are? It's like the number one rule of being a vampire: you don't try to turn someone who's been dead more than a minute."

"I thought the number one rule of vampiring was 'do not sparkle'," says Sierra.

"That too." I nod at her.

Ashley laughs.

"Come on, Sarah, you know the first rule of vampire is not to hunt where you live." Dad rolls his eyes at me like an overly patient math teacher dealing with a high school freshman who can't do long division.

The worst part is, he's probably right. Vamps have been following that rule for thousands of years. So much so, I almost wonder if leaving a pile of drained corpses right in our front yard might actually be good cover. The hunters would never imagine we'd attack people where we live. No, I'm being strictly theoretical here. I am not going to kill-feed, and even if the world turned upside down enough for me to do that, I definitely wouldn't litter the yard with bodies. Mom would lose it. I'd be grounded for two whole centuries.

Sam holds the small object he's picked up closer to his eye. Blix leans forward off his shoulder to also get a close look at it. The imp whispers. Sam nods, then lowers his arm before facing us. "Something broke his control over the demon inside the sefil. I don't know why it attacked us, but it wasn't sent here on purpose."

"A grenade," says Ashley.

"What?" blurts Mom.

"You know, a hand grenade." Ashley pantomimes pulling a pin and throwing a grenade.

"That's not what I meant by what!" Mom fans herself. "I mean, what are you doing around explosives? I don't want you girls touching that stuff."

Dad and I exchange a conspiratorial glance.

"Mom?" I whisper. "Do I get a pass whenever Wolent wants me to burn out a vampire nest?"

As if suddenly remembering I had a ten-pound bomb in the house not too long ago, Mom nearly faints. "Oh, my. Sarah… did you have to remind me about that?"

"Sorry." I nibble on my lower lip.

"It's different… somehow." Mom keeps fanning herself. "Hand grenades? Where did you get one of those?"

Ashley swipes her hair off her face. "It wasn't ours. Some jerk tried to throw it at us, but he blew himself up."

"Ahh." Dad chuckles. "I can see how that might be a distraction in his ability to control a summoned minion."

"You go to throw the grenade at the vampires," says Sierra. "Oof, natural 1. Critical failure. You blow yourself to shit."

Mom gasps.

Sophia's face turns red. She's grinning, but a little too embarrassed at Sierra brazenly cursing right in front of the parents to laugh out loud.

The D&D reference is more than enough to get Dad snickering and willing to overlook the bad word. It's too awkward for Mom to yell at her with him right there laughing at what she said, so Mom stews in silence. Good for Sierra, she didn't swear specifically to annoy Mom. It just kinda happens sometimes. And besides, the line demanded the word.

"He kinda exploded everywhere." Ashley grimaces. "Bloody gloop all over the place. Really weird."

Mom buries her face in her hands muttering to herself about 'this isn't really happening.'

"Sorry." I fidget.

"Stop apologizing for things that aren't your fault." Mom lowers her hands and takes a breath. "I just need to find a way to cope with our new normal."

"So..." Ashley twists around to look at Sam—who's mostly behind her. "You're sure the guy lost control of the demon when he blew himself up?"

Blix nods.

I'm nothing short of astonished some sod managed to control one of those things, says Dalton in my head.

"Blix?" I ask. "Are you sure that vampire had control over the sefil? Or did he just think he did?"

The imp chatters and chitters at Sam, sounding like a demonic chipmunk version of a college professor doing a presentation on ancient Sumerian demonology. Sam listens, nodding occasionally.

"Yeah," says Sam.

The rest of us—except Chloe, who's too preoccupied with skull fragment poking—exchange glances. Like, the imp just spoke for two full minutes and that somehow translated to 'yeah.'

"Just 'yeah'" I ask. "Blix was talking for a long time."

Sam smiles. "Yes, but he was explaining stuff I already said. The guy made the sefil on purpose using a demon he'd already summoned.

Those guys are occultists. They'd been playing around with black magic for a long time."

Fecking reckless morons, mutters Dalton. *Letting one of those things loose on the world could've doomed us all.*

I blink. Seriously? Like, one sefil would kill every vampire on Earth?

If it was allowed to kill a sufficient number of us and grow powerful, it's theoretically possible. Far more likely it would do something so egregious the mortals rose up and wiped us out. They see one sefil, they assume all of our kind are mindless, bloodthirsty monsters.

"If those sefil things are so dangerous, why'd they make one on purpose?" Dad flips open the cooler next to him and grabs a can of iced tea from the ice water inside.

"Same reason that motivates the bad guys in any movie where there's some cult trying to destroy the entire world." I puff at a stray lock of hair that's just refusing to stop falling over my eye.

Sam translates Blix's answer. "Wanted to see if he could and because he's a dumbass. He thought he could control it and keep it from going nuclear."

"Ouch." Dad cringes. "They always think that, don't they? Right up until they lose control."

Mom glances at him.

"You should've seen them, Dad." I laugh. "They looked like something out of a movie. One dude had 'satan' tattooed across his forehead."

He sprays iced tea as my comment strikes in mid-sip. Once the coughing subsides, he tearily laughs. "Good grief. Are you serious or pulling my leg?"

"Serious," says Ashley and I at the same time.

"Wow." Dad whistles.

Ashley giggle-snorts. "She called the guy *Methestopheles.*"

Mom stares at me.

Dad tilts his head.

I explain how the dude was so skinny, with only three teeth left and a sunken face, he totally looked like a meth-head who'd become a vampire occultist. "The name just kinda hit me."

"The big, bald redneck-looking guy with the beard, she called Beelzebubba," rasps Ashley between fits of laughter.

"You've gone too far," deadpans Sierra. "The puns have violated the ancient laws. You must face consequences."

"I know, right?" Sophia rolls her eyes, then smiles.

Sierra shakes her head at me. "You're not an Innocent. Dad cursed you into starting a new bloodline that's incapable of resisting the urge to constantly drop horrible puns."

Dad beams with pride.

"Okay, serious time." Sierra sits up straight. "Why did that thing come after you guys if you set it free? Shouldn't it like… thank you?"

"Eek. I had no idea we had a sefil around or that we set it free. That could've been bad." I grimace.

"Umm." Ashley rubs her neck. "It came after us because it's evil, violent, and mindless."

"So are Philadelphia Eagles fans, but they're not barging into our campsite trying to strangle you," says Dad.

Ashley and I stare at each other. It's weird for Dad to make a sports reference. He's developed a small repertoire of sports jokes to poke Grandpa's buttons, but we are not the target audience. I don't understand sportsball. The Littles don't get the joke either, and ignore it.

"I mean…" Ashley gestures randomly at the forest. "It saw us at the place those vampires lived. Probably followed us here. Maybe it was smart enough to understand we are vampires and it might've been afraid we'd try to stop it before it ran off to do whatever."

Sarah, you may wish to consider permanently destroying the one who made it. If he made one on purpose, he's going to do it again.

I wince. Dalton is right. There aren't too many things bad enough to get the entirety of undead society agreeing that a particular vampire ought to be destroyed. The list is short: deliberately acting to expose vampires' existence to mortals, making a *sefil* on purpose, and willingly joining a SKA band. In all seriousness, though, the *sefil* thing is bad enough to get men like Stefano Bianchi nervous. As soon as I go anywhere near Arthur Wolent, he's going to see in my head that I had contact with a *sefil*. If we *don't* destroy the guy responsible, he'll be disappointed in us, perhaps even angry. Since the guy does have a soft spot (for some reason) for me, he'd probably only send me back here to finish what I should've done in the first place.

As distasteful as it is for me to think about perma-killing an immortal, it would not be the first time I've done so. I ended Scott for good. Granted, he wasn't really a full vampire. He was a tortured soul condemned to an eternity of suffering... even before he rose as an undead. The bomb I dropped off at Anselme's little conclave most certainly nuked several vampires for good. Lime-hair guy made a *sefil* on purpose. The thing he set loose on the Earth came within inches of killing my parents, as well as Ashley, and me. I'm sure it wouldn't have simply left Sophia, Sam, and Chloe alone, either. It's still strange it didn't kill Dad when it had the chance to.

Mortals are of little use to them. It smelled you, Ashley, and little Chloe. Wanted to consume the three of you first.

Ugh. So, it basically threw my father aside like a kid pushing green beans out of the way to go straight for the microwave dinner brownie.

Essentially, yes. If it had succeeded in consuming the three of you, it might have simply toddled off in search of more vampires. Of course, it also might've murdered everyone it saw just for laughs if no vampires happened to be near enough to smell.

Comforting... not.

Yeah. I am totally willing to kill that guy... again.

Society will be proud of me for it, or at least nod in acceptance that I did what any self-respecting vampire should do in this situation.

"Okay." I glance over at Ash. "Feel like helping me do some cleaning?"

"Cleaning? There's a mess in the trailer?" Mom blinks.

I fidget.

"Not that kind of cleaning, dear." Dad pats Mom on the hand. "I believe she means 'cleaning' in the sense of *Leon*."

"Who's Leon?" Mom glances at him, then back at me.

"Duh, Mom. The movie?" Sierra rolls her eyes. "She's gonna go assassinate someone and melt the body in a bathtub full of acid."

Mom—not taking her seriously—frowns. "Oh, yes. I remember. Ridiculous premise. Who did they think would ever find it believable that someone trained a preteen girl to fight and kill?"

Sierra gives Mom a look while standing there somewhat conspicuously in a 'hi, I know how to use a sword' sort of way.

Dad covers his mouth to hold back laughing. Both Sophia and Sam give Mom a 'wow, really?' stare.

It takes about eighteen seconds for Mom to realize that Sierra is not only a preteen girl who's been trained how to kill, she's actually done it. Granted, she's only 'killed' zombies and vampires. As far as I am aware, she's yet to end a mortal's life—and I'm going to try to keep it that way.

"Well, Mom." I offer a whimsical shrug. "I guess our family is unrealistic."

She stares at me, horrified. "Wait, you mean to tell me you are really going to kill someone?"

"Not exactly." I stand, then look down at my feet. Yeah, this is gonna require sneakers. "He's already dead. I just, umm, need to make him *deader*."

16

CLEANUP, AISLE SIX SIX SIX

Many things about my unlife have left me awestruck, baffled, or thrilled.

No one will ever be able to claim vampirism is boring. The most shocking thing to happen thus far on our vacation is not being attacked by a sefil. It's Dad suggesting that Ashley and I bring Sam with us as we go to permanently destroy a vampire. Cody and Ben Peters would be so damn jealous. Yeah, this isn't exactly the sort of field trip most ten-year-old boys go on while camping with their families in the woods. Executing vampires is a pretty niche hobby, after all.

Predictably, Sierra was pissed and immediately began demanding to know why he gets to go with me, but she can't.

Mom wasn't too happy about the idea, either.

I can't argue Dad's rationale. My little brother did—more or less—destroy the sefil by snapping his fingers. The boy can kill demons with a nerf gun. Our present vampire problem consists of demon-summoning crazies. According to Dad, it would make no sense for us not to bring our most formidable defense to bear against the Forces of Evil™. It took him reminding Mom of what happened with the sefil and how easily Sam was able to get rid of it to calm her down. Dad's afraid—though he's not showing it—that some other demonic thing will pop up and hurt me or Ashley. He's more than willing to go with us, too… but Dad's a bit too big and heavy for either me or Ashley to carry while flying.

One of the weirdest feelings I've ever had post-vampirism is believing that my little kid brother might literally be able to protect me. Things aren't supposed to work this way. I'm eighteen (technically nineteen), he's ten. I'm supposed to do the protecting.

Ugh, magic is so weird.

So, yeah. We're bringing Sam with us. The boy borrowed Dad's red headband. Mom decided to begrudgingly tolerate this after Ashley and I reassured her all the vampires would still be unconscious and helpless. Slight nervousness in Dad's eyes told me he's worrying about the same thing I am. What if this guy made more than one sefil? Here's hoping Mel doesn't get annoyed at Sam interrupting her vacation again.

We fly to the house by the algae-covered lake. Sam clings to my back, loving every minute of it. The kid adores flying, even though he —wait. He *can* fly on his own. Sorta. Olmaz gave him summonable wings. I can't remember if my kid brother can jump into the air from the ground or his wings are merely for gliding. He's been pretty responsible insofar as keeping them hidden from public view and doesn't whip them out too often. You'd think most kids his age would go hog wild and fly all the time. His biggest problem right now is it's only possible to fly unseen at night, and he's not allowed out after dark. Odd. This would be a perfect opportunity for him to bust out his wings. Not only are we in the middle of freakin' nowhere, we're in another state. If anyone did happen to see us, we'll be hundreds of miles away in a few days.

Regardless, the boy is happy to cling to my back.

We land a few steps from the porch. The house is pretty much in exactly the same state as we left it.

"Wow, what a dump," mutters Sam.

"*Eem neeba.*" Blix whistles.

Gonna guess that's demonic for 'sure is' or 'and how' or something along those lines. When even a demon thinks you live in a hellhole, that's a problem.

"Okay, how do we do this?" Ashley smiles at me like we're about to start an innocent craft project. "Do we need to destroy all of them or just the one guy?"

I shift my weight from leg to leg. "Good question. We know the green-haired guy made the sefil, so he's definitely gotta go. Not sure about the others."

Society would consider them all part of it, says Dalton.

"Yeah... accomplices to the vampire apocalypse," I mutter.

"What apocalypse?" Ashley blinks at me.

I head up the steps onto the porch and in the front door. "Sefil. I realized why 'polite vampire society' is so terrified of them."

Ashley follows me in, close at my heels. "The soul-eating thing?"

"Yeah. Dalton said they get more powerful with each vampire they consume. Eventually, they'd become an unstoppable monstrosity that devours everything in its path."

"If they eat enough vampires, they turn into Disney Corporation?" Ashley whistles. "That's bad."

I chuckle. "Something like that."

"Wow." She whistles. "Would've been nice of him to tell you that before we ran into one."

I was rather hoping you never saw one. Didn't seem important to bring up.

Fair enough. These things are supposed to be rare, right?

Quite. Even the craziest of our kind are hesitant to make one willingly. The few that have occurred throughout history have generally been accidents or desperate fools.

Desperate fools? Isn't that on purpose but being a moron?

Somewhat. I mean that in the sense of a vampire trying to 'save' a mortal they are fond of, but too much time has passed and they unknowingly bring forth one of those things.

Oh. Ick. Bad enough they lost someone they love, but to watch a demon hijack the body of someone you care for—and then being forced to destroy them? Eek.

"I don't see anyone with green hair," says Sam.

"He exploded." Ashley points at the gory skeleton draped over the couch.

It appears somewhat meatier than before. Seems the fleshy bits are already in the process of regenerating.

"Oh, wicked." Sam goes wide eyed and rushes over to check out the body.

Blix, perched on his shoulder, chatters almost continually.

Ashley approaches Beelzebubba and stomps on the table leg sticking out of his head, inflicting more brain damage.

I stare at her.

"What?" She shrugs like she didn't do anything incredibly creepy or morbid. "Don't want him waking up and attacking us."

"Right..." I sigh. There's something inherently wrong about watching Ash casually stomp a guy's brains in. This is a girl who cries when kittens mewl in pain while receiving their vaccination shots.

Guess Methestopheles is mine. I peer down at him. Looks like he caught a few significant bits of grenade to the face. He's down to only one tooth. That explains why he's still out cold. My education on hydrodynamic physics is a bit lacking, but as close as he was to the grenade going off, I'm sure the shockwave from the blast probably pulped his brain inside his skull.

"Guys..." Sam looks up at us. "Blix is saying at least one other demon was summoned here."

"Eep!" Ashley spins to look around. "Is it still here?"

Sam shrugs. "No idea."

"Damn. I really should've gotten some latex gloves first." I gingerly grab onto lime-hair guy's remains (a blood-wet skeleton covered in raw hamburger) and lift it off the sofa. "Hey, Blix. You're sure this guy made the sefil on purpose?"

The imp nods, then babbles.

"He said these guys didn't really understand what the sefil could do if it was allowed to feed on souls." Sam picks up Slash's broadsword in both hands, ogling it. "They just thought they had a demon they could control as a weapon. We're lucky it hadn't been too long. The sefil wasn't powerful enough to break free and eat these jerks."

Ashley drags Slash's body over to the other two in the middle of the room. "Did he really control it or was that thing just letting him think so while it gathered power?"

"I have a theory." Sam smiles.

Blix folds his spindly little arms and peers at him in a 'go ahead, let's see how wrong you are before I explain' way.

My brother play-swings the broadsword gradually back and forth. It's so big and heavy for him, it nearly takes him off his feet. "I think they probably had some degree of real control over it. Otherwise, the sefil would've eaten their souls."

"*Naalu orba.*" Blix goes wide eyed.

Sam smiles to himself. Seems he was right, or at least close enough to right for the imp not to correct anything.

"Did it eat their souls after the guy blew up?" Ashley waves at me. "Put that mess down. Don't stand there holding it. You're dripping blood everywhere."

I drop the bloody skeleton atop the other vampires. The clattering squish it makes upon landing is the opposite of pleasant. Ashley and I get to work looking for the remainder of the vampire, as the blast disintegrated his entire right arm and most of the ribs on that side. Bone fragments are scattered all over the place. Yeah, sure, vampires aren't flatworms. We can't fully regenerate if even one finger survives. Pretty sure we only need to destroy the brains to keep them dead for good. The three best ways to permanently destroy a vampire are: sunlight, fire, and acid.

Since we forgot to bring several gallons of industrial grade hydrochloric acid with us on our camping trip, we'll need to use one of the other options.

"Hmm. What do you think?" I ask of no one in particular. "Drag them outside and wait for morning or build a funeral pyre?"

"Fire." Ashley nods once. "Anything unpredictable could happen between now and sunrise. Feel kinda bad ruining the house, though. Should we move them outside?"

"This place is a dump." Sam sets the broadsword down, seeming tired of holding it up. Swords are infinitely cool to boys his age, but his arms can only endure so much. "Burning it would be an improvement."

Ashley scrunches her nose. "The house would burn big. Might start a forest fire. Let's be safe."

"Conscientious murder." I snap my fingers. "I like it."

"It's not murder." Sam laughs. "They're already dead. This is environmental maintenance."

Can't believe I'm laughing, but here we are. Can't believe they made so many *Fast and Furious* movies, but, again, here we are. Ashley and I get to work carrying the demon-occult vampires out in front of the house, where we can burn them safely. She grabs arms, I grab legs, and we haul them one at a time out the door. It's not that we aren't strong enough to lift the bodies alone. Just... working together is much less clumsy and minimizes close contact. While we do this, Sam explores the living room like a small detective, investigating various clusters of occult-looking objects. These guys have loads of candles, some books, weird bottles of unknown substances, and dead small animals. For all I know, the jars of brownish crud with stuff floating in it is month-old coffee used as an ash tray. Probably not. Vampires don't generally smoke, nor do they drink coffee. These guys were *not* Innocent, so wouldn't have anything remotely resembling food here. Yeah... that stuff in the jars is either really old, or it's 'occult slime.' I don't wanna know.

We save Beelzebubba for last, since he's going to be the most difficult to move.

It's so weird and surreal lugging dead vampires around. Can't help but imagine the two of us in some bizarre, morbid comedy movie about Wednesday Addams going to college. We're moving into (or out of) a dorm room and relocating her collection of corpses. Even though neither Ashley nor I need to rest or breathe, we pause to take a break when only Beelzebubba is left to move.

"We're stalling," says Ashley.

"Yeah. Guy's huge."

"Not like he's heavy to us." She raises her arms and lets them fall against her sides. "It still feels crazy weird being this strong. I don't need Dad's help to open jars anymore."

I laugh. "Therein lies the irony of the universe."

"How so?" She raises an eyebrow.

"Vampires are strong enough to open jelly on our own... but we don't need normal food anymore."

She overacts sighing at the sky. "So not fair. Hey, speaking of not fair, would we get in trouble if we mind-controlled clothing designers to start putting real pockets in our stuff?"

I ponder this for a moment. "Tempting, but I think society would notice women's clothing having pockets as being unnatural. They'd probably call it satanic."

Ashley snaps her fingers in fake disappointment. "Drat."

"Oh well. Let's get out of here." I head back inside.

Ashley follows.

Sam, holding a bit of paper, walks around the shredded couch toward us. "The demon that might still be here is from an incomplete summoning ritual activated before it was finished."

Ashley and I exchange a guilty glance. Oh, shit. Did we set something loose when we read that scribbled nonsense on the back of the scroll?

"The scroll?" I ask.

Sam is about to say something when a metal bar flies upward from the debris on the floor and nails him between the legs. The soft *thump* of the hit precedes a faint squeak coming out of his nostrils. His 'oh, that's not good' expression might have made me laugh if not for seeing my little brother in pain.

Without a word, or any further noise, Sam drops the paper scrap to cradle his groin, buckles at the knees, and falls to the floor.

The offending pipe swings itself up as though an invisible man wielded a baseball bat and intended to bash Sam's brains out onto the rug.

Oh, hell no.

I dive forward, grabbing the middle part of the maybe three-foot-long pipe as it swings down, pushing it past my brother so it smacks an empty spot of rug. Don't have much leverage while flying, so I swing my feet down and try to wrestle the pipe away from the invisible force holding it. Our tug of war lasts only three seconds before the pipe jerks back from me with enough force to throw me across the room. My hands slip off the old metal, covered in plastery dust.

Flight allows me to catch myself and stop before going face-first into the wall by the fireplace. By the time I flip over to face the damn thing again, it's already poised to crush my brother's skull. I kick-launch myself off the wall toward him, despite being too far away to get there in time. Ashley swoops in for the save, grabbing the pipe. She widens her stance; rather than try to pull the pipe away from the invisible man, she's pushing back against its swing.

A tenth of a second before I get there, the pipe flings her aside, then rears up again, trying to whack Sam.

I grab it at the height of the arc, pushing back as if attempting to shove an invisible attacker away from my little brother. Sam still hasn't moved since he hit the ground. He's gotta be aware of this pipe trying to smash him in the head, but he's not reacting. His face is red, but other than that, he looks as calm as a meditating monk.

Expecting the pipe to toss me again, I focus on holding it away from Sam while being ready to flow with any attempt to fling me aside. The way it's moving makes me imagine an invisible man swinging it like a club, but I'm not hearing any footsteps moving with us. No, there isn't an invisible demon here. This is just energy in the pipe, like a poltergeist. Now that I'm aware of what it's going to do, it's not too difficult to use my flight power to control the situation and stay on the pipe. It tries to hurl me away twice, but I simply glide around in a circle, keeping my grip on the old metal scrap.

"What the hell is going on?" yells Ashley.

"Probably that other demon," I grumble. "Blix?"

The imp pops his head up out of a pile of debris in the corner and chatters.

"What did he say?" I glance at Sam as the pipe swings me in circles.

Ashley ducks my flailing legs, then lunges in and also grabs the pipe. Between the two of us, we're mostly able to hold it stationary. Damn thing is getting pissed. Not sure what 'it' is, but the energy in the room is taking a serious turn to the dark and angry. The mood is somewhere between telling Dad and Sam that DC Comics is better than Marvel and Sierra overhearing some adult say that girls have no business playing video games.

"Sam?" I yell. "What did Blix say?"

The boy continues to stare into space.

Blix bursts out of the debris pile and fly-zooms off down the hall, deeper into the house.

"Wow, that's not normal." Ashley bites her lip. "It didn't hit him *that* hard. He shouldn't still be paralyzed."

"We have no way to know how bad it feels to get whacked in the balls." I grunt, struggling to hold the pipe away from smacking me in the face.

"Umm. Can't be as bad as childbirth," says Ashley.

I stare at her. "Have you ever had a baby?"

"No." She rolls her eyes. "You know that."

"Then you still have no frame of reference."

Ashley again looks at him. "Should we, umm... like check him out to make sure he's not seriously hurt?"

Even if I could get past the massive awkwardness of what she's suggesting, we can't exactly do it while this pipe is trying to kill us all. Worse, if he thought he might be hurt, Sam would be totally okay with me or Ashley 'examining the injury.' Somehow, his complete lack of embarrassment makes it ten times worse for me.

Sam meeps.

"Is that a yes or no?" asks Ashley.

Hmm. Maybe I can avoid the cringe entirely by peeking into his head. Sure, I'll experience the same pain he's experiencing, but it's much less embarrassing. No sooner do I start to concentrate on looking into his head, the damned pipe seems to sense my shift in attention. It wrenches itself down in a twist, slipping away from my hands with enough force to fling me to the floor. My face crushes a long-empty plastic soda bottle, launching the cap across the room like a bullet.

Ashley then whacks me in the side of the knee.

Well, *she* isn't really doing it. The damn demon-possessed pipe did it all by itself, but she's holding onto it so it *looks* like she did it.

"Ack! Sorry!" yells Ashley.

At least, she made a blurry sort of noise that I assume is her apologizing. Can't hear her too well thanks to an explosion of blinding pain. Feels as if my leg got blown off at the knee by another hand grenade. I'm about to start screaming when my eyes come back into focus on my *intact* leg. There are only a few little scrapes where the pipe made contact, and a smallish bruise. I picked a bad night to wear shorts. Something tells me having denim between my skin and the pipe wouldn't have made any difference. The injury is really minor. I've done worse to myself walking into things. Only, for no plausible reason, it freakin' hurts like crazy.

"Aww, fffff..." I swallow the f-bomb, grab my knee, and curl up on the floor, rocking side to side while sucking air past my teeth. Now, I totally get the knee pain joke from *Family Guy*.

An aurora of agony undulates inside my knee. It's unnatural. Oh, that explains things. I emit a shuddering wheeze. My experience at being on the receiving end of vampire claws helps me hold this pain at arm's length. It's bad but not *that* bad. My memory of much worse pain pushes this strange effect out of my awareness. In a moment, my leg no longer feels as if it had been mauled, rather a dull throbbing ache like one of the many times I rammed my knee into my bedpost, or desk, or doorjamb.

And. Ugh. A guy taking a hit in the nethers is painful enough from an ordinary pipe. No wonder Sam can't move. The thought makes me extra pissed off at this thing for causing magically amplified pain to my little brother.

Snarling, I mentally force myself to sit up.

Sam meeps again.

Blix comes racing into the living room, one arm up over his head. He's holding an amulet or something with a long gold chain trailing behind him in the air. The floating pipe loses interest in Ashley as well as Sam. It zooms after the imp, dragging Ashley around like a human kite for a few seconds until she loses her grip and faceplants the wall beside the fireplace, her body horizontal five feet above the floor.

The imp races by above me, chattering and waving the amulet.

"Oof," mutters Ashley as she floats away from the wall. She hangs there horizontal for a few seconds, shaking off the disorientation of a face-first meeting with drywall, then rotates upright and sets down on her feet. Bits of plaster dust fall from her chest and legs.

When an invasion of imps descended upon Cottage Lake, it became quite clear that blunt force didn't bother them much. It's as though the little bastards (I exempt Blix from the term 'little bastards') were made of spongy rubber. Mom walloping them with her giant iron skillet only stunned them. Blix running away from the pipe probably means it *can* hurt him. Safe bet it's the same paranormal effect responsible for the unusually severe pain. It honestly didn't bonk me that hard in a physical sense.

Blix zooms over me again, chattering feverishly.

"What?" I rasp, rubbing my leg. "I don't understand you."

"Break," squeaks Sam.

Ashley reaches a hand out. "Gimme. Sarah can't stand up right now."

Sam groans and shoves himself up to sit, staring at me with concern. He hadn't been crying before, but sitting up to check on me pushes past some threshold and sets the tears streaming down his face. Still, his expression is remarkably calm.

"I'm okay," I wheeze. "Just a whole bunch of amplified pain."

Ashley chases Blix around in circles. "Amplified pain?"

"Yeah." I cringe and straighten my leg. "Like being forced to listen to William Shatner sing a cover of an entire Linkin Park album nonstop."

The pipe stops chasing Blix for a moment. I get the sense of the entity animating it cringing in horror at what I said.

"Wow," mutters Ashley. "Are you sure you don't just want me to kill you, so the pain stops?"

"Hah." Cringing, I rub the spot where it hit me.

Blix pulls an abrupt 180-degree midair turn. The pipe swings itself at him. Like a tiny airplane with horns evading the arm of King Kong, the little guy barrel rolls out of the way and zooms over Ashley, dropping the amulet to her. She swipes it out of the air, grabs it in both hands, and snaps the medallion in two pieces as easily as if she broke a giant cookie.

A flash of crimson light paints the room red for a tenth of a second. The pipe tumbles over and falls to the floor as if dropped. My leg stops hurting. Sam gasps in a huge breath. He pushes himself up on all fours and crawls over to me.

"Sare, you okay?"

"Yeah. Just bonked me on the leg." I look him over. Except for being red in the face, he doesn't seem hurt. "What about you? That looked really painful."

"It was, but I'm okay now." He peers down at his jeans. "It hurt so much I didn't really even feel it."

"That doesn't make any sense." Ashley tosses the amulet bits aside.

Sam wobbles to his feet. "Sure, it does. My brain refused to process it."

I stand, leaning all my weight on my left leg while raising and lowering my right, working the last bits of soreness out of the knee. "Don't suppose you know what just happened?"

"Other demon." Sam gestures at one of the amulet fragments. "The summoning bound it to that amulet."

"Umm. Is it gone for good?" I explain the scroll we found and the writing on the back.

Blix chatters.

Sam winces. "Yeah. He thinks you guys might've accidentally summoned it when you looked at the occult writing. They didn't finish it, so instead of getting a really nasty, powerful demon bound to specific instructions, it ended up being pretty weak and annoying."

"Demonic poltergeist." Ashley walks over and grabs Beelzebubba by the ankles. "C'mon, let's finish up and get out of here."

"Good idea." I hobble over and grab his arms. "Umm, how are we going to light them on fire?"

Sam waves in a 'no problem' gesture. "I got it handled."

Ashley and I shrug at each other, then lift the big guy and haul him outside to the pile o' dead vampires.

We drop him in place, then step back. Sam walks gingerly out of the house, still clearly not having fully recovered from taking a steel pipe to the groin. He stops at the base of the porch steps and stares at the bodies. For a moment, I half expect him to turn into Drew Barrymore's character from *Firestarter*. He's got that same creepy little kid about to do something paranormally bad type stare.

A moment later, a flamethrower effect appears from thin air on the other side of the body pile. The shimmering dark crimson fire briefly illuminates the face and shoulders of Max, our 'pet' hellhound. Ashley and I involuntarily take two rapid steps back. This fire is a bit more dangerous than ordinary earthly flames. Remember how I said crematory ovens are much hotter than a campfire? Well, my kid brother found a way to bring a portable crematory oven here.

In a mere three minutes, there's nothing left of any of these guys but a dusting of ash on the dirt. There's less chance of them getting back up from that than Pee Wee Herman returning as an A-list celebrity.

"Thanks," says Sam.

A distinctly canine warble comes from the empty space next to my brother. He grins, squirms, and jostles around like an enormous dog is affectionately nuzzling him. So... so... strange.

Soon, the last bits of red fire disappear.

"Welp." Ashley glances at me. "Guess we're done."

"Looks like it." I stretch my right leg out again. Knee is still sore. Ugh. How long is that going to take to heal?

"Back to camp?" Ashley swings her arms back and forth.

"Yeah."

Sam shuffles over to me. "I'm glad the camp is kinda far away from this house."

"Keep the evil at a safe distance." Ashley nods.

"Well, yeah. But… I don't really wanna walk now." Sam manages a weak smile. "Oh, hang on a sec."

"What's up?"

He shuffles back into the house. "Be right back."

Ashley and I exchange a glance of confusion.

Sam reappears a moment later, carrying the broadsword Slash tried to kill Ashley with. What is it with boys and swords? The darn thing is almost taller than he is, but he appears to have claimed it. Whatever. I'm the overly permissive big sister. Mom can argue about it if she wants. Dad will surely take Sam's side here and approve keeping the sword, but not necessarily allowing the boy to have it in his bedroom until he's older. I mean, the thing looks authentic—not a cheap prop—and it's probably expensive.

I pick him up. "Are you sure you're okay?"

"Yeah. Just sore."

Blix lands on my shoulder and chatters.

"He said we'll be fine in like an hour." Sam exhales. "Not real pain."

"Did we destroy that demon?" asks Ashley.

Blix gives her a thumbs-up.

"Good. Last thing I need is something else following us back to camp." I turn in place, surveying the area. No sign of any more vampires, demons, or any ill-tempered sasquatch. There isn't even a Girl Scout with a bad attitude looking for overdue cookie payments. Feeling momentarily safe, I lift off, carrying my brother.

Ashley glides up alongside us, smiling at the wind in her face. It's hard not to love flying. Below us, the forests of Northern California remain quiet and placid. Maybe there is a sasquatch looking up at us, maybe not.

What are the odds the rest of our vacation will be calm?

Yeah, I know. But I can hope.

17

UNSAFELY HOME AGAIN

Color me surprised.

Nothing paranormally weird or even conventionally dangerous happened over the next five days of exploring the redwood forests. Ashley and I did return to visit Portia and let her know the details of what happened to Jesse Stroud. She knew about the diabolist vampires but didn't take them seriously, believing their occultism no more dangerous than a bunch of edgy art-school students who paint pentagrams on the walls of abandoned buildings.

Anyway, we're back home.

Some people think the purpose of vacations is not so much to enjoy the vacation itself but to make you appreciate home all that much more. Could be. I'm guessing the person who said that is like me, a homebody, the tragically uncool vampire who runs back under her parents' roof rather than taking unlife as a free pass to explore the world, free of responsibility or attachments.

Whatever. I don't care what anyone thinks of me. I never let social standing affect me in high school, and I'm not about to let undead peer pressure change me, either. Paolo and Stefano can look down their noses at me all they want; I'm still not going to abandon my family. To be fair, they are kinda chilling out lately. Neither one of them expected me to actually follow through with delivering Wolent's giant bomb. I've shown I can 'take orders' and do what needs to be done.

For the time being, I don't waste much time thinking about vampires or supernatural nonsense. This is a 'time to be normal' moment. I'm relaxing on the couch in our living room with Chloe, trying to find something worth watching. Chloe keeps nudging me to put *Frozen* on again. The way little kids have of being able to watch the same movie over and over and over and never get tired of it? That's her. She's that age. 250 years from now, she'll still be watching *Frozen*… unless some other kids' movie comes out and replaces it.

Heck, in 250 years, will movies still even be a thing? Did children 250 years ago want the same story read to them over and over? Two and a half centuries from now, we'll probably be able to project our consciousness into a fake reality and *experience* movies like memories. *Total Recall* anyone?

Hmm. Would such technology work on vampires? Guess I'll find out if it ever happens.

Nothing jumps out to catch Chloe's attention, so I put *Frozen* on again. She's thrilled, almost as if she'd never seen it before. An eternal seven-year-old is a bit like the joke about a goldfish with a three-second memory span. It's easy to keep her entertained, but I'm going to be in for a *lot* of repetitiveness. Not that big of a problem for me, really. I signed up for this job—watching Chloe that is—knowing how kids her age can be. I mean, what kind of monster would I be to choose the ability to have a social life over a little kid's continued existence? Even worse, I don't even want a social life. And as far as repetitiveness goes, *hello*… I'm still playing freakin' *Skyrim*.

There are two kinds of children. One type will sit and watch a cartoon in complete mesmerized silence. The other type sings along with every song and parrots every spoken line. Guess which type, Chloe is. Yeah, she's not the silent one. I have the sad thought she's making up for her former life when she fearfully had to stay as quiet as possible. At least she's on key. If we didn't have to, like, keep her entire existence hidden from the world, she'd probably make it to the finals on AGT. The absolutely ridiculous idea of starting up a VGT—Vampire's got Talent—show gets me laughing.

Chloe spares only a half second of a weird look at my unexplained laughter before ignoring it and continuing to sing along with Elsa.

This is one of those moments any parent would consider a precious memory. I do, too... despite not really being her mom, and the moment not being quite as precious as it would with a mortal child. We have forever to repeat this scene.

Speaking of forever... I wonder how much longer the road trip tradition will go on? Are the 'rents going to want to do it when the Littles are all adults? Will we even be able to get everyone together? Will the Littles even become adults? I half chuckle, half wince at the last question. It's perhaps a manifestation of my worry something about my crazy unlife will hurt them, but it's as much not knowing what the heck Sophia did.

Dad would be positively thrilled if Sierra and Sophia remained tweens forever. He had enough awkward problems dealing with me going through the teenage years, boyfriends, and all the associated uncomfortable things dads find uncomfortable about raising girls. As fathers go, he handled it well. He'd love to keep thinking of his kids as innocents. Or maybe I'm romanticizing it too much. He'd be proud of them for growing up. Question is, will they?

In my mind, our Family Road Trip morphs from us piling into the Yukon to a literal caravan of vehicles as Sierra, Sophia, and Sam all bring their own cars plus families along for a cross-country adventure of epic proportions. Yeah, I don't see that happening. Sierra's totally not interested in getting married and having kids—which probably means she'll be the first of my sibs to do so. Sophia's going to be bashfully afraid of boys right up until the moment she isn't. If I had to guess, she's going to find one guy she *really* likes and that'll be that. They'll either end up married for the rest of their lives or she'll give up on romance entirely after losing him.

Just guessing.

Sam, I dunno. If he doesn't hurry up and get a girlfriend the day after he turns fifteen, Uncle Hank will declare him gay. The episode with the pink dress didn't help that. But... good thing is, no one but Uncle Hank gives a shit about his opinions.

And, crap. I'm doing it again.

My mind is wandering around a bunch of what-ifs and drifting into the maudlin aspects of eternal life. This means something is bothering me. It's not only that the remainder of our vacation happened without a problem. It's also not from any lingering issues regarding my meeting with Arthur Wolent, where I told him about encountering a sefil and destroying its creators. The real problem is I don't know why I'm anxious. Despite being home, some indefinable energy around me is preventing me from fully embracing the feeling of safety and security home should provide.

It can't simply be the looming dread that comes hand in hand with the tail end of summer.

Fall is a metaphor for death in a way. Long days of care free play are about to end, drowning in the morass of school and responsibility. At least, that's how kids think. Mom and Dad don't really have much of a reaction to the end of summer. Jobs don't take a three-month vacation for adults. Like most parents, they sorta look forward to it. Schools get to babysit the kids for most of the day, pressure off them. Can't complain though. I'd rather be permanently frozen feeling a bit down over the last two weeks of August than have to deal with a day job. Especially as an immortal. The nine-to-five thing is only tolerable because there's a promise of retirement at the end. For a vampire who never gets old? Eek. Eternal cubicle dwelling is a fate worse than death.

Something's wrong, and I don't know what. It *might* be pure nerves. It's possible I'm so used to things going crazy that a few days of everything being normal and fine is making me superstitiously think the Universe will take revenge. But... I can't say for sure. It's often difficult to tell superstitious worry apart from inhuman intuition. I'm almost certain this is more tangible than my overactive anxiety.

Our road trip ended in the most bizarre way imaginable: completely normal. I almost can't believe the days went by without me having to get into a fight with a sasquatch or even an ill-tempered squirrel. Sophia was super bummed at not seeing any faeries. Mom's glad to be home. She's not really a fan of camping. However, she'll tolerate it once every few years to make Dad happy. Mom did insist that in the event a road trip happens next year, we go somewhere civilized with museums or fun things to do.

So, yeah. Home.

It's fairly late in the afternoon. Sam and Ronan went to Daryl's. The girls went with their friends to a pool party. Ashley headed back to her mom's place to spend time with her. As tight as the two of us are, we don't need to spend *every* waking moment together. I mean, it's not like we don't have forever. As uncomfortable as it was for me to get past the idea of her becoming undead, it does eliminate the sense of depressing urgency to enjoy the time I have with her.

Wolent, for his part, sat through my story of the sefil with a strange facial expression. The only way I can think to describe it is the look that might be on a man's face if he watches a giant bus slam into a wall three feet away from his daughter and she walks away without a scratch. He was predictably upset over Jesse Stroud's destruction, but had no outlet for it. The entity responsible for it—as well as those who summoned it—are already all destroyed. About all he could do was spend twenty minutes grumbling about California being a 'vampire wild land' and worrying out loud that sooner or later some idiot down there is going to doom us all. Us being vampires.

Making matters a little more nerve-wracking for me, Dalton's been telepathically cautioning me about keeping Mel as secret as possible. He's worried that if other vampires learn my kid brother could basically snap his fingers and kill them, his life would be in danger. I'm not too worried. Honestly, it isn't Sam who has the power to do that. It's not like he can *force* Mel to destroy any vampire he points at whenever he wants. Besides, the boy isn't going to run around flaunting he's got a succubus on speed dial.

Also, Wolent certainly knows about Mel already. I have no doubt he's seen her in my thoughts. Couldn't help but think about her while telling him what happened in California. He doesn't read my mind out of lack of trust. It's merely faster and more efficient for him. Besides, if I ran into any important or dangerous vampires I don't recognize, he would see them in my thoughts and know exactly who's causing problems.

The movie's almost over when Mom comes in the front door, back from work. She pauses behind the sofa while I give her the current status update. Chloe perks up when I pass along that Sophia and Sierra are at a pool party. Once our briefing ends, Mom goes to the kitchen for her usual habit of calling each Littles' cell phone and checking up on them. She's not obnoxious about it. Every day when she's home from work, she'll call everyone with an 'are you okay, do you need anything, don't forget dinner in about an hour' type thing. Assuming, of course, they're out somewhere. If they're home, she doesn't bother calling for obvious reasons.

"I wanna go swimming," says Chloe.

Her tone isn't bratty, demanding, or whiny.

Oof. Umm… "I'll try to think of a way to take you swimming."

"It's not hard. Child plus water equals swimming." She grins.

"I mean…" I squeeze her hand. "You know we really can't be seen in public or we'll need to move every two years or so. People can't see you not getting bigger."

She huffs. "Yeah. I know. I don't wanna get in trouble. Didn't say it's *possible* for me to go swimming, just that I want to. Never did swimming before."

"Never?" I blink.

"No." She swishes her feet side to side, tapping her big toes together. "My parents were buttheads."

This we knew. 'Buttheads' is putting it extremely mildly. "Do you even know how to swim?"

She stares at me like I just asked her if the sun exists. "No, but it isn't like I can drown anymore."

Ashley breezes in from the kitchen, carrying a bowl of popcorn. "She's got a point. We could go to the lake tonight." She flops on the couch beside me, holding the bowl out in front of me so Chloe and I can reach some. "Only like a week of summer left."

I blink at Ashley, surprised she's back already.

"Oh, no." Chloe grabs her face in mock panic. "Only a week? We should hurry and have fun before I gotta go to bed early for school nights."

Ashley and I sputter into laughter... and get into a comical discussion about a fictional world where vampire children are so numerous they have legit schools. We construct a *Harry Potter*-ish type fantasy, talking about the sorts of classes they'd teach. It's funny for a while until we start getting bogged down in the details, like would the kids keep repeating the same grades over and over since no one's getting older?

Once the giggling subsides, I nudge Ashley. "You're back fast. Is your mom okay?"

"Yep. She's good. Actually going on a date tonight with some guy from her office." Ashley wags her eyebrows. "She hinted they might be going back to the house after, so I am keeping my distance."

"Good for her." I wag my eyebrows. "Are you gonna check the guy out?"

"Eventually, yeah." She tosses popcorn in her mouth. "If she dates him for more than a week."

This is pretty epic news. Mrs. Carter hasn't even accepted an invitation out for coffee since Ashley's bio-dad left. I can't help but wonder if she's having a reaction to her daughter going vampire. Could be positive, as in she no longer feels like every ounce of her waking energy needs to be devoted to protecting her child. Could be negative, as in such a reminder of mortality has her looking not to be lonely in a romantic sense before she gets too old for it to be possible. I'll be cautiously optimistic for the time being and be happy for Mrs. C.

"Lake?" asks Chloe. "Can we?"

"Well, it'll be dark and not too likely anyone will see us out there at night." I tap a finger to my chin, then grab a handful of popcorn. "Why not?"

18

THE WORRIES OF MODERN UNLIFE

I t's creeping up on four in the morning.

I'm stretched out in the bathtub enjoying a nice, warm, relaxing soak. The trip to the lake went well. Chloe had a blast. Despite never having been swimming before, being able to fly kinda trivializes things. Flying in air and flying in water aren't terribly different from swimming. Ash and I did try our best to show her how to legitimately swim to make the experience more authentic. I really hope the sound of her laughter never gets old. There are precious few things in the world made of pure innocence, like a child's laughter.

Anyway, the tub is mine now.

I gave Chloe a bath as soon as we returned since the lake water has a certain aroma to it better off not being allowed to seep into hair. Yeah, she's always going to be seven and always going to need at least some degree of supervision in the tub. I didn't exactly have to scrub her like an infant, but one doesn't leave kids her age unsupervised in the bath. Or… maybe not. I mean, she said so herself, it's not like she can drown. She's also not yet reached the age where she demands privacy.

Ugh. My unlife is weird. I have questions Dr. Spock can't even answer.

A few minutes of relaxation comes to a begrudging end as another worry woodpeckers into my brain. Happily replaying a joyful Chloe playing in the water makes me think about having only a week of summer left. This gets me thinking about school again and how Ashley decided to stop going to college now that she's a vampire. For her, this is a permanent summer vacation: no school, no job, no responsibilities ever again—other than helping me watch Chloe.

The two of us have chewed a hole in the wall and escaped the rat maze.

Of course, the reality outside the boundaries of the video game called mortal life can be scary, too. We can only minimize risk so much. However, really... the Forces of Evil™ have better things to do than come looking for two teen girls who just want to have fun.

... and now I'm humming Cyndi Lauper.

Yes, I know who she is. Thanks, Dad. He loves all Eighties music.

This makes me wonder if things had been different and I grew up into my forties, would I be permanently stuck in the 2000s the same way he's fixated on the Eighties? Meh. Unanswerable questions shouldn't be asked. It would be easier to explain why the Kardashians are famous or why anyone cares what movie critics think about movies.

Ash has a point. Maybe I should stop going to college. It's really just a waste of money. I'll never actually use whatever education I get. Day jobs and careers don't work for vampires. If I dropped college, the end of summer wouldn't feel so much like a looming end of fun times.

I mull this idea for a while but can't quite get past how sad it will make my parents. They need that little bit of plausible deniability that some portion of their lives is still normal. Eldest kid in college is the expected route life would take. I'm going for their sake more than mine. And, yes, I know, that's a horrible reason to do something like college. But I don't care. It's not like I'm wasting four years of my life. It's four years I won't notice gone and that will mean everything to Mom and Dad.

Suppose I could peek into their heads to see if that's actually true. Maybe they aren't so wound up on me going to college and their need for me to do so is all in *my* head. I mean, they're going to get the same effect when the Littles go to college. Not like I'm their only kid, merely the eldest. Yes, the ethical thing to do would be come clean and ask them, but if I ask, then they will suspect I don't really want to go… and that will make them sad, too. If, of course, they care as much as I think they do.

Ugh.

My brain isn't ready for this conflict, so it makes me think about why Ashley becoming a vampire is simultaneously awesome and sad. She had hopes and dreams for the future—and just tossed them aside like no big deal. Then again, I had hopes and dreams for the future, too. At least she had the choice to do something else. Unlife just kinda fell on my head. No, this is not me regretting what happened. Seriously. Growing old, having a family, career and so on vs. eternal youth and a carefree existence? Seems like a no brainer, right? But emotions make no sense.

Somehow, the little fact that Ashley *died* needles at me. I should be sad about it. But I also shouldn't. She didn't stay dead. Well, she did, but you know what I mean. I shouldn't be all morose over the abstract idea that she technically died. Reality is, I won't need to watch her get old and die. We are both frozen in time, forever just out of high school.

Huh. Frozen. Is that why Chloe likes the movie so much? Is she making a punny statement about us being vampires? She hasn't been in this house long enough to inherit Dad's punnery.

Maybe these things feel strange to me because I'm the age I am. The 'rents—especially Dad—would jump at the chance to be eighteen again. Wait, no. Dad would prefer to be twelve, not eighteen. Eighteen had too much responsibility. People expect eighteen-year-olds to get summer jobs. My father misses the days when his biggest worry was which video game to play or which movie to watch next. Every kid— my parents included—couldn't wait to grow up. I remember being ten and demanding to get old enough to drive like *right now*. I don't regret not being ten anymore. I'm happy where I am. It's gotta be different past forty, some kind of 'you don't know what you have 'til it's gone' type thing.

Like, Chloe will never feel weird about not growing up because she has no way to understand what she's missing. Can't miss what you don't know, right? And seriously, never being interested in boys (or girls, whatever) is only going to uncomplicate her life. Existence was so much simpler when all the drama in my life came from which plushie got the prime spot under my arm at night. The other animals tended to get jealous.

Yes, I'm talking about kid-me pretending. I feel, given the weird nature of my life at present, I need to qualify that my stuffed animals were not, in fact, alive and did not, in fact, get jealous. As long as I am responsible as a guardian, Chloe's in for an eternity of simple happiness.

I swish around in the warm embrace of a lavender-blueberry bath bomb.

Out of nowhere, my thoughts leap back to the moment the sefil began inhaling my life force. My stomach does an immediate backflip. Like some girl in a horror movie, I curl up in the tub against the wall, staring at the bathroom door. The mood in the air is so ominous, I expect the door to fly open at any second to reveal the monster, returned.

For a full minute, I sit there motionless, not even breathing.

The sense that a malignant presence is lurking just outside the door waiting for the right moment to attack me is impossible to ignore. It's too real to be my imagination. At least I'm already naked. Vampire fights are deadly to fabric. Claws, knives, supernatural strength, and my bad luck do one heck of a number on my wardrobe. Maybe I should just dump shampoo all over myself so I'm hard to get a hold of.

I can't imagine how the hell that sefil came back to life, but if he's here, my only chance is going to be running.

The doorknob turns.

In an instant, I'm no longer a vampire, but an ordinary girl about to be Norman Bates-ed. I'm too scared to even scream as the door opens.

… and it's Sam.

As soon as my brain processes it's my little brother staggering half-awake into the bathroom and not some demonic force, the sense of supernatural terror dissipates as fast as a light switch going off.

"Sorry, Sare," whispers Sam, trudging straight past me to the toilet.

I can't reach the shower curtain without uncurling myself. Sitting in a ball waist-deep in opaque purple water offers a reasonable degree of modesty. Besides, Sam isn't looking at me. He's almost sleepwalking.

The sound of him peeing is almost deafening.

It's awkward, but I'm not *too* embarrassed. One does not share a house with three siblings without getting used to bathroom barging. I fold my arms across my chest and wait, staring at the little sparkly bits of bath bomb floating in front of me. Soon, a flush announces he's finished.

"Sam?" I whisper.

He pauses halfway to the door, still not looking over at me. "Yeah?"

"Did you sense anything weird and demonic in the hallway?"

"No." He yawns. "But I'm also not all the way awake. Why?"

"Thought I felt something bad watching me."

The boy wipes his eyes, yawns, then turns his head toward me. He's clearly exhausted, but the expression of protective concern on his face shines through it being so late. "I'll check."

"Thanks."

He nods once, then walks out, closing the door behind him.

I uncurl and exhale.

The bathroom once again feels normal. An unknown power violated the sanctuary of my most relaxing place, my inner bath bomb sanctum. This cannot go unanswered. Rather than scared, my mood plunges into anger. Since it's impossible for me to relax again tonight, I get out of the tub, flick the drain open, and grab a towel.

I'm at a loss to explain what happened, but something *definitely* happened. The Universe wouldn't dare let us have five days of uninterrupted vacation unless it was saving up a big paranormal whammy for later. Yeah, I should probably go ask someone for help-slash-advice.

Question is... who?

19

A PARENTAL SHORTFALL OF CINEMATIC PROPORTIONS

Vampiric sleep is awesome.

Not the actual sleep itself since it's not something I'm aware of, barring the occasional way-too-vivid dream. The awesome part is how it's impossible for me to lie awake for hours staring at the ceiling whenever I'm worried, anxious, emotional, or overtired. As soon as the big, fiery ball of nope peeks over the horizon, I am *out*.

By the way, I found out, courtesy of Dalton, that we aren't necessarily tied to the clock as far as sleeping goes. The concept of hours, minutes, and seconds is entirely of human invention. Being essentially magical creatures, we are subject to far more primordial laws—and I'm not talking about the rule where two guys cannot stand at adjacent urinals in an otherwise empty bathroom. I mean really primordial, planets and galaxies type stuff. It's the position of the sun relative to the Earth. This is why vampires all experience sleep based on the sunrise of where they happen to be. If it were purely clock based, all vampires in the world would pass out at the exact same moment regardless of the sun.

That would be mildly inconvenient.

Anyway, the Universe generally has its crap together and does stuff in sensible ways... except for how it loves to mess with me. In the last few minutes before falling asleep last morning, Ashley and I got to talking like we so often do while 'having a sleepover.' And yes, she's like a human cat, prefers to share a bed with me rather than sleep in her bedroom. As kids having sleepovers, her bedroom wasn't in the house like it is now—long story—but she also wasn't a vampire. Remember that nest of jerks I bombed? Well, there's a reason the phrase 'vampire nest' is a thing. Some part of our deep inner psyche, the part that's not from human origin, has a definite pull to sleep in groups. Maybe it's where the whole association between bats and vampires came from.

Kinda like how if you put more than one woman in the same house, our plumbing tends to synch up with each other? Putting more than one vampire under the same roof usually results in a scene straight out of the morning after a frat party in the Sixties. Thankfully, it's just Ashley, Chloe, and myself, so we don't look like the fallout from a wild college sex party. And by that, I mean boys and girls tangled in a mass pile of bodies with derpy facial expressions and no semblance of order.

Nah, it's just the three of us tangled in a derpy pile of bodies.

It's gotta be a defensive mechanism. Vampires sleeping together increases the chances that anyone who messes with us during the day will regret it. Sure, they might destroy one of us, but the others will wake up and shred them. Unlike medieval times, we are not facing any serious risk of random superstitious idiots stopping by with a sharpened stake and the will to use it. We have a normal house protected by the veil of innocuousness—as well as a large hellhound. On a conscious level, we are not afraid of being attacked while sleeping.

Subconscious brains—even among the undead—don't listen to reason and they don't take no for an answer. They're like toddlers... or telemarketers.

Oh, right, back to talking to Ashley before we passed out. I've decided not to be confused by the Universe anymore. I used to wonder how a girl like me who did everything right, followed all the rules, and tried to be as nice and kind as possible (though admittedly, I could've been more aware of Ashley's wants and had been somewhat bitchy to the Littles over the last two years of my life). But hey, what teenager *isn't* subject to fits of mild brattiness? Nothing I did was, in the grand cosmic scheme of things, truly bad or abnormal for a girl my age. Yet, fate still turned me into a vampire. Used to say it was like the health and fitness nut who busts their butt to live perfectly only to get some nasty terminal disease at age thirty-five.

Anyway, I've changed my attitude. Vampirism is a reward. At least, to me it is.

This is the attitude we're going into eternity with. The Universe decided to reward us with being forever teenagers experiencing the absolute best time of life in perpetuity. I'd remark 'stay positive, right', but we're serious. This isn't me trying to blow sunshine up my own backside. We're at the perfect stage of life. *Some* responsibility that lets us feel like an adult when we want to... but still young enough to where actual adults will often let us slide on stuff because 'we're just kids.' Few people in society would have much to say about a couple girls who look sixteen lounging around doing nothing. Certainly not as socially unacceptable as a girl in her thirties still living at home with the parents and not working.

So yeah, we have it pretty damn sweet.

Of course, some mysterious Force of Evil™ out there is threatening the everlasting happiness of being a teenager.

I wake first.

It's normal to envision two absolutely dear friends and their adopted kid co-sleeping to be this cute, adorable scene. For the most part, it is. But, this is also our reality so there is derp involved. I regain consciousness to find Chloe's foot in my face and Ashley drooling on my shoulder. Well, not really drooling. She would be if she were mortal. While the two of us are quite capable of doing that while awake, asleep, our bodies stop pretending to be alive.

Ashley's hair is a wild mess. She's got one arm up over her head, mouth agape. I'm still not sure how in the heck Chloe moves. The kid almost never seems to be in the same position she was in before we pass out. Uh oh. Is she having vampire nightmares about her former life? *Can* vampires wake up from bad dreams the same way mortals do? Hmm. I am probably being overprotective. The kid looks completely at ease. She just sleeps hard, fully committing to unconsciousness as deeply as Dad commits to memorizing Eighties trivia.

I reach a hand out from under the blankets, grasp her ankle, and move her foot out of my face. After sitting up, I lift her off the mattress, spin her around to orient head-toward-pillow, and set her back down tucked against Ashley.

Alas, being awake allows my mind to spin with worry all over again. I can't sit still, nor stay in bed. I strip out of my long T-shirt, wrap myself in a towel, and hurry to the end of the basement for a quick shower. Ash and Chloe are still sleeping when I sneak back into my room and finish drying off. Feeling a bit weird today, so I grab a plain white sundress from my closet, pull it on, and head upstairs, my hair still a bit damp.

The aroma of freshly baked cookies hangs in the stairway leading up from the basement to the kitchen. It's an unusual fragrance, somewhat close to apple pie but not really. Whoever baked didn't make chocolate chip—they did something more exotic. Ooh. Score another big win for vampire life. I can eat *all the cookies* and not care about anything more than how bizarre they'll feel coming out. No calories, no diabetes, nothing... well, nothing except for feeling greedy and rude to my family for hogging them all. I have no intention to gorge myself, merely being amused at the notion of doing so wouldn't affect my waistline at all.

Then again, I have Dad's genes. I probably could've eaten a scary number of cookies and not gained an ounce, even as a mortal. Some people are lucky like that. Others can look at a photograph of a cookie and gain half a pound.

I emerge from the door into the daylight-warm kitchen to find Dad hovering by the counter nibbling on a cookie. A tray of said cookies sit in front of him, partially covered by a dishtowel. They look a bit strange, no two are exactly the same size. Some almost look like tiny burritos—a thin layer of cookie material wrapped around a light brown fruity filling. Interesting. They smell good, though.

Dad stops gnawing on his cookie to stare at me.

Yeah, it's the dress. While I'm nowhere near as avoidant of them as Sierra, my usual MO is T-shirt and jeans, or shorts. Me wearing a dress isn't so rare as to cause an obligatory joke about 'what's the occasion,' though. My father simply raises an eyebrow.

"Hey," I say, wandering over to the tray and sniffing. "Someone baked?"

"Obviously," mumbles Dad around the cookie. "I'm assuming we did not experience spontaneous cookiegenesis."

"Spontaneous Cookiegenesis sounds like the name of the kawaii babymetal band Sophia's going to start when she's a high school freshman."

Dad snort-laughs.

Not sure what's funnier to him: the name, or the suggestion Sophia—who is not musically inclined as well as intensely shy—would start a band.

"Hon, try to bite one of these."

I study the lay of cookies in the tray, searching for my victim. "That was my plan already."

He waits, watching me.

"Why are you looking at me like that?"

Dad gestures at the tray. "Just… try one."

I select a somewhat undersized, quite sloppy looking, cookie. One that I'm sure Sierra or Sam would ignore for being a reject. Smells fine, just looks ugly. Thinking little of it, I raise the cookie to my mouth and bite—on stone. Okay, not exactly stone. It doesn't hurt my teeth, nor is it absolutely rock hard. There's a bit of give, but I can't seem to bite through the cookie no matter how hard I try.

When I pull it away from my mouth to examine the tiniest of tooth indentations in the cookie material, Dad gives me a 'that's what I thought' face.

"What's going on?" I glance between him and the tray. "Is this some kind of cruel prank? Wonderful smelling cookies we can't eat?"

"I'm wondering that myself." Dad chomps on his cookie like Scrooge McDuck checking a gold coin for authenticity. "This reeks of Sophia."

Of the kids living under this roof, she is by far the most prone to spontaneous acts of bakery. Even if these cookies did not exhibit any unusual properties, she would be the most likely suspect.

"Sophia?" calls Dad. "Got a minute? Can you come to the kitchen, please?"

I squeeze at the cookie in my fingers. Feels normal. Squishy enough to be a cookie rather than a hunk of concrete. The thing doesn't weigh any more than a cookie this size ought to. Again, I try to bite it and my teeth come to a halt like a millimeter deep in the dough. The flavor is good, too. Kinda Fig Newton like. I think Sophia tried to bake homemade versions of those things. Smelling and sorta-tasting it is making me hungry... and it's getting frustrating the cookie won't let me bite it.

Clattering and thudding come from the deck out back. I look over at the sliding glass door as Sam and Ronan wander into view. The boys are both wearing swim shorts, mud, and grass bits. Seems they've been horsing around in the lawn sprinkler. Even without my mental powers being online at the moment, I can read their intention clear as day. They want snacks... and probably smelled the cookies from the yard.

Sam grabs the door and pulls it open. Both boys step into the house, shivering slightly at the transition from late-August outdoors to air conditioning while soaking wet. Neither hesitate for longer than it takes to inhale a savoring breath of the aroma, then rush over.

"Oh, there's cookies," says Sam in a nonserious attempt to pretend he hadn't noticed them already. He grabs one. "What's for dinner?"

"It's not even four yet," says Dad. "Dinner's a ways off."

Ronan grabs a cookie.

The boys bite them at the same time... with similar results. Sam and Ronan exchange a look, then stare at Dad like this is some prank of his creation. Blix appears in a puff of greasy purple smoke on Sam's shoulder. Wet, bare, bony skin doesn't make for the most stable perch.

The imp begins to slip off him as soon as he appears—but quickly wraps his tail around Sam's neck for support. My brother doesn't seem to notice or care, so the little guy can't be squeezing too hard. The imp has the frenetic energy of a sugared-up toddler mixed with the agility of a capuchin monkey as he seizes the nearest cookie on the tray for himself. The only critter in this house that fiends more for snacks than my little brother is Blix.

He raises the cookie to his mouth in both hands, opens cartoonishly wide, then chomps down hard. I'm expecting something straight out of Tom & Jerry—where Blix's teeth promptly shatter and fall out of his mouth, leaving the cookie intact. Lucky for him, that doesn't happen. However, the imp has no more success at biting the cookie than any of us. He emits a bewildered warble, then tries again, gnawing desperately on the enormous (to him) pastry like a rat trying to chew its way out of a cage.

The boys also get to work trying to bite off a hunk of their cookies.

It's truly bizarre. Chewing on these things—or trying to—is not uncomfortable. Bits of the outer dough are flaking off in my mouth, but it's damn near impossible to penetrate the cookie interior.

"What's this talk of cookies?" Sierra marches in from the living room, and pauses, watching the five of us struggling to snack. "What the heck are you dorks doing?"

Dad, leaving his cookie jutting from his teeth, wordlessly grabs a fresh one from the tray and hands it to her as if challenging her to do better.

Not one to back down from such a thrown gauntlet, Sierra swipes the cookie from his outstretched hand. She holds it up as if to say 'this is how you bite a cookie.' Her overconfident demeanor evaporates within seconds of tooth-to-cookie contact. WTF could not more obviously display on her face if she had the letters tattooed on her forehead.

All of us stand there bewildered and gnawing for a minute or two.

Sophia hurries in. "Sorry, I was in the bathroom. Did you call me?"

Dad plucks his cookie away from his mouth. "Yes. Did you bake these?"

Sierra frowns. "Failed baking experiment?"

Sophia clasps her hands behind her back and twists side to side, making her dress flare a little. She seems eminently proud of herself. "No. They're doing exactly what they're supposed to."

"Umm." Sierra bonks her on the head with the cookie. "Why did you make inedible cookies that smell so good? That's mean."

"Aww, they're not inedible." Sophia laughs. "You're just not doing it right."

Dad eyes the cookie, then my littlest sister. "What, exactly, did you do here?"

"I made Fig Non-Newtons," says Sophia past a huge grin. "The harder you bite them, the harder they become."

Sam bursts out laughing.

Sierra gives her a flat look. "Nerd."

A look of mission in his eyes, Dad raises his cookie to his mouth. His teeth sink into the cookie at an excruciatingly slow pace. It's almost as painful as watching Uncle Hank eat a ham sandwich. However, he does succeed in biting a piece off.

Sam and Ronan also attempt gingerly biting their cookies, having similar results. Hmm. I try again, applying the most minimal jaw pressure. This time, the cookie behaves more like a normal cookie and I'm able to bite off a hunk. Alas, chewing it suffers the same resistance to pressure, so I'm forced to eat in geologic time.

"Mmm. Wow." Dad smacks his lips. "Tastes amazing. The slow tooth penetrates the shield."

The Littles, plus Ronan, peer quizzically at him.

Dad shakes his head in disappointment.

I raise one hand. "I got it."

Sierra swallows her first successful bite of Fig Non-Newton. "Soph, why the heck did you make these? They're obnoxious. Nothing that tastes this good should be so frustrating to eat!"

"Umm." Sophia shrugs. "To see if I could... but mostly for the pun."

Dad beams with pride.

"Nerd," deadpans Sierra.

"Yep." Sophia grins. "I am."

"It seems I am yet again reminded of a catastrophic failure in my parental responsibilities," says Dad. "You guys up for a movie tonight? I need to introduce you to *Dune*."

Expressions on the kids range from mild curiosity to 'sure why not.'

I raise an eyebrow. "Are you going to inflict the six-hour director's cut on us or the theatrical release? Or the new one?"

Dad rubs his chin. "Still deciding."

"Hmm. I need to see someone about a demon, but I guess it can wait a night." I fold my arms. "Hopefully."

Sam peers up at me. "What about a demon?"

A cognitive disconnect keeps me standing there in silence for a few seconds since my eyes and brain don't agree. My grass-and-mud-covered scrawny little brother looks as ordinary as it gets for a suburban kid. No part of his outward appearance suggests he'd be anything even close to an authority on demons. But... I can't think of anyone off the top of my head who'd be better able to answer my questions. And sure, it's less what Sam knows and more what he can translate from Blix. Still, it's crazy to think of my kid brother as a resource for demonic information.

Especially when he's giving me his most earnest 'I want to help' stare.

"Okay... crazy as this sounds..." I pluck a bit of grass off Sam's forehead. "Maybe I don't need to go hunting for a vampire expert on sefil."

Dad cringes. "Why are you still thinking about that thing? Didn't Mel destroy it?"

"She did," says Sam.

I nod. "Yeah, but... last night... I had this strange feeling some dark presence was hanging over me. It's only an unexplainable feeling, but it sure felt like that thing wasn't quite done with us. Is there any chance it might come back?"

"Eep!" Sophia clings to me.

Sam glances at Blix, who's still trying to gnaw on one of Sophia's pun cookies. The imp shrugs his wings. "I dunno too much about those kinds of demons, but we could ask Olmaz."

"That works." I flap my arms. "Saves me the trouble of having to go somewhere."

Dad tosses the last hunk of his cookie into his mouth. "Sophia, be careful with these. They're obviously unusual. Consider them a controlled magical substance, not for public knowledge."

"Okay." She nods.

"Nothing to worry about. We got secrecy handled." Sam grabs another two cookies, handing one to Ronan. "There won't be any left by tomorrow."

CLOSET CONSULTANT

We could make all sorts of jokes about Sam's closet.
I don't, though. The mood isn't there, since I'm too worried about demonic vampires. Also, they're a bit played out.

Sam opens the door to reveal a rather ordinary closet full of games, toys, action figures, and some clothes. He shuts the door in an almost ritualistic fashion, concentrates a moment, then opens it again. Even though I expected something weird to happen, an involuntary gasp slips out of me at the sight of his closet containing a cave. Where before had been carpet littered with Star Wars toys and PlayStation accessories is now a manhole-sized opening into a black-walled cave tunnel.

My brother walks down into the passage as casually as if we'd just opened the hatch stairs to the attic. Wait, no. He's a little more hesitant about the attic. Dunno what it is about attics; they're scary to kids. Heck, even I still feel a twinge of unease going up there.

Ronan follows him in. He lets off a faint yelp and starts hopping from foot to foot like he's on a hot beach in the middle of the summer. I brace for discomfort and take a cautious step in. The smooth stone under my feet is almost painfully warm. It's not quite 'scream and run' hot, but standing still for too long will most likely result in burns. Both boys are still barefoot in their swim shorts. Sam, oddly, doesn't seem to care or notice the heat. Ronan jumps on me like a little kid insisting on being carried. He's also ten now—his birthday was like a week ago on the seventeenth. But, he's so small and skinny he could pass for eight. Carrying him isn't exactly a burden.

Fortunately, this demonic demi-plane lacks something highly important: the sun.

Not far from the portal, I come online. This enables me to float off the ground and stop cooking filet of sole. Even though I am online and it's dark (ish) here, the temperature is *less* comfortable than daytime normal. Feels like about 118 degrees or so if I had to guess.

Sierra and Sophia, overcome with curiosity, join us as well—but upon watching Ronan doing the hotfoot dance, they hesitated at the opening long enough for Klepto to fetch their shoes from downstairs. Mom can't be upset at them for wearing shoes in the house since we are no longer technically in the house.

Sam leads us down the passage, which feels as if it's descending at a moderately steep angle. It's not threatening to make anyone fall, but it's the sort of drop where if anyone did trip, they'd go rolling for a good distance before being able to stop.

Blix stretches his wings out, basking in the ambiance of this place.

Sam looks fine. Ronan, myself, and the girls are already sweating from the heat. Hmm. I guess if the demons have decided to really give my brother an extended lifespan, letting him be tolerant of infernal heat is a small door prize by comparison.

It takes us about ten minutes of walking to reach the bottom of the passage. The tunnel we've been following opens into a huge chamber. Howling wind comes from the left side where the room simply stops existing. It's like we're on a balcony of some fantasy castle—or a fortress on the desert planet Arrakkis—staring out at a vast expanse of featureless grey desert. Somehow, there's still cave-like ceiling above us and on all sides other than the left. It's easily a two-hundred-yard-long open gap. No posts, rock formations, or anything solid supports the ceiling. This chamber should not exist. It's in defiance of physics.

But, yeah. Hell. Or something similar to it. I shouldn't expect demonic demi-planes hidden in my kid brother's closet to follow logical rules.

"Olmaz?" asks Sam. "Do you have a few minutes? My sister wants to ask you something."

Ronan clamp-squeezes me. The boy doesn't look nervous, but he's definitely acting like it. Concerned, I peer into his dark emerald green eyes. Swear, this kid is so adorable. He's going to grow up into a real long-haired pretty boy. Go figure he also likes learning how to play guitar. Fingers crossed the future is kind to him. Pity that hair bands are kinda out of fashion. The kid's two decades late to Earth.

He *is* nervous but not scared. Apparently, the last time the boys came down here, Olmaz appeared suddenly and scared him into jumping off the ledge. Ack! Well, we're decently far away from it now, plus I got him. When I squeeze him back a little tighter, he seems to relax.

A column of inky black smoke bursts up from the ground nearby. Sophia jumps, startled so bad she falls on her butt. Sierra merely makes fists. Sam smiles.

The smoke plume widens and stretches out until it forms a humanoid shape with great batlike wings. Olmaz is pretty much what most people would expect at the word demon: huge, muscular, and bare-chested. He's not crimson, though. His skin's a dark charcoal grey color. Two large, black horns extend up from his temples. His face is quite human. Between his beard and quirked eyebrow, he's giving off vibes somewhere between the huge, scary biker dude who's really a nice guy and an almost whimsical Viking.

And yeah, he's dressed the part. Looks like a heavy kilt made of leather adorned with skulls... straight out of the in-game art for *Diablo*, only he's much friendlier. Still trying to wrap my brain around the concept of demons being nice. According to Sam, they're more or less just like humans: some are good, some are jerks. Also, as with humans, it's the jerks who get most of the airtime on the news, so to speak.

Normally, when something jump-scares Sophia and truly startles her, she'll start crying. If she feels like the person startled her on purpose and got a laugh out of it, she'll cry harder because they're being mean to her. For a second or two, it seems like she's about to cry... but she sits there on the ground in complete silence, gawking at Olmaz the way a middle-aged single woman might gawk at Jason Momoa if she just randomly collided with him in the street and got knocked on her butt.

"Hello, Samuel." Olmaz sweeps his arm while offering a half-bow of welcome.

"Hi." My brother returns the bow. "Thanks for seeing us."

Olmaz waves dismissively. "Oh, it's a pleasure. I do adore having company. It's nice to have someone to talk to who isn't begging for mercy or screaming."

Sophia gasps. Spell mostly broken, she scrambles to her feet. But hey, at least she's not crying.

"He's teasing," whispers Sierra.

"Partly." Olmaz examines his fingernails. "I do enjoy making mortals scream, though I don't resort to the banal cruelty of torturing them with fire or pain."

Sophia fidgets, then asks in a mousy-whispery voice, "What do you do to them?"

"Ever go to sit on the toilet and find out too late the seat is up?"

She blushes.

"I see you have." Olmaz chuckles. "That whole 'leaving the seat up and not noticing it' thing is my pet project. It is but one of the ways I elicit the wonderful screams of torment from mortals."

Sierra looks about ready to attempt punching him.

Sophia blinks. Her fear's evaporated to confusion.

"Is that all you do?" asks Sierra in a challenging tone.

"Oh, quite not." The big guy's deep voice releases a resonant chuckle that seems to echo off over the desert to infinity. Maybe to infinity and beyond. "Some of the most beautiful screams come from people racing to stores minutes from closing time, only to watch an employee lock the door when they're ten feet away from grabbing the handle."

"Ooh." Sam cringes.

"People scream about that?" Sierra scrunches up her nose. "Really?"

"The entitled ones do." Olmaz chuckles. "Some who think everyone in the store needs to put their entire day on pause to attend to their wants."

Sierra whistles. "Oh. So, you're tormenting Karens in tedious, frustrating, non-life-threatening ways that leave no lasting damage."

Olmaz stretches his hand out, examining his long, black claws. "I prefer to think of it as performing a necessary function of the universe."

"Yeah, but you make donuts go stale too fast sometimes, too." Sam sighs. "That's kinda mean."

The demon shrugs in a 'it is what it is' kind of way. He doesn't seem particularly proud of rapid pastry spoilage, though I get the sense he doesn't regret it. This guy also claimed to be responsible for USB connectors. Specifically, how we try to plug one in, it won't fit, so we flip it over, still won't go in, so we flip it over again back to the way we originally held it and then it works. Pointless tedium.

"Umm, Olmaz?" I ask. "Can you help me out with answering a question or two, please?"

"Of course, Sarah, sister of Samuel." He bows to me.

Sierra gives me side eye and mouths 'sister of Samuel' with a question mark at the end.

No, I don't think Sam's got any sort of royal presence here. He's merely the point of contact between me and the demons.

"Had a crazy scary situation a couple days ago..." I explain what happened with the sefil, the vampire occultists, and my strange, ominous feeling while sitting in the bathtub last night.

"How are you not sweating?" whispers Sierra to Sam in the midst of my explanation.

He shrugs. "I think they like me. Maybe it's because of the wings."

The 'I want wings too' look lasts on Sierra's face for about 2.33336 (repeating) seconds before she dismisses it with a shiver. Association with demons still bothers her to a point, no matter how nice they are. Good. She should be happy with whatever Sophia's enchantment did to her. Besides, the two magics might conflict and do something unexpected.

"Hmm." Olmaz taps a claw to his chin in thought. "Once one of my brethren has infiltrated a mortal's dead remains to become this creature you know of as a 'sefil,' they will certainly try to go back."

"Back?" I blink. "You mean, it's not destroyed?"

"M'len D'lar only destroyed the physical body." Olmaz gestures at the landscape around us. "Demons cannot be truly killed in your world except in highly unique and specialized circumstances. When she disintegrated the body, the demon residing within returned to its home plane."

"Hell?" asks Sierra.

He tilts his hand at her in a so-so gesture. "What humans refer to as 'hell' is, in reality, many multiple demi-planes sandwiched together, each containing varying degrees of torment, boredom, emptiness, bleakness, or whatever happened to gather there... or Kansas."

Sierra gives him a flat look. "That sounds like school."

"Aww, c'mon. School is fun." Sophia nudges her.

"Sure, for a nerd." Sierra folds her arms.

"You're a nerd, too." Sophia thrusts her arms out to either side. "You play video games all day and love comic books and Japanese animation."

"That makes me a geek, not a nerd." Sierra scratches an eyebrow. "Nerds go to college at fourteen and build nuclear reactors in their garage when they're twelve."

"I'm not going to build a nuke reactor." Sophia rolls her eyes.

"No, but you have magic, and that's more destructive." Sierra snickers.

Ronan leans his head against mine. Poor kid looks tired. He's overheating, I'm sure. We probably shouldn't spend *too* much time in here.

"Okay, so this thing wants to come back." I adjust my grip on the boy to compensate for him not holding himself up as much. He's gradually in the process of passing out.

Olmaz nods once. "Yes. He's out there somewhere and, from the sounds of it, fairly angry."

I squirm. "Why is he angry at me? I didn't destroy him."

"'Tis a fairly simple explanation." Olmaz smiles, revealing coal-black teeth. "Mel is far too powerful for that demon to exact any sort of revenge on. You are—under the correct circumstances—a helpless target."

Great. I frown. I'm the little kid who gets beat up even harder because her older sister slapped the heck out of the bully.

"Do we need to worry about him?" asks Sam. "Isn't he stuck, unable to cross over for a while after being killed?"

"Correct." Olmaz smiles at Sam in the manner of a proud teacher. "Unless some other vampire up there is careless and gives him the opportunity to leap into another sefil, it's unlikely you have much to be concerned about."

Sam ponders for a few seconds. "But he's stuck in timeout for being killed, right? How can he come back over so fast?"

"It's not quite so simple, Samuel." Olmaz chuckles. "Mortal lawyers are not the only ones who delight on manipulating the smallest of technicalities for their own purposes."

Sierra huffs in a 'no kidding' sort of way. "Demons are the originals. Where do you think lawyers get it from?"

"Be nice," whispers Sophia. "Mom's a lawyer."

"I'm not being mean. I'm being literal." Sierra wipes at the sweat dripping from her nose. "The power to manipulate the wording of legal documents to get them to say what you want them to say without technically lying is a form of magic. Mom's special, but not all lawyers use their great powers for noble ends."

Time to bite my lip. As kids, we view Mom with a certain degree of heroic infallibility. Truth be told, most of what she does is protecting a corporation. Can't really call that 'noble'. It's not bad either, just... is. I'm sure if Mom ever ran into a situation where the company did intentional harm to some group and asked her to cover it up, she'd quit. "Yeah, Mom's sense of ethics is strong."

"So..." I peer at Olmaz. "The demon responsible for that sefil is trying to come back... and it might do so *if* someone is careless enough to do a late Transference? That's the only way?"

Olmaz shakes his head. "This one will be waiting at the edge of the planar boundary looking for the first opportunity to jump across. It could be another sefil or some mortals summoning him by name. An intentional effort on the part of mortals to bring him back would circumvent the"—he glances at Sam—"timeout period. Honestly, both are quite rare. It's most likely your greatest worry over the next few decades is a minor uptick in demonic nuisances."

"What, like telemarketing calls or door-to-door missionaries?" I ask.

The big guy laughs, making all the air in my chest vibrate. "Ahh, missionaries. I wish I could claim that one as mine. Alas. The nuisances could take various forms, most of which will seem relatively harmless initially. The true danger would only become apparent much later on."

Sam grins. "Sounds like Dad trying to cook."

"Hey!" calls Dad's voice from the proverbial heavens.

I picture him sticking his head in the portal from Sam's closet, wondering where we went.

The Littles stare upward, gasping in surprise.

Sierra smirks. "We shouldn't be surprised he can hear us. Dad's got a direct line here to get his jokes."

Olmaz claps himself on the leg, chuckling. "I tease you, children. That was not really your father."

Sam finds this funny and cracks up.

"Hmm. So, you don't think this demon is a serious problem for me to worry about?" I ask.

"Likely not." Olmaz pats me on the shoulder. "You fear what it almost did to you. That, my dear not-quite-mortal, is only possible through the manifestation you call a sefil. If this demon were to return to the mortal world in any other form, it would not be so dangerous."

Well, that's something, at least. I don't need yet another reason to keep looking over my shoulder. "Cool. Umm, just in case... is it possible to permanently kill demons?"

He wags his giant eyebrows at me. "It is, but to do so is incredibly complicated and requires skills humanity has mostly abandoned as mythology."

"You mean magic." I set my hands on my hips.

"Something like that." He flashes a knowing smile. "You will, of course, understand why I am not inclined to go into details."

I nod at him. Makes total sense to me. As an immortal, I wouldn't feel comfortable teaching someone how to permanently kill me either. "Yeah. No problem."

It's fine. We don't need to know the 'proper' way to kill a demon for good. We have a Fuzzydoom. Worked on a butt-old vampire. It is perhaps excessive to throw Fuzzydoom at door-to-door missionaries, but something tells me he'll work just fine on an enraged demon bent on revenge.

Ronan's about to collapse straight out of my arms.

"Thanks for the advice." I bow at the big demon. "I think it's about time for us to return home. The heat's getting to the little ones."

"I'm ten," says Ronan in a somewhat delirious tone. "I'm not a 'little kid' anymore."

"You're barely as tall as Olmaz's knee. You are little." I peer at the demon. "I'm not much taller than his bellybutton. To him, I'm little, too. It's a matter of relativity."

Ro looks at me like I'm a dork.

Can't say he's wrong.

"Very well. A pleasure to have this conversation with you, Sarah, sister of Samuel."

The Littles chuckle.

Great. They're going to be calling me that for months.

Kill me now.

21

AT THE CORNER OF UNCOMFORTABLE AND HILARIOUS

Whatever floats through the mind of a disembodied demon must have swayed in the other direction. For the remainder of the day, nothing dark or ominous occurs. No crazy moods in the house. Our life feels normal. The Littles hung out with their friends, played video games, played in the back yard, came in for dinner, we watched *Dune* with Dad (the original theatrical release with Sting in it) and went about our night like ordinary people.

Well, ordinary people who get seriously into a debate about the addition of 'weirding modules' to the story. Sophia and Dad are upset since those things aren't mentioned in the book. Sierra called Sophia a 'weirding module' for having such a strong opinion. We're pretty much back to normal.

It's later that night. Tilloa stopped by to hang out since we haven't seen her in a while. Not entirely sure why, but she's mildly afraid of Chloe. I think it has something to do with how, in her mortal life, the *Ring* movies scared the hell out of her. Crazy how some things which aren't on the surface very scary to look at can stick in a person's psyche. A pale-as-heck girl with long, black hair is just sort of an immediate fear trigger for Tilloa. Dad has a strange one, too. He generally likes horror movies, but the first film to really scare him when he was a kid wasn't, in fact, a horror movie at all but *Terminator*.

He's over it now, but as a little boy, he had a phobia of skeletons. That part in the movie where the terminator robot loses its skin and it's just a metal skeleton chasing Linda Hamilton through the steel factory? Yeah, gave him nightmares. He spent weeks as a kid afraid to get out of bed at night for fear a silver skeleton was lurking around every corner of the house waiting to get him. To be fair, a skeleton moving on its own (metal or not) is way scarier than a little girl with color saturation deficiency. So far, I have not told Chloe that Tilloa is afraid of the girl from the *Ring* movies. She'd throw on a white nightie, let her hair fall over her face, and sneak up on Tilloa just for laughs. To her, it wouldn't be mean. Perhaps Tilloa wouldn't flip out as much as I thought, but better off not taking the chance.

Anyway, the four of us head to Seattle looking for a meal and a way to bust boredom.

It's not super late, at least not late enough to the point where anyone seeing Chloe outside would call the police on us. Honestly, these days? I'm not so sure anyone would bother. Someone seeing a seven-year-old outside past midnight would probably just roll their eyes and not want to get involved. Not saying I'm going to roll those dice. I'll have her inside before eleven.

Ashley thinks we could use porphyria as an excuse if someone asks about Chloe. We could say she sleeps during the day so she's not, in fact, up after her bedtime. Not sure anyone would buy that, though. Our best option is to avoid scrutiny at all.

As we fly toward downtown Seattle, my stomach twists in a knot. It's not a severe, crippling knot. More like the type of knot one ties in the drawstrings of their sweatpants to keep them from falling off while taking the garbage to the curb... just enough to hold things up for five minutes.

I'm anxious about what sights and thoughts may await me within the mind of whoever I end up feeding on. It's silly of me. What are the odds I'm going to encounter *another* kidnapper, child molester, killer, or generally psychotic freak? Pretty low, right? One would hope. My brain starts threatening me with guilt for not running around intentionally reading everyone's mind and hunting for bad people. That would not only be ridiculous, it's an easy path to attracting too much notice to vampire kind. The Universe will tolerate me playing superhero on occasion, but not as a full-time job.

Except for us *flying* into Seattle in search of blood to drink, we talk and laugh like a bunch of ordinary young women out for a good time. Granted, Ash and my idea of a good time is tragically lame (as Tilloa puts it). She's way more of a social creature than we are. She likes parties, bars, night clubs, and so on. The woman is extroverted enough for all of us. Tilloa's also got the fashion sense. We're like two LL Bean models going out with the woman from the cover of Vogue. Dunno if it really is, but her outfit looks expensive. She's rocking the Christian Dior (or whatever it is) while Ash and I are totally in Marshall's territory, me in a midriff-baring Sonic the Hedgehog T-shirt and jean shorts. Ashley's got her black unicorn T-shirt and a short blue skirt. The cute cartoon uni has a knife taped to its horn and the words 'I will cut you' below it. The two of us opted for flip-flops. It's warm out, even at night. Well, warm for Seattle. And flops are easy to carry while flying. We kinda *have* to carry them or we'd lose them. Upside: flip-flops are cheap. If we lose them, oh well.

Tilloa's boots look like they cost about $900.

Chloe's just a normal kid in an off-white romper type dress. She couldn't be bothered with shoes at all tonight.

There's a strange line with kid fashion, a wide variety of prices and styles seem 'normal,' but at some point when you start dressing your kid in clothing that appears obviously high end, it becomes weird and pretentious. Even when celebrities do it, it comes off as odd. What kind of person spends $1,200 on a dress/outfit their child will wear a couple times before they outgrow it? It's just like flaunting that you have more money than sense.

Right, tangent alarm, Sarah. Back to reality.

We land downtown and take up a position in the shadow of some trees near the parking area for a sports bar type place. It's not long before a group of guys who appear to be a party of friends emerge from the place and start heading for their car. One can't walk without help. Three are having a little trouble walking. They don't look *smashed*, but they're clearly in no condition to drive. The fifth friend appears entirely sober and a little on the geeky side. Not that his buddies are total jocks, but their designated driver looks like the sort of guy who truly doesn't mind skipping the alcohol.

Yeah, I'd be him if our roles were reversed. Yes, I know, I'm bad at teenagering, but I never really understood the point behind drinking. It's expensive, we'll get in trouble for it (at least until age twenty-one), it doesn't really even taste all that great, and if you have just a little too much, it punishes in the morning. Me? I'd rather keep the money.

But, I know I'm lame.

When the guys are close enough, we move in.

Chloe gets the designated driver. She's too little for alcohol. Tilloa, Ashley, and I each choose a guy of our own, plus there's an extra man (the most inebriated) we leave waiting in Derpville while we bite his buddies.

One or two other people arriving or leaving the sports bar pass by at a potentially awkward distance, though don't seem to notice what we're doing in the dark. If they saw any hint of people standing there, they likely assumed we're engaged in a public display of affection. Maybe they assume we're hugging friends we haven't seen in a while before everyone goes to their respective cars.

Don't really care why they ignore us. They do, and that's all that matters.

Nothing wonky in my guy's head. He's normal... and in a bit of a rush to get home so he can read to his son before bedtime. Aww. I needed that. This guy's a good dad. Eek. I'm glad Chloe didn't get him. She might be jealous. Then again, she adores Dad, so... she's either come to terms with her horrible bio-father or decided to ignore that he ever existed. Or... maybe Aurélie did a little tinkering in that head.

I wouldn't complain if she did. Chloe does not need to remember years of abuse.

We feed without any complications—shocking, I know. Nothing for Follows Rules Girl to get her panties in a knot over at all. These guys aren't even trying the 'hey I can drive' nonsense. They know they've had too much and are letting Mike drive everyone home.

Heh. That's another law of the universe. In any group of guys numbering more than three, there is guaranteed to be at least one named Mike.

"Guys," whispers Chloe.

We look over at her.

She's fly-levitating so she can reach the neck of Mr. Designated Driver. Two little fang holes seep blood. The way she's holding him, it's like she's trying to show us the bite.

I detach my fangs from my guy's neck. "What? Is something wrong with him?"

"No." Chloe grins. "It's open Mike night."

Ashley moans into her guy's neck.

Tilloa continues feeding from her man, staring at me, her brows a bold, flat line of 'you gotta be kidding me' over her eyes.

"Oof." I whisper, then wink. "Stop playing with your food."

She grins before resuming her meal.

Soon, we're done and send the guys on their way.

"Open Mike night," mutters Tilloa. "Good grief. It's time for an intervention. Your home should be designated unsafe for children."

"Why?" I quirk an eyebrow at her.

"The punning is contagious." Ashley snickers. "And too late. She's already caught it."

I start walking across the parking lot, leading Chloe by the hand. "Speaking of home… we should either head back there or find something fun to do where people won't notice her outside so late."

Ashley and Tilloa follow. All of us, even Chloe, are on the same page. We're heading for a more secluded spot from which we can take off. That, or, if we randomly stumble across something fun, we'll stop to check it out. Having a child along with us definitely serves as a damper on potential activities. We can't really bring her anywhere public without risking unwanted attention. And no, this is not me complaining. I'm completely happy spending all night at home. The out here doing something fun thing is ninety percent for Tilloa's benefit.

We're about two and a half blocks away from the sports bar, passing a tinier dive bar type place, when a voice calls out from the left.

"Hey, Red," yells a guy. "Niiiice legs. Do they go all the way up?"

Some dude and his two friends loitering on the street corner start making noises at us, mostly Ashley. They're checking me out, too. Neither guy is paying much attention to Tilloa, which is weird. Of the three of us, she is easily the most traditionally pretty. I mean, the girl's seriously got movie star looks. She also happens to have big time Lara Croft 'I will kick your ass six ways from Sunday' energy, too. They're probably scared of her. Ashley and I look about as threatening as a pair of pet hamsters someone made little Paddington Bear costumes for.

"What's your name, sweetie?" yells the other guy, staring right at me. "So cute. C'mon over here and I'll show you how to use those lips."

Ashley doesn't even look over at the men, just keeps on walking. I really should follow her example. I turn away.

"Where are you going?" yells one.

"Hey bitches, think you're too good for guys like us?" calls his friend.

Chloe whirls to glare at them. "Eat a dick!"

The men are stunned for only a few seconds before the one who initially catcalled Ashley scowls. "You kiss your mommy with that mouth, brat?"

"No, but I kissed yours," shouts Chloe.

I facepalm. There's no way in Hades she has any idea what 'eat a dick' literally means. It's crap she heard her jackass parents say.

"Ooooh!" calls the other dude. "Getting owned by a little kid."

The target of Chloe's verbal slap seems considerably less amused.

He takes a step toward us, jabbing a finger at me. "You should teach that kid some manners before someone else does it for you."

I totally understand how Ash and Chloe's first meeting with the vampires in Crescent City turned into a brawl.

Chloe lets go of my hand and advances three steps on the guy. "Who's gonna teach me manners? You? Bring it, bitch boy."

The guy, still like fifteen feet away from us, looms at her.

She reacts to this attempted intimidation by stomping toward him.

This is not going to end well. I dash after her and grab her hand, pulling her back. The guy and his buddies start chuckling. They seem to think the kid wasn't serious. Their second mistake would've been thinking she wasn't a threat. Honestly, I doubt she would've done anything more than get in his face and insult him. She knows what the consequences of vulgar displays of supernatural power could be. Still, escalating a situation like this only makes an accident more likely.

I scoop her up. She leans around me to give the guy the finger... holding her arm (and middle finger) out until we break line of sight around the next available corner.

"Subtle," says Ashley. "Real subtle."

"Oops." Chloe frowns. "Sorry. They said mean things to you guys. I didn't like that."

"It's all right. Nothing happened." I kiss her atop the head. "In the future, though, just ignore idiots like them."

We're all quiet for a while as we walk. Eventually, I set the kid down on her feet and resume leading her by the hand.

"Umm," asks Chloe. "What's a dick and why is it bad to eat one?"

Ashley bursts out laughing, her voice echoing off the buildings of Downtown Seattle. Tilloa cracks up, too.

Dammit! No one prepared me for this. How am I supposed to answer a question like that coming from a kid her age? How would Mom handle it? My brain hits me with the mental image of me, Sierra, or Sophia, aged seven, ambushing her with the question. The imagined reaction on Mom's face gets me cackling with laughter.

Chloe watches us lose it for a moment, then sighs. "Why are you all laughing? What's so funny? Bad Mommy said that all the time when guys made her mad and they didn't laugh."

I cough. "Well, umm... Ash?"

"Bail!" She holds her hands up. "All yours."

"Ti—"

"Not touchin' that with a ten-foot pole." Tilloa waves me off. "That's a question only Mom answers."

Gee, thanks guys.

"Okay, umm." I shift my jaw side to side, thinking for a way to explain without making things worse. "Well, you know that word that Mom really hates?"

Chloe tilts her head. "The one that starts with c?"

Ashley and I both wince.

Tilloa goes wide eyed.

"Ack, no. Not that one. The one she hates a little bit less."

"Oh, you mean 'fuck,'" says Chloe in a matter-of-fact tone.

Tilloa face-palms.

Ashley starts giggling uncontrollably.

Some random guy going by on the other side of the street whirls around to stare at us. He shakes his head and mouths 'wow' at her.

"Take a picture, it'll last longer," yells Chloe.

The guy turns away and walks a bit faster. A woman going by us gasps.

Ashley, finally in control of her laughter, squats down to eye level with the kid. "Kiddo, honey, we really need to talk about your manners."

She points at the guy. "What about his manners? It's rude to stare."

"Uh, true. You got me there." Ashley scratches her head.

"Anyway, that thing you asked about..." I fidget. Hopefully, the kid buys the simple explanation I'm about to try. "No one really eats them. It's a figure of speech. Means the same thing as 'f you.'"

"Oh." She makes a face of contemplation. "Then why not just say 'f you'?"

"Some people don't like that word. They want to convey the same meaning and use less-bad words."

Chloe rolls her eyes. "Wimps. The world would be a lot less stupid if people just said what they meant."

"Indeed." I chuckle.

"So, no one eats dicks?" asks Chloe. "And you didn't tell me what it is."

Tilloa emits a strangled gurgle.

"Aaaawkwaaard," singsongs Ashley.

"It's nothing you need to worry about," I say.

"Oh. Sex stuff." Chloe frowns. "Eww."

Ever want to just slip into a dimensional vortex and fall out of existence? Yeah. That's me.

"You don't know..." Tilloa stares into space.

"Nope. No one talks about it to me 'cause I'm too little. But they get weird and squirmy like you guys are being, so I guess it's that stuff. Why is it such a big secret?"

"It is." I give her hand a squeeze. "It's like vampires. Mortals can't find out about vampires or the whole world will collapse. Same goes for kids and the icky stuff. We're not allowed to talk about it."

She stares at me. By some miracle, my comparison of vampire secrets to adult secrets satisfies her. "Okay."

And just like that, she forgets all about the entire conversation. Or at least acts like it never happened.

Whew.

Tilloa pantomimes a Neo-from-*The Matrix*-dodge. Yeah, seriously. I dodged a hail of bullets.

Ashley bursts out laughing again.

Oh, good grief. She's imagining Neo dodging a hail of... other things. Wobbly, rubbery things in a multitude of pastel colors.

No, I can't read her mind—anymore. I just know Ashley.

"Sorry," says Chloe a few minutes later, out of the blue. "I'm tryin' ta stop cussing so much, but sometimes, people are just so dumb and annoying I can't help it. Big stupid deserves bad words."

"Hah." Ashley laughs. "I can totally relate."

It's hilarious to me because it's so true. Ashley isn't the biggest fan of swear words. She doesn't hate them like Mom does, but she does try to avoid them because they just feel 'mean' to her. When something's driven her to the point of swearing, things have gotten serious.

Fingers crossed nothing will go off the rails enough for her to drop an F-bomb any time soon.

22

BETTER WEIRD THAN DEMONIC

O ur girls' night out was a reasonable success.

Post-feeding, we hit a night club of Tilloa's choosing. Well, sorta. I mostly lurked outside with Chloe while Ashley and Tilloa went inside to do whatever it is people going to nightclubs do for fun. Bringing the kid into a place like that would've been a serious project for no worthwhile return. Can't say I've spent too much time inside clubs. What little experience I have with them almost entirely revolves around running messages for Wolent or my one failed attempt to steal a spyglass for Dalton. However, I am sure there is nothing inside those places even remotely entertaining or appealing to a kid Chloe's age.

I'm fine staying outside with her. I'm basically our designated driver.

We amused ourself exploring rooftops and messing with some people in an apartment by tapping on their windows... windows that no one should have been able to reach from the outside without a bucket lift or giant ladder.

Not the most mature moment of my unlife, but it was kinda funny.

The nightclub visit lasted a bit over an hour before Tilloa and Ashley emerged. We ended up going to Tilloa's small underground apartment in the 'vampire condo' place. It's trendy and kinda industrial looking, the sort of thing the rich corporate bad guys from Dad's movies like to live in. But... we don't have to worry about noise levels waking up the family here.

A few minutes after I've flopped on her plush white sectional sofa, my phone rings. This is probably not going to be good. Telemarketers don't call this late, so it's almost certainly vampire related. If it isn't vampire stuff, it's my family, or Hunter, or Michelle with a serious emergency. Maybe it's just Mom randomly waking up in the middle of the night and calling to see if I'm okay since I'm not in the house.

I pull my phone out of my pocket and hold it up to look at the ID. It reads 'unknown.' Good sign it's a junk call. I hit the button to stop the ringing... and it starts right back up. Ugh, fine. Whatever.

"Hello?" I say after flicking the slider to pick up the call.

A male voice bursts from the speakerphone, hurling rapid-fire words at me in a harsh-sounding foreign language. The intensity of it makes me lean back from the phone.

Ashley, Tilloa, and Chloe stare at me.

"What?" I shout over the barrage. "Who is this? What are you saying?"

"Is he cursing at you or saying something nice?" Ashley tilts her head.

"I can't tell." I wince at the phone.

"Oh, then it's probably German." Ashley nods.

"Sorry, whoever you are. Gotta be a wrong number." I hang up. "Unbelievable."

My phone rings again. This time, it seemingly answers the call all by itself. The German screaming of indeterminate emotional context resumes.

Chloe shakes her head. "Someone needs to calm the f down."

Okay, she's trying. She said 'f' the letter, not the whole word.

"Yeah, I do think that's German." Ashley leans closer, listening. "Do you know any German?"

"Only a few lines from *Du Hasst*," I say.

"Ooh, I love that song!" Chloe jumps off the sofa and starts headbanging, flinging her dark black hair around like a pom-pom. "Dooo... Dooo hasst!"

Ashley and I exchange a look. It's impossible to watch a seven-year-old headbanging to German heavy metal and not feel weird about it.

"*Ich hasse euch nicht! Ich brauche eure Hilfe!*" shouts the man on the phone.

"Whoa," whispers Tilloa. "I think he understood you."

"Well, I don't understand him." I sigh.

Chloe stops headbanging and gazes at our shocked expressions. "What? We did this song in music class."

Ashley covers her mouth, eyes wide. "Wow. Really? What are you, in first grade?"

"Yeah... I was." Chloe laughs. "I'm teasing. The older boy who lived next door to us liked this kinda music. He played it so loud I used to hear it in my room."

"How do you say 'I don't speak German' in German?"

"Umm, if you knew that, you'd be lying because you'd know some German." Ashley wags her eyebrows at me.

"Now is not the time for Minor Technicality Girl to make an appearance." I stab a finger at the air. "Do you know anyone who understands German?"

"No, but I have Google." Ashley pulls out her phone, fiddles at the screen for a moment, then speaks in a somewhat hesitant tone, clearly reading, "*Langsamer. Wir verstehen kein Deutsch. Wie müssen einen Übersetzer verwenden.*"

The phone falls silent.

Ashley and I exchange a look.

"Did that work?" Tilloa kicks her boots off, then sits there rubbing her feet.

Swear... why are the expensive shoes always uncomfortable? You'd think the more a set of boots cost, the more comfortable they'd be.

"*Ich bin der Geist in der Lampe,*" says the phone.

"You're the ghost in the lamp?" I blurt.

Ashley gawks. "You know German?"

"No, but that one's kinda obvious." I chuckle. "Oh, wow… at that museum. They had this old as heck desk lamp from like the 1940s. Supposedly, it's got the spirit of a German spy in it who tried to kill Churchill."

"*Nein! Nein, ich habe nicht versucht, Churchill zu ermorden!*" bellows the ghost.

Ashley stares at her phone, helplessly. "Umm. How the heck do you spell any of that? I have to type it in."

"Umm," I say. "Can you talk slower?"

Word by agonizing word, the spirit—seemingly at great effort—slows himself down, speaking a word or two at a time. Thanks to Google having some degree of auto correcting, we manage to achieve a degree of communication.

Chloe perches on the sofa between me and Ash, watching intently. She seems to be having fun merely listening and watching this crazy back and forth.

Unless we're experiencing a translation error, it seems that the ghost trapped in the desk lamp wants me to help him escape the lamp. He's been trying to find me ever since I took Sam there to free Mel from the jar she'd been stuck in. This guy insists he is not an assassin. He also claims the lamp never belonged to Churchill, never being closer to him than in the basement of a building he may or may not have visited an upper floor of.

Hmm. It normally doesn't take a whole lot of effort to convince me to help someone in need, even a ghost. However, the last time I went to 'steal-slash-save' a spirit from unwanted confinement, things got super complicated. Mystics were involved, and it was an all-around unfun experience for everyone involved, including the ghost. That being said, Coralie *is* happier now than she was in the basement of the mystics' lodge.

In this case, though, something tells me if I decline to help the ghost, he will pull the modern version of 'Henry the Eighthing' me. That movie where the ghost keeps the woman up all night long by constantly singing Henry the Eighth? Same concept, only angry German barking coming from my phone constantly.

He hasn't threatened to do that, but... safe assumptions can be made.

If this dude's name is Klaus, I am going to laugh until tears come out of my eyes. Of course, if that *is* his name, I'm not going to be able to hold back the possessed goldfish jokes.

"What's your name?" I ask.

"*Wie heisst du?*" asks Ashley.

"Tobias," replies the ghost. "Tobias Krüger."

Ashley gives me side eye. "Good thing it's not Fred."

I stifle a laugh. "Or Klaus."

She blinks.

"The goldfish from *American Dad?*" I roll my eyes.

"Oh." She cackles. "Yeah, that would've been funny. Wasn't he evil?"

"I think so. Really evil, but had no way to do anything." I shift my gaze to the iPhone screen, showing a call in progress from an unknown number. "Are you a bad guy?"

"*Bist du ein Bösewicht?*" asks Ashley, reading off her Google page.

"*Nein, nicht so sehr.*" The ghost sighs.

"Sare?" asks Ashley.

"*Nein. Sehr. Ess, ehh, aitch, arr.*"

Ashley types at her screen, thumbnails clicking. "No, not so much? So, you're kinda sorta a bad guy?" Realizing he likely doesn't know what she said, she starts typing.

"*Nein. Ich war bei der Bundeswehr. Ihr Engländer betrachtet mich als Feind, aber ich bin nett.*"

She stops typing to stare at my phone. "I think he answered me, but... he doesn't know English?"

"Guys." Chloe flails her arms. "If he was a spy, wouldn't he *have* to know English? He'd suck at being a spy if he couldn't pretend to be English."

"*Das Mädchen hat recht. Ich verstehen English, aber aus irgendeinem Grund kann ich es nicht mehr sprechen. Es ist höchst ärgerlich.*"

I rub the bridge of my nose. Wow, is this frustrating. He and Ashley go in circles for a few minutes before she says he's trying to say he's a nice guy, but because he was with the German Army, we consider him a bad guy. He also seems to think we're English. Oh, and he repeatedly insists the lamp did not belong to Churchill. It's like a thing with him. He doesn't let it drop until we all say out loud that we believe him the lamp was not Winston's.

Ashley can't help herself and says, "Wiiiinstooon," in a deep voice like the spirit in *Ghostbusters*.

This confuses the ghost.

Understandable. Pretty sure he hasn't watched many movies.

"Okay. Tell him... wait. He understands me, just can't reply in English. Gah, that's gotta be so frustrating."

"Ihr habt keine Ahnung," rasps the ghost in a soft, beleaguered voice.

"Right... okay, so I believe you. And honestly, even if I didn't, you're still a ghost that's trapped in a desk lamp. That's gotta suck no matter who you were in life." I exhale. "So... problem is, I have no idea how to get you out of there. Let me talk to some people and I'll call you back?"

"Diese Lampe nimmt keine eingehenden Anrufe an."

"What?"

"Diese Lampe nimmt keine eingehenden Anrufe an."

"No, not you. I heard you. I'm asking Ashley what you said." I glance at her.

She types... then bursts out laughing.

I raise the Eyebrow of What.

Still laughing, she slips words in between chuckles. "He said his lamp doesn't take incoming calls."

Ugh.

"Okay. Give me like an hour and call me back?"

"Ja. Mache ich."

The call drops.

"So surreal," I whisper.

"Did that just happen?" Tilloa gives me a cockeyed glance. "Did we really just spend like forty minutes on a phone call with a ghost stuck in a lamp who can only speak German?"

"Either that or we're all on the same trip." Ashley makes a goofy space-cadet face while twirling her finger around by her ear.

"No, I'm pretty sure it happened." I lower my arm—and phone—into my lap. "Gotta say, though, I much prefer this kind of weird than having a demonic vampire monster try to drink my soul."

"No doubt." Ashley points at the ceiling. "What now?"

"Gonna start by trying to make this easier." I call Aurélie. As usual, she's happy to hear from me. Even though she looks like she's barely a day over twenty years old, she's got the reaction of a little old lady who's thrilled when anyone young takes time out of their day to talk to her. Pleasant conversation about this and that eats about twenty minutes before I realize it. Finally, I get to what I wanted to ask. "Do you know any vampires around here who speak German?"

"Only one. Eleanor St. Ives."

"Eep." Chloe shakes her head rapidly. "No. Please, no."

I put an arm around her and pull her close. "It's okay. You don't need to go anywhere near her. The 'rents can watch you until we get back."

"Where are you going?" Chloe calms in an instant.

Here we go. I purse my lips. "To break into an occult museum, apparently."

Ashley blinks. "Wow. You're really going to do it?"

"I guess. This guy's going to nag the crap out of me until I either destroy or help him." I sink into a deep slouch. "Wouldn't be the first time I went to steal a trapped ghost. I am about as close as it gets to being a professional trapped ghost rescuer."

She and Tilloa laugh.

"Gah. So weird. But hey... I love weird. Weird is better than deadly."

23

MY SIRE'S PROGENY

The next chapter in my surreal unlife unfolds in ways I never imagined.

Tilloa agreed to keep an eye on Chloe while Ashley and I fly to Olympia. Specifically, we're going to the 'House of Mysteries' museum. I do have mixed feelings. This situation is a bit different from the mystics keeping Coralie hostage. The family who runs the little paranormal oddity museum seem to be nice people. They are not keeping Tobias prisoner to exploit him for personal gain. Okay, maybe they are in a way. I mean, his presence there contributes to the genuine eeriness in the air and they do make money exhibiting this stuff. They are not, however, forcing him to do anything or trying to use him directly the same way the mystics attempted to make Coralie see the future for them.

Honestly, the Blackburns—the family who owns the museum— might not even know for a fact his ghost is real. Maybe one or more of them are 'sensitive' enough to detect there's something unusual with the lamp, but as to it containing a real ghost, who knows? I'd imagine if they were capable of interacting with spirits, Tobias would've been yelling at them asking for his freedom. The reason he's fixated on me so much is I am perhaps the first person in many decades he's become aware of who can hear him. It's as if he's stranded on a deserted island and I'm the first boat he's seen in the distance. So, yeah, his desperation is completely logical.

We land in the vicinity of Capitol Lake. The area's got some nice trees which are good for concealing vampire flight. This spot is not far from the museum. It's easy to walk out of the small grove and onto the sidewalk acting casual. It's after two in the morning now, so anyone seeing us outside would probably react. Both Ashley and I have the 'blessing' of vampiric cuteness, so we look younger than we are. I'm being sarcastic. Most vampires get supernatural beauty. We have powers of radiant 'aww.' Le Sigh. At least my T-shirt isn't baggy. I'm not the type of girl to flaunt her assets—not that they're of a size to be flauntable—but in a snug enough shirt, my boobs are obvious enough to tell the world I am not, in fact, eleven years old. They might convince a distant observer to consider me sufficiently adult to be outside at this hour. Maybe not.

There are a lot of hormones and stuff in our food. Many girls who are actually fifteen or sixteen get mistaken for being in their twenties. Sierra even has a classmate or two who looks way more developed than twelve. So, yeah. It's anyone's guess how a person will react to encountering us out by ourselves at this hour. Good chance anyone seeing us will mistake us for runaways. Anyone approaching us is going to be trying to help—or trying to take advantage of us.

Thankfully, we are mind readers… and far from helpless.

However, the street is quiet and empty.

The museum is on Tenth Avenue, an ordinary building like any other commercial storefront on a downtown city street, except for the décor. It's part fortune-teller, part crazy prop from an offbeat movie that tries to be scary but comes off as funny. I half expect there to be a mechanical fortune-teller machine in here that grants wishes but ends up 'monkey-pawing' whoever it makes a deal with.

It's dark inside, which is good. The place closes at midnight. Two hours and thirty-nine minutes after closing, there shouldn't be anyone left inside other than the ghosts or whatever else might be haunting the place.

And yeah, all the little hairs on the back of my neck are standing upright merely from me being close to the door.

"Ooh." Ashley shivers. "This museum's got legit mojo."

"Something like that." I nod. "There's at least one other real ghost in here. She likes to play the piano. So, if it starts up without warning, try not to freak out too much."

She gives a thumbs-up. "Sophia's the one who jump scares."

"Right. You just hide behind pillows as soon as the soundtrack gets ominous." I poke her in the side. "You don't jump scare because you're never actually looking at the screen when the jump scare occurs."

Ashley sticks her tongue out at me. "Okay, so what's your plan?"

"Go in, grab lamp, bring it to St. Ives to translate."

"Think she'll help?" Ashley cocks her head to one side, giving me a 'really' squint.

"Maybe out of experimental curiosity." I offer a helpless shrug.

"Uh huh." Ashley sets her hands on her hips. "Mrs. Science Fangs is not going to be able to get a ghost out of a lamp."

I can't help but chuckle. Grown adults do not call people 'Mrs. Science Fangs.' Ahh, Ashley. Please never change. Oh, wait. That's right. You won't. I hug her.

"What?" She asks, squeezing me back.

"Nothing." I grin at her. "Just a moment of feeling happy."

"We're about to commit grand larceny. You should be nervous, not happy."

I roll my eyes. "There is no way that lamp is worth enough to qualify as *grand* larceny. Besides, I'm only borrowing the lamp."

She raises both eyebrows. "Borrowing?"

"Yeah. Once the ghost is out of it, I'll bring the lamp back. If we get lucky, the Blackburns will never know it went for a walk."

"Who are the Blackburns?" she asks.

"The people who own this place."

"So, you're saying this is not stealing. Are you trying to convince me, or yourself?"

I shrug. "Depends on your opinion of the transubsantiative rights of the ethereal."

"What?"

"Heh. I dunno. I just made that up. Do ghosts have personhood?"

"Good question." She taps one foot for a few seconds. "I don't think so. At least, not in a legal sense. People don't believe ghosts are real. We'd have to prove they're real before lobbying for legal protection."

We stare at each other, then say, "Too much work," simultaneously.

I turn my attention to the door. Without even thinking too much about the stupidity of trying the knob, I do so... and the door opens. Wow. What are the odds they forgot to lock up when they left? Not good. There's no way I am *this* lucky. First, the random house we chose in Crescent City had an open back door, now here? That I'm not acting for personal gain only goes so far to push the wheels of fate in my favor. The door being unlocked most likely means one of the owners is still in the building. I suppose it might be possible Tobias— or some other spirit inside—unlocked it for me.

We hurry inside to avoid anyone happening by and seeing us.

Inside, the place is as I remembered it. A veritable wall of 'otherness' slaps me in the face. The charge of supernatural energy in the air is so strong it makes me cringe a bit, as if I'm walking into a store at the mall where they have the music up way too loud. The green glass lamp sitting on the old-fashioned desk near the middle of the giant room turns itself off and on in a repeating cycle. It's as close as Tobias can get to waving at me and yelling 'I'm over here.'

I take two steps forward, then stop to peer back at the door. It's not until I'm looking at it that I understand what's bothering me. The silence. My ears are telling me there is no one else in the building. My brain refuses to believe the owners would've been careless enough to leave for the night and forget to lock the front door.

"What?" whispers Ashley. "Why did you stop?"

"The door wasn't locked." I shift my weight to one leg, folding my arms. "Trying to figure out why."

She makes an 'oh okay' face at me and stands there patiently.

Looking at her sets off a thought cascade. She inherited some form of charm powers from Aurélie. When I'd been the only Innocent vampire around, I didn't have anyone to compare myself to. Any weird abilities would've seemed normal for the bloodline. Ashley and I are clearly not the same in regard to powers. While I do seem to possess the ability to project harmlessness as sort of a defensive mechanism, she takes it to the next level, effectively becoming invisible when she wants. Not literal invisibility. She's still there, but mortals and vampires just ignore her existence unless she does something that specifically pisses them off or gets their attention. I can't do that.

She also seems to have the ability to sweet-talk bears, but who knows where that came from.

It's kinda charm related. So perhaps all that is Ashley mixed with what she got from Aurélie and produced an unexpected side power. I'm calling it a power because people don't just walk up to bears, treat them like big dogs, and send them on their way without being mauled.

Anyway... since she obviously got stuff from Aurélie, there's a more than zero chance I inherited things from Dalton. He's a Lost One. The Old Guard vampires, like Aurélie, don't really have a common theme in their abilities. They range from charmers to being physically strong, to mystics, to other things. Lost Ones, however, tend to share a suite of similarly themed talents all revolving around stealth and such. Dalton can make security cameras ignore him, for example. I'm sure he's got a supernatural ability to pick locks. Getting into places he's not supposed to be in is kind of his thing.

If life happened to be one of Dad's D&D games, Lost Ones would totally be the rogue class.

I glance back and forth between the door and Ashley. Crap. I *am* Dalton's progeny. I think I just picked a lock without even trying. Weird... it never worked before. Can't say I *tried* to make a lock open by sheer willpower at any point, even tonight. I just grabbed the knob and opened the door like I somehow just expected it would open for me. Reminds me of how illusions work in D&D. If I successfully disbelieve the door is locked, it isn't locked. Deeper and deeper I go into the rabbit hole.

That's how it works, luv, says Dalton in my head, sounding like a proud big brother.

So, I did?

You did.

The house in Crescent City, too?

Aye, lass.

I stare at my fingers. Great. Now that I know I can do it, I'll be so nervous it'll never work again.

He laughs. *That's the trick. Just act like you belong walking into the place and reality will oblige.*

Right. Easier said than done. If the trick is *not* thinking about it, I'm screwed. Follows Rules Girl can't help but be nervous whenever she's breaking the rules. Except, I just did it now. Hmm. Is it because I really do intend to bring the lamp back? There's no malice here, only trying to help someone. Breaking into this place doesn't make me feel guilty. In fact, I wanted to disturb as little as possible.

Could be. You may want to get on with it, though. The first rule of legerdemain is not to dawdle. The longer you are somewhere you shouldn't be, the greater the chance something will go pear shaped.

Right. Got it.

"Explain later," I whisper. "Nothing to worry about."

Wow. How about that? As much as I've constantly said how badly I suck at being a thief, I guess I kinda am one. Or at least a spy. Sneaking into places doesn't *always* mean stealing. I spin around and hurry toward the recreation of 'Winston Churchill's Desk.'

Ashley scurries along behind me, gazing around. "Whoa. This place has some seriously messed up vibes."

"Yeah. It does. Try not to touch anything."

The piano in the back right corner begins playing all by itself. Ashley and I jump-cling to each other like a pair of skittish schoolgirls. At least neither one of us screams. A few seconds after the music starts, a spectral woman appears seated on the piano bench, playing.

"Is that Moen?" asks Ashley, her voice shaking.

"What?"

"The composer," she mutters.

"You mean Mozart?" I shake my head at her. "Moen's like a faucet or something."

"Duh." She crosses her eyes. "I meant to say Mozart. No idea where Moen came from."

The pianist ghost shows little reaction to our presence, though she does give off a noticeable air of being pleased with herself. Yeah, she wanted to startle us on purpose. Maybe not the freakout and scream reaction she'd been hoping for, but she should know better. One, I've been here before, and two, we're vamps. So what if we jumped? Even when someone's expecting a sudden loud noise in an otherwise quiet environment, they're going to jump when it happens. That's normal.

Not like we're ridiculous ghost hunters who go looking for evidence of the supernatural, then freak the hell out and run off screaming when they get exactly what they're looking for in the first place. So dumb.

Right, as Dalton would say, time not to dawdle.

I fast-walk over to the desk. The lamp appears to be made of dark green glass and brass. It very much looks like something from the 1940s. Other than the power cable—which is kinda ratty and in obvious need of replacing—it's in good condition if a bit dusty. It's also not plugged in, yet still turned on.

"So cool." Ashley picks up the prong end of the power cord.

In the grand scheme of everything we've witnessed on the supernatural end of things, a light bulb glowing while it's not connected to electrical power is super tame. But, sometimes, it's the small things that are neat.

"Is this the right one?" Ashley brushes her fingers across the lamp.

"Tobias?" I whisper.

"*Ja*," says a disembodied voice.

I gently pick the lamp up and gather the cord. "Yep. This is it."

Know what's weird? Other than like… *everything* these days? As soon as I lift the lamp, the mood in the room changes. It's as if a dozen other spirits are overjoyed Tobias is leaving. If he's spent the past however many years he's been here constantly bitching about his predicament, no wonder they're glad to see him go.

Ahh well. Happy to help.

"Let's get out of here," I whisper.

Ashley jogs to the front door and holds it open for me.

We get five steps away from the place down the sidewalk before someone behind us yells, "*Stop.*"

My heart nearly launches itself up into my throat. It's not easy to sneak up on a vampire. Our ears are really sharp. But someone did. And we got caught. I stop short, but Ashley keeps going like she didn't hear the guy.

Relax, lass. Tis only me, says Dalton telepathically.

Ack. Cripes. I practically melt into a puddle of nerves. You scared the shit out of me.

Ashley spins to peer back, raising an eyebrow. "Sare?"

"Just Dalton talking in my head." I exhale hard. "Thought someone caught us."

"Oh." She turns around, looking at our surroundings. "We're clear."

Wasn't intending to make you brick it, luv. Re-lock the door so they don't know anything happened. Also, be right charitable of you to stop anyone else from blagging the joint.

Umm. Yeah. I scoot over to the door. How does this work?

Grab the handle. Want the door to lock.

It can't be so simple. I do as he says, staring at the door while making faces like the wizard guy from *Conan the Barbarian* when he tried to get that weird magical doorway to open.

This is going to sound obnoxious, says Dalton, *but stop trying to make it lock and merely tell it that it's locked.*

I'm way too anxious about being caught and getting in trouble to calm down. His telepathic yell set off all my anxiety about breaking rules. I stand there, staring at the door for what feels like twenty minutes. At some point I'm not even sure when, the knob stops turning when I jiggle it.

You got it, luv. All set.

This is going to take quite a lot of practice. This Lost One power requires a degree of blasé confidence about breaking into places that I might never be able to conjure easily. If anything, it'll keep me from abusing it and getting in real trouble. Might only work for me if I believe I'm doing something noble. Heh. I can live with that.

"C'mon," I whisper to Ashley exactly the way I did when we 'vandalized' the whiteboard at school. "Let's get out of here."

24

POLITE SOCIETY

O f all the places in the world, one of the last places I ever expected to visit willingly is St. Ives' laboratory.

Figured the odds of me doing that were about the same as taking a day trip to a Chinese prison labor camp somewhere in outer Mongolia, but hey... here I am. She is remarkably polite and willing to talk to me. One would almost think we hadn't gotten off on the wrong foot. No, I do not take any blame for that. She wanted me to give her something I didn't own and got angry when I didn't. That, to me, is not reasonable.

But, as far as she seems to be concerned, she's past it.

We—and by that, I mean myself, Ashley, St. Ives, Pascal Ivanov, and two of her hipster henchbeards—are standing around a plain steel table in one of her lab spaces, all staring at the desk lamp. It's been about a half hour of poking and prodding thus far. St. Ives cannot apparently see or hear the ghost. The woman is old enough to peer into my thoughts, so she's been doing that to 'hear' Tobias and effectively translate.

Without the need to clumsily rely on Google and thumb-typing Ashley's best approximation of how to spell German words, communication is much faster and more accurate. Evidently, Tobias Krüger really was a spy during the war.

"You said you weren't," I blurt.

"I said I was not a spy who attempted to assassinate Churchill," replies Tobias via St. Ives' translation. "I was merely a spy, and I did not try to kill anyone. This lamp didn't belong to the old bastard, anyway. It sat on a desk in the basement where the codebreakers worked. Also, I did not die to a gunshot."

Ashley fidgets. Her body language says she's a little nervous and freaked out by the topic of death, but her facial expression is pure curiosity. "How *did* you die?"

Tobias heaves a sigh, then speaks in a somewhat embarrassed tone. The light bulb flickers in time with his words, kinda like the car in *Knight Rider*. "*Ich habe mich an einem Stück Brot verschluckt, als ich Mittagessen gegessen habe.*"

Eleanor's android-like demeanor cracks a little. One corner of her mouth lifts in an attempted smile. "He asphyxiated on a piece of bread while eating lunch."

Wow. I blink. "Seriously?"

"*Ja,*" laments the spirit.

Poor guy.

"Does he know why he..." Ashley blinks. "Wait. Sorry. Forgot he can understand English. Do you know why you got stuck in this lamp?"

St. Ives translates the response. "He isn't sure, but suspects it's probably due to it being next to him at the time of his death. His face lay pressed against the base for over an hour until someone discovered him. I am no expert on spiritual matters, but it is possibly related to the presence of electrical current within the lamp."

"Are you sure you're not a bad guy?" asks Ashley.

"Do you think he'd admit it if he was?" I ask.

"*Ich war mit unserer Regierung nicht einverstanden, aber musste Befehle befolgen.*"

St. Ives raises an eyebrow. "That didn't work too well at Nuremburg."

"What did he say?" I glance at her.

"He didn't agree with the government, but had to follow orders."

"Oof." Ashley cringes.

"Yeah, the 'following orders' defense didn't work." I also wince.

"*Was ist in Nürnberg passiert? Das habe ich nicht mitbekommen,*" says the lamp.

"He doesn't know about Nuremburg. One moment." St. Ives speaks in German for a while, likely explaining the war crimes trials. Better her than me. I kinda brain dumped most of history class already.

"*Oh. Ja,*" says Tobias in a flat tone. "*Ich verstehe, wie es dazu kommen konnte.*"

Ashley and I peer at Eleanor expectantly.

"He said he can certainly understand how things led to war crimes trials."

Ya think?

We talk for a little while more through Eleanor. Tobias claims not to have been on board with the war and exploited his English fluency to obtain a post as a spy in London. This allowed him to avoid combat and not participate in anything he deemed as evil. While he did send information back to Germany to maintain the illusion of doing his job, he edited things to be useless or misleading. He even suspected British Intelligence was on to him, knew he fed his commanders bogus information, and had been about to approach him about becoming a double agent officially. Alas, he perished before they made contact with him due to a highly unfortunate mishap involving a cheese sandwich.

He's convincing enough that I shift from wanting to help him mostly to avoid being incessantly nagged for the next few centuries to wanting to help him because I want to help him. Problem is, St. Ives is absolutely clueless when it comes to the best procedure to evict a spirit from an old desk lamp. At least she helped us understand the situation.

I'm going to break my rules about involving the Littles in the weird stuff and go to the next reasonable source for help here: Sophia.

She's close at hand, easily available, and would be happy to help.

Heck, she freed a genuinely evil ghost from a soul jar because she felt bad for him. It's not going to take much convincing to get her to pop the cork on poor Tobias. He really does seem like a genuinely nice—albeit woefully unlucky—man.

"Regarding the child Chloe," says St. Ives.

Here we go… I face her, ready for an argument. Not going to start off being impolite, though. Diplomacy works better for me. If that fails, I'll fall back on my youth. Wait, no. Pleading won't work on St. Ives. The 'aww but Mom' technique only works on people with functioning emotions. To sway Eleanor, I'd need to concoct a logically sound, scientifically intact argument.

Crap.

"Uhh, I'm not sure poking and prodding her is going anywhere. Last time we were here, you basically microwaved her. Can we please stop?"

Ashley steps up beside me. "Microwaving children is generally frowned on in polite society."

"Yes." St. Ives raises a hand as if to tell us to slow down. "I was going to tell you that my research has hit a dead end. I do not believe the change is reversible. Other than some folkloric drivel claiming the process of becoming a vampire might be undone if the sire is killed before the progeny has a chance to take a mortal's life—which by the way is complete nonsense—there is no information out there on the subject."

"Oh." I offer a hesitant nod, trying to process the meaning of what she's saying.

She's giving up trying to 'fix' Chloe. This could be good or bad. Also, go figure there isn't any info on how to reverse vampirism out there. I'm guessing most vampires wanted the change, so they wouldn't change their minds after. Ones like me who had it dropped on them also probably feel like I do. After getting more or less used to it, this is awesome. Why would I want to go back to being mortal? The moody, self-hating, 'I miss the sunlight' type vampire has got to be a Hollywood construction. Sure, there are probably a handful of vamps who have buyer's remorse, but it's hardly common.

Eleanor holds her head up as though she's giving a speech to a board of scientific review. "I intend to speak with Mr. Wolent about my findings. Chloe is likely beyond reversal at this point. Too much time has passed."

Again, I nod. Yeah, pretty much what I figured. One way process. Hmm. Sophia might be able to change her back into a mortal... but this is Sophia. She'd have about the same odds of turning Chloe into a bunny rabbit as she would making her mortal again. Not worth the risk, and I'm sure the kid prefers to stay as she is. We have similar attitudes about that. For me—and Ashley as well—it's freedom from living in a world where we have to be afraid of every shadow. Young women just do not feel safe the way men do. We don't go outside alone at night. We don't go to the bathroom in a public restaurant alone, we're always looking over our shoulders. Mom ushered me into the dark reality of life when I was around ten. Overnight, the world went from no big deal to a scary place.

Chloe doesn't know about that sort of thing yet. She is happy to be a vampire because it means no grown men will terrify her into hiding under her bed for hours ever again. She doesn't have to be afraid of adults anymore.

Sigh. Now I want to zoom home and hug her.

"Thanks," I say just over a whisper.

Eleanor rests a hand on my arm. "Relax, Sarah. I am cautiously willing to vote for allowing her to remain among us as long as she behaves. You and she have proven over the past few weeks you are at least minimally capable of making an effort to conceal her existence."

I twitch. Was that a backhanded compliment or is she being genuine? Hard to say. Whatever it was, I'll take it.

"She will." I exhale in relief. "Only real problem is her temper and... colorful vocabulary."

"Indeed." Eleanor glances at the lamp. "There is, unfortunately, nothing more I can do for your spectral associate."

"Understood." I pick the lamp up. "Thanks for your time."

She nods in a manner that makes me think I owe her a favor now. Okay, fine. As long as it isn't going to require me hurting someone or stealing something from an innocent person, I might as well do it. Life, even unlife, requires compromises. Vampires don't last long on their own. We need friends.

Even prickly ones with no senses of humor.

She starts to turn away, but pauses long enough to make an odd face at me. I almost picture her saying 'I *do* have a sense of humor, it's merely too refined for normal people to comprehend.'

Again, I almost catch her smiling.

25

PHONE HOME

There's no way I'm dragging Sophia out of bed at nearly four in the morning for this.

Tobias is stuck in a desk lamp, but he's been there for a long time. One more day won't matter. With regrets to the Blackburn family, I take the lamp home. My intentions have not changed. As soon as the spirit is successfully separated from the desk lamp, it will go back to the museum. It might not be paranormally significant anymore, but it's still a genuine 1940s-era lamp that *was* in a British government building during the war. It's unlikely to be priceless, but also has to be worth something.

We go home by way of Tilloa's place, hurriedly retrieving Chloe before racing as fast as we can fly back to Cottage Lake. Wow. I really need to stop playing chicken with sunrise so much. Mom's already awake by the time we go in the sliding door from the deck. When I say 'awake' I mean not in bed. Her mental state at the moment isn't quite there. She's standing by the sink, absentmindedly attempting to bite one of Sophia's pun cookies. Mom's not having any success at it, and seems to be caught in a loop of confusion her sleep-saturated brain isn't able to handle. It's like watching someone experience a proverbial glitch in the Matrix. She haz cookie (spelled with a z). She bites cookie. Cookie doesn't break apart. This does not compute.

I pause long enough to say, "The slow tooth penetrates the shield" before zooming downstairs.

Mom is probably going to stand there thinking on my bizarre comment for a good ten minutes. When she wakes up a little bit more, she might get the *Dune* reference, which will cause her to seek out Dad and ask for clarification. And yes, she's going to think her daughter is weird. I know. I own my weirdness.

Once in my room, I set Tobias down on my desk. We're not cutting things *so* close there's no time to change. Ashley, Chloe, and I swap our clothes for comfortable sleepwear—oversized T-shirts—and pile into bed.

THINGS RARELY GO QUITE TO PLAN.

I intended to pester Sophia about the lamp first thing once I woke up, but she's not home. Evidently, the girls are all over at Priya's house. Cool. The kids deserve to have fun. They aren't beholden to the demands of the supernatural underworld.

Sam, Daryl, Jordan, and Ronan are hanging out in my brother's room. Sierra is on the PlayStation in the living room. (Shocking, I know). It's also raining like a freakin' monsoon out there. Sam and his friends are a bit strange. They like spending time playing outside. To hear the 'rents talk, that attitude is not normal for 'kids today.' I always figured Ashley and I were on the introverted side. Didn't realize it's a generational instinct.

I settle in for a nice lazy day at home. Alas, the sheer fact of it raining buckets demands otherwise. To make a long and tedious story short, from the time I wake up until almost seven in the evening, I'm zipping all over the place, getting soaked. It's daylight so... car, no flying. Probably shouldn't complain *too* much. Driving in a car is much less exposure to the rain than flying. Though, it is late August, so I wouldn't get too many weird looks going around in a bathing suit.

People have accused me of being derpy sometimes, but I am not so dumb as to wear a light-colored shirt while going on out on a day like this. Why does that matter? Because I hate bras. Never cared for the medieval torture devices. Becoming an undead has freed me from the last remaining thread of 'maybe I should deal with them.' Let's just say 'sag' in thirty years is no longer a worry of mine.

Scott once told me I never had to worry about sag because they weren't heavy enough.

Grr. Great. Not only do I spend hours doing errands, I'm angry most of the time, too, thinking about that jackass. I'm glad I ripped his head off and burned what remained of him.

Anyway... do some shopping errands for Mom, pick up some dry cleaning for Dad, schlep Sierra to her sword class and sit there watching that for an hour, race home. Well, not 'race.' It's raining way too hard to drive in any way that could be described as 'racing' anywhere. Sierra might be abnormally tough thanks to Sophia's magic, but she's still my kid sister. I go full grandma.

I picture Robert Downey Jr. saying 'you never go full grandma' in an overly serious voice and make myself laugh.

Sierra glances over. "What?"

She is, of course, being self-conscious and thinks I'm laughing at her for something. Before I can even answer, she leans forward to check her face in the door mirror. Seeing nothing out of the ordinary, she resumes staring at me.

"Long story. Not you."

Sierra smirks. "As slow as we're going, you have time to read War and Peace before we get home."

"Heh. That's kinda what I was laughing at..." I chuckle. "Couple days ago, I found a bad guy while feeding. His friends were going to hurt a woman, so I got involved."

She nods in an 'of course you did, and I expect nothing less of you' way. "Okay. Why is that funny?"

"It wasn't. But..." I explain Ashley making the 'going full superhero' joke... and how that became a 'full grandma' joke in my head.

Sierra is not impressed. Oh well, not every joke can win. I thought it was funny. Made myself laugh, so that's good enough for me.

The remainder of our conversation on the way home is about demons... specifically the one that may or may not be trying its damndest to come bite me in the ass. Sometimes, the Universe isn't fair. Monster tries to kill me, fails to do so, and it's carrying a grudge at me for not simply rolling over and dying. Go figure. It's debatable how culpable I am in the matter. The sefil didn't exactly just happen to stumble across me completely by chance. We did go out looking for the people who murdered Wolent's emissary to Portia Ward. It could be argued they started it by attacking our guy. Whatever. Semantics won't help. Not like one can reason with the utterly unreasonable. This demon is basically an addict who got a taste of paranormal-grade heroin (sefil soul feeding) and we cut him off from it. Diplomacy does not work on addicts, toddlers, demons, and people like Uncle Hank.

My kid sister is still upset at being forbidden from fighting the sefil. I do my best to explain how the thing was kicking *my* ass, and she only would've gotten herself killed. On some level, she does understand. It's still not a fun pill for her to swallow.

We're talking about vampires and relative power levels when I pull into the driveway at home. Sierra is pretty sure she's going to stay about the same (power level wise) for as long as the magic lasts on her —which may well be permanent. Me, on the other hand, will eventually become an elder and pull ahead of her. This is, of course, assuming nothing blows me up or eats me before a few centuries go by.

Cheerful thoughts, right?

We make a mad dash for the door, futilely dodging rain that's falling in sheets. Really no point to it. I should've just walked. The only difference it makes to run is Sierra ends up out of breath plus soaked, as opposed to merely soaked. She goes upstairs, I go downstairs to dry off. Once I've had some quality towel time and put on dry clothing, I grab the lamp and jog upstairs to Sophia's room. She should be home by now in anticipation of dinner any minute.

Sure enough, I walk in on my kid sister in the middle of something magical. She's got various scraps of construction paper, yarn, and crayons set up in a ritual circle around where she sits cross-legged on the rug. Kinda looks like it's witchcraft day in kindergarten arts and crafts.

She's concentrating intently on a big piece of paper covered in blue crayon writing in the style of ancient runes. It looks like a prop from a medieval fantasy movie. Hope she said 'klaatu, verrata, nicto' before she picked it up.

I lean against the doorjamb.

After a minute or two, she glances over at me, then smiles. "Hey, Sare. What's up?"

"What'cha doing?"

"Trying to add a couple more weeks to summer. It ended too fast," she says in total seriousness.

I gawk. Oh heck. This isn't going to end well at all. "Uhh, I thought you liked school."

She shrugs. "I do. It's for Sierra."

"She asked you to do this?" I raise an eyebrow, taking a step into the room.

"No. She's just scared of being in school." Sophia makes a gun-shaped hand gesture.

Grr. "I hate this so much. I want to kick someone's ass really bad for making Sierra terrified someone's going to randomly shoot up her school at any minute, but... who do I blame?"

"*Die Puppenspieler einer gescheiterten kapitalistischen Gesellschaft, die Profit über menschliches Leben und Glück stellt,*" says the lamp in a fatigued sort of tone like he's tired of explaining the same thing again and again.

I peer down at... him? It? I'm not really looking at the ghost of Tobias Krüger at the moment. He's not visible. I'm looking at the lamp, which is an 'it.' He's inside it, so I'm still not sure entirely sure which pronoun to use. This is the only case in which a pronoun ought to be complicated: a person (more or less) and an inanimate object inhabiting the same physical space. The line is blurry as to which of them I refer.

"Wow." Sophia stares. "The light flickers when he talks just like that old TV show Dad loves with the talking car."

"Yeah. Either someone in the prop department was bored and had some extra wiring... or the filament in the bulb is responding to fluctuations in the electromagnetic energy of the ghost when he talks."

"Nerd!" yells Sierra from her bedroom.

Sophia and I laugh.

"Why do you have a talking lamp?" Sophia tilts her head, draping one side of her long blonde hair down to the rug by her knee.

"It's not a talking lamp. It's a ghost trapped inside a lamp." I walk the rest of the way into her room and sit on the floor nearby, careful not to disturb her Crayola ritual circle. "Kinda hoping you might be able to set him free."

She squirms. "The last time I let a ghost out of something, it caused problems."

"Yeah. True. This is different."

"How?" She nibbles on her lower lip, eyeing the old, green lamp.

"This ghost wasn't put in here on purpose for being bad. He just kinda got stuck somehow."

Sophia gingerly reaches out and touches a few fingertips to the top of the lamp. "Oh. Okay. Yeah. He doesn't feel bad."

"So, you can get him out of this thing?" I ask.

"I've learned that it's not a great idea to make definite promises about magic." Sophia pretends to crack her knuckles. "I can probably do it, but something strange might happen."

I smile. "Stranger than a ghost stuck in an old desk lamp?"

Sophia exhales. "Good point. Okay... Here goes."

She holds both hands out over the lamp like it's a campfire and she's cold. I sit there holding it, trying to stay as still as possible while simultaneously being ready to jump away and pull Sophia back from an enraged void octopus or some other magical calamity. Klepto—who up until this moment had been peacefully napping on the bed—perks up to watch. It's kinda odd how a kitten is capable of conveying emotional moods via facial expression. It's ever so subtly beyond normal like the way the characters in *Zootopia* are animals but emote like humans. It's not natural, it shouldn't seem so believable, but it does. Thankfully, the kitten seems confident and curious.

Over the course of the next three minutes, as Sophia's expression becomes increasingly serious and focused, a faint, glowing nimbus begins to exude from the lamp. At first, it looks like a ghostly copy of the lamp is expanding outward from the physical object, like an enlarging hologram superimposed over reality. Twelve seconds after the 'ghost lamp' appears, it abruptly collapses from a transparent lamp copy to a much brighter, softball-sized orb of light.

As if gathering a big soap bubble, Sophia coaxes her fingertips around the spectral mass and ever so gently tugs it away from the lamp. One tiny phantasmal thread remains connected to the lamp for another minute or two while she makes a series of annoyed faces at it. Finally, the thread snaps, allowing her to collect all the spirit energy between her hands.

It's throwing off a surprising amount of light. Anyone outside in the back yard looking at her bedroom window would think she's playing with one of those powerful construction lights you can hang nearby while doing projects. Dad got one of them a couple years ago. I think he used it once. Maybe twice. Oh, and he also *insisted* on getting like a two-mile-long extension cord for it. Because, you know, our house is so big. Okay, it's not really two miles long but it's way in excess of anything practical. What is it with dads and getting into a competition about who has the longest extension cord they will never practically have a use for?

Sophia looks up at me, her face cast in shadows like she's about to tell a scary campfire story with a flashlight under her chin. "Umm. Something isn't right."

Crap. I should've known there would be a catch. Bracing for the news we've just unleashed a dangerous monster on the world, I ask, "What happened?"

She squishes her hands around the ectoplasmic mass like a kid who picked up something sticky and can't let go of it. "It's stuck to me. I'm trying to release the ghost into being just a ghost, but I can't get this sticky stuff off my hands."

The first time Ashley was alone with a boyfriend for more than ten minutes, I got a text 'how do I get this stuff off my hands?' Of course, at the time, I had no idea what Ashley was talking about. Sophia's comment is *entirely* innocent, but it reminded me of my friend's awkward moment. No idea why she asked me. We were both clueless. I hadn't even seen a boy with his pants off yet, much less touched one. It's kinda hilarious now to think about. The guy... wanna say his name was Tristan or something... talked her into using her hand on him. She had no idea the 'dragon would breathe' so to speak. Caught her off guard. Amazingly, she wasn't grossed out at all.

Right. Pushing that thought out of my head. Sophia's here. I don't want to explain why I'm fighting the urge not to laugh. She's not ready to hear that stuff yet.

"Sare?" whispers Sophia. "Oh, poop. You won't be able to answer me. You don't know about magic."

"Want me to call Darren Anderson?" I pull my phone out of my pocket.

"Umm. Maybe." She looks around for a few seconds, then leans toward me, shoving the glowing orb at my phone. The ghostly orb light flashes for a split second, then disappears. "Okay, that worked... for now."

"Ich bin mir nicht sicher, ob das hier besser ist." Tobias' voice comes out of my phone's speaker.

Also, the screen unlocks itself, leaping to Google Translate. 'I'm not sure this is any better' appears on the right side.

"Ooh. Neat." Sophia grins.

"Wie interessant. Es gibt Fotos." (How interesting. There are photos.)

"Ack!" I blush. "Don't look through those!"

Sophia raises an eyebrow at me. "Did you take pictures of Hunter you wouldn't want Mom to see?"

My face gets redder. "Not like that! Just... super cheesy."

"What's that mean?" Sophia leans back, one eyebrow raised.

"It means we were acting like lovesick romantic dorks and the photos are embarrassing." I can't look at her. No, I'm not lying. There are no nude photos on my phone. Mom would kill me. We do, however, look like promotional stills from an incredibly lame romance movie. Fully clothed. Well, maybe he's showing some pectoral, but the pictures are nothing that couldn't be shown in public... except for being morbidly embarrassing.

"Sorry, Mr. Ghost," says Sophia. "There's something weird going on with your spirit energy. I dunno what it is, but it's like you *have* to stick to something."

"Mew, mew," says Klepto before making this warbling sort of noise that's part purr, part meow.

"Oh, maybe." Sophia nods at the kitten. "It's possible you weren't *trapped* in that lamp as much as you wanted to stay there."

"*Unmöglich! Ich versuche seit Jahrzehnten, dieser verdammten Lampe zu entkommen.*"

I tilt the phone screen around to read: 'Impossible! I've been trying to escape that damn lamp for decades.' Yeah, well... people try to quit smoking for decades, too... and fail at it. "If this need to attach yourself to electronics is a psychological hangup, it might be beyond even Sophia to fix. We're going to need a ghostly therapist. Where the heck would we find one of those?"

"Hollywood," deadpans Sophia without hesitation. "Across the street from the 'plant happiness counselor,' between the dog psychiatrist and the Himalayan salt crystal healing spa."

"Plant happiness counselor?" I blink.

She waves dismissively. "Yeah, this woman thinks if she goes to people's houses and spends an hour or two saying nice things to their houseplants, they'll grow better."

"*Die Menschheit ist dem Untergang geweiht,*" says Tobias in a defeated tone.

I peer down at the screen. (Humanity is doomed.)

Well... I'm hoping Sophia's just making a joke and there isn't really someone out there working as a professional plant happiness technician. Wow. "So, what do we do now?"

Sophia stretches. "Go downstairs. It's almost time for dinner."

I smirk. "I meant with the ghost."

"He's gotta live in your phone for now." Sophia abruptly starts laughing.

"Uh oh. That's not good. Why are you laughing?" I fidget.

"ET phone home."

The ghost is silent. Probably because he's from the 1940s and has no idea what ET means.

"He's not an alien." I shake my head.

"No... ET as in ectoplasmic Tobias." Sophia points. "And the phone *is* his home."

Sierra appears, sticking her head in the doorway from the hall. "You are both nerds."

"Ich fühle mich, als hätte ich einen Witz auf meine Kosten verpasst."

I peer down at the screen. (I feel as if I have missed a joke at my expense.) "Not really. She's making light of the situation, not you... and it was honestly a real stretch."

Sophia raspberries at me. "You don't need the old lamp anymore. I gotta do some research on what to do next. I'll do it after dinner, or the next time I can borrow the big book."

She's talking about the *Tome of F Knowledge*. I should probably be worried. It's not like Sophia to break rules or do things she's not supposed to do. However, for some reason, she has no qualms about helping herself to that book whenever she needs—and whenever Darren Anderson and the other mystics there won't be aware she borrowed it. Maybe it's got something to do with the book essentially being sentient. She doesn't see it as steal-borrowing an object, merely sneaking away to talk to someone.

Whatever. I decide to trust her good nature. It's probably going to bite us in the ass, but it'll have Nerf fangs.

Oh well. Tonight, I'll be taking the now-ghostless lamp back to the museum. I'm sure they've noticed it gone missing by now. But, when it mysteriously appears, they'll probably mistake it for a supernatural event. Hang on... I'm a vampire. Technically, anything I do is a 'supernatural event.'

Heh.

"Guys," calls Dad from downstairs. "Dinner!"

I stand and stuff the phone in my pocket.

"*Uhh, das ist... intim,*" mumbles the ghost.

Huh? I pull the phone out again. The translation says 'uhh, this is intimate.'

Wham. Zero to super blush in an instant. It's as if I just stuffed a man's head into my pocket and had his face pressed against my butt. Ugh. This is awkward. How am I supposed to put my phone in my pocket when it's become a sentient man? The back pocket is gonna smush his face against my backside. Front pocket isn't as tight but it's even more squirmy. Dammit. Guess I carry it in my hand for now... or dig out a fanny pack. Oh, wait... I do have a belt clip for this phone somewhere. Dad got me one since he thought the new phone was 'the size of a surfboard' and wouldn't be pocket-carryable. I've proven him wrong even if it is a bit cumbersome.

Here's hoping Sophia can hurry up and set him free for real.

26

DISASTER IMMINENT...
TOMORROW

A few days later, and I still have a ghost in my iPhone.

Ashley's blasé to it, having no qualms about changing while the phone sits on my desk. We don't know for sure if Tobias can 'see' in a traditional sense. But even if he can, it doesn't bother Ashley. One, he's a ghost. All he can do is look. Two, he's a ghost. Ghosts could follow us into the shower to watch and we'd never know.

Well, maybe we would now since we're vampires. But I mean... you know that fake rule out there about the number of spiders a person swallows in their sleep? There's a less-fake rule. The average person has zero privacy from curious ghosts. Over anyone's lifetime, they'll probably be peeped at in the shower or while having sex dozens of times by bored ghosts. Yeah, I'm making certain assumptions. Maybe ghosts lose the part of humanity that gets a thrill out of carnal pleasures—even if they can only watch.

I dunno. Personally? I've been dropping a T-shirt or something on top of my phone before changing.

Sophia says she's working on it. Evidently, the big book is in use or at least being watched, and she can't get to it yet. If she hasn't been able to do anything in another couple days, she promised she'd approach Darren and ask to use it.

So, anyway, it's Labor Day weekend, officially marking the end of my second summer as a vampire. Crazy to think about it being only two years. Well, two years and two months, give or take a week. Time flies when you keep getting caught up in supernatural catastrophes.

As always, Dad is making a big production of the holiday.

We're mostly all outside in the backyard. It's slightly overcast but still warm enough to be comfortable—I mean for the mortals. I'm *too* warm. But hey, I'll take 'uncomfortable summer heat' over burning alive. It's not even painful anymore, merely 'ugh.' Ashley and Chloe are visibly less at ease out in the daylight, but it's not so bad either one of them has thrown in the towel and run inside.

The Littles, Chloe, and Ronan are zooming around the yard in bathing suits, playing with a sprinkler and a Slip N' Slide. Whoever invented that, by the way? Who got the idea that a few seconds of careening helplessly out of control along a water-soaked sheet of plastic would be fun? I mean, 'careening helplessly out of control' is a metaphor for life in most cases. But, yeah, it's definitely a win with the kids. They love it.

Mrs. Carter is here as well. So is Mrs. Lawrence, Hunter and Ronan's mom. They and the Sheridan grands (Mom's parents) are sitting around the big round table on the deck sipping iced tea and talking about random adult things. Dad's parents are in Maui or something and couldn't make it this year. Uncle Ricky—Mom's brother—is hanging out with Dad over by the grill talking about guy stuff. Ashley and I are bumming it on the two folding loungers. She's stretched out and relaxed. I'm draped on top of Hunter—who is not wearing a swimsuit. Ash and I are doing the bathing suit thing, too, even though we literally *can't* tan anymore, nor do we have any interest in frolicking in the sprinklers. It's just tradition. For the past... oh, as far back as I remember, the Labor Day Weekend cookout is to be spent in a swimsuit all day long—at least for kids. Time used to be I'd be right out there jumping in the sprinklers, too. I'm a bit old for that now—but still kid enough to where it feels like I ought to be in a bathing suit. Putting on real clothes for this feels too much like I've become a stuffy adult and have to sit there talking about jobs or politics or whatever else they're rambling about.

Speaking of politics, Uncle Hank is *not* here—to everyone's delight.

Ashley and I are neatly settled between kid and adult in our own space. It's comfortable here.

Well, mostly. Ashley will be much happier in a few hours when the sun is starting to vanish.

Chloe's tolerating it amazingly well. The kid has to be operating on *Bugs Bunny* logic. Like, she doesn't really understand the sun can hurt her, so it doesn't. Like how the gorilla could fly with concrete wings until Bugs pointed out he's breaking the law of gravity.

Mom, on her way back out to the deck from the kitchen with more iced tea, pauses by us, leans close, and whispers, "Sunbathing vampires? My, my. What *is* the world coming to?"

We chuckle.

Hunter starts to give off a mild sense of awkwardness at having Mom right there. We're not doing anything, but I am in a bikini and laying on top of him.

"It's like tradition or something." I examine my fingernails. "It would feel too weird *not* to have a bathing suit on today."

She smiles, then gives the grandparents side eye. "You are planning to do something about my parents seeing Chloe?"

Oof. I mentally cringe at some bad thoughts. Ashley and I are stuck at eighteen. Sad as it is to think about, my grandparents will likely be gone before so much time has passed that it's super weird to them we haven't changed at all. They're both in their early sixties now. If they make it to their nineties, that's about thirty more years. It's rare for an almost-fifty-year-old woman to look as young as I do now. Maybe they'll notice. But at ninety, they probably wouldn't be able to notice, anyway. Ugh. Is that mean to say? Not trying to be mean, just practical. My point is... Chloe, being only seven right now, is going to be a tiny bit more obvious about not growing older. The grandparents will definitely realize there's something extremely weird about her even two years from now.

Worse than the sad thoughts that my beloved grandparents will die someday is realizing Mom just basically asked me to play with their minds.

I nod at Mom. "Yeah. As soon as it's dark."

She starts to walk over to the table with the tea, but hesitates, looking back. "What are you going to do?"

"Give them a compulsion not to pay attention to the fact she's not getting any bigger. To them, it'll seem normal and expected... I hope."

"You hope?"

I offer a weak smile. "Yeah. Never tried to do a compulsion like this, so it might take me a few tries to fine tune it perfectly."

"Oh. That's all right." She makes an appraising sort of frown-smile like she tasted something she expected would be awful but it's rather good. "Elegant solution. Much easier than trying to get them to forget she exists."

"Yeah."

She stares down at the tray she's carrying. "It does feel so strange giving you permission to mind control my parents."

I nudge her, smiling. "Relax. It's not mind control. Just a mental block. Some parents see their kids as little children no matter how old they get... so I'm not really doing anything unnatural here."

Mom's mood brightens. She laughs. "True. Remember to be in bed by eight, sweetie."

I give her a 'ha ha very funny' smirk.

She breezes over to the table, sets the tray down, and joins the adult conversation.

Dad and Uncle Ricky have been away from the other adults, leaving Grandpa Sheridan the only guy at a table of women. The two of them have been making the Jedi master and padawan jokes all afternoon in regard to grill cooking. Yes, my father has grill implements styled to look kindasorta like lightsabers. He wanted to get a giant steel death star for a grill, but Mom said no. She also shot down the grill shaped like an AT-AT walker. So, he settled for an ordinary one.

Hunter, Ashley, and I talk about random stuff, sounding and feeling pretty much like normal teenagers finally.

My gaze randomly happens to shift to the group of kids by the Slip N' Slide two seconds before Chloe takes a running leap at it. The instant she lands on the yellow plastic sheet, she practically disappears, launched as if shot out of a cannon. In like a quarter-second, there's a Chloe-shaped hole in the fence and she's way off in the woods behind the house. It happened so damn fast, none of the adults noticed. They jump at the *bang* of her hitting the fence but somehow fail to notice the cartoonish-cutout of an upside-down child, arms and legs flailed to the sides, in the wood. It's so surreal, I initially start to laugh thinking it's an illusion. Hmm. No scream-crying in the distance. Either Chloe isn't hurt badly at all... or she's really messed up.

"Whoa," whispers Hunter. "Did Chloe just go ballistic?"

"Oops," whispers Sophia. "Too much slippery."

I'm about to fly into an absolute panic and go running after Chloe, but before I can even sit up, the kid is once again standing at the front of the Slip N' Slide as if time just rewound itself. Sophia glowers intently at the yellow plastic sheet, her expression screaming 'c'mon, c'mon, c'mon!' Chloe flings herself at the water slide again. This time, she goes spinning along it in an ordinary manner, except she's cruising a bit too fast to be normal. She ends up tumbling onto the grass at the end of the slide. She's giggling and laughing. Okay, that's fine. It probably won't result in broken bones.

The hole in the fence is gone.

Two possibilities exist.

One: Sophia overamped a slippery spell on the waterslide and created a child-launching railgun capable of hurtling seven-year-olds at supersonic speed. Then, realizing her error, rewound a few seconds of local time to tweak the enchantment before Chloe got up close and personal with Mach 3 a second time.

Two: I hallucinated the entire episode.

It's pretty much impossible for someone outside Sophia's 'inclusion zone' to realize the difference between a momentary hallucination and one of her time oops take-backsies. For my own sanity, I'm going to dismiss it as a fleeting bizarre daydream. Fortunately, I've discovered that injuries Innocent vampires sustain during the day *do* heal... eventually. We're stuck injured until the sun goes down, but after that, we're good. So, I don't need to be overly paranoid during the day.

Anyway, the afternoon is relaxing.

Even though I don't need normal food, it smells wonderful and I fully intend to have some. Hey, gotta act normal, right?

Dad adores Labor Day Weekend. He's got a ceremonial Yoda grilling apron he only wears once a year, today. Judging by the aroma in the air, the food is almost ready. Thanks to his acute attunement to 'the Force,' my father also senses it's about time. At least, that's how he refers to his ability to smell... and years of experience grilling. We like to tease him about his cooking skills, but it's ninety percent nonsense. He really is pretty good at grilling. It's 'inside cooking' where he runs into some issues. Those issues are primarily due to laziness, guesswork, and experimentation. Like he doesn't really care about the differences between thyme, oregano, or rosemary. They're all 'green flaky stuff' he might randomly add to whatever.

My father opens the lid of the grill to examine his masterpiece.

A six-foot-high geyser of dark crimson flames belches upward, coalescing into the approximate shape of a buff male torso, head, and arms. From this apparition of flames, a deep, resonant voice thunders, shaking the deck. "Prepare to know the pain of eternal suffering!"

"No kidding," deadpans Sam. "Dad's cooking."

Dad slams the lid shut with a dull *clank*, tamping out the fiery thing, then glances back over his shoulder at everyone as if hoping no one noticed that. "Uhh, wee bit too much lighter fluid. Last time I buy the cheap brand."

The girls all stare at the grill in varying degrees of scared. Sam has this unimpressed smirk on his face. Ronan's wide eyed. Hunter whistles, his breath warm on my hair. Uncle Ricky is examining his vape wand, no doubt wondering if he mistakenly loaded the 'extra strong THC' instead of ordinary flavor. Mom, Mrs. Carter, Mrs.

Lawrence, and the grandparents are frozen, jaws agape. Our backyard has fallen into complete silence.

I sigh at the clouds. Some people want to be rich, want power, to be famous... all I want is normality. Why is that so damned hard?

"Umm, Jonathan?" asks Mom in a hesitant voice. "Are you trying a different hot sauce this year?"

Dad turns to his right to look at the kids in the yard. "Sam, did you do something to the grill?"

"Nope." The boy shakes his head.

"Not me, either." Sophia grimaces. "The last time I tried to get rid of the essence of purified evil, I flushed it. Mistake. Do *not* recommend."

Grandpa Sheridan gestures at the grill. "What the devil is going on?"

"Nah." Sam smiles at him. "Just a minor demon, not a devil."

Mom facepalms. "Funny prank, Sam... but that's enough."

My brother tilts his head as if to say 'what are you talking about, I didn't do it.' A second later, his eyebrows tick upward and he gets this 'oh, okay, I get it' expression. "Hang on, Dad. Let me turn off the projector."

Sam runs across the yard, up the deck stairs, and goes into the house. No idea what he's actually doing, but—miraculously—the adults all seem to believe the line about a projector being responsible. Maybe they think it's one of those crazy Halloween type things that makes it look like real ghosts are in the windows.

My little brother reemerges from the house after thirty seconds, races over to the grill, and pretends to fiddle at something underneath. He might be legit checking for demonic problems, but he's definitely *not* disabling a prank device. Finally, he stands up and backs away. "It's okay now."

Dad tentatively lifts the lid two inches to peek inside, then, seeming relieved, opens it the rest of the way. No weird manifestations erupt. The food looks undamaged. Whew. I study the expressions of the adults. Things appear iffy, but nothing a little mental eraser won't fix once the sun goes down.

I eye the grill. It's gotta be that demon from the sefil. He's going to be seriously annoying, I bet. Yeah... this problem is going to bite me in the ass. Oh well. Can't really do much about it right this second. Besides, I've got a few years before his influence in the mortal world will be capable of more than scary parlor tricks. No reason to rush around in a panic.

May as well sit back and enjoy the holiday.

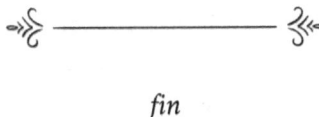

fin

ACKNOWLEDGMENTS

Thank you for reading *Vampire Innocent 16!* Sarah's story will continue soon.

Additional thanks to Lee Sheridan for editing. Also, thank you to Dr. Micky O'Brady for sanity checking the German lines!

ABOUT THE AUTHOR

Originally from South Amboy NJ, Matthew has been creating science fiction and fantasy worlds for most of his reasoning life. Since 1996, he has developed the "Divergent Fates" world, in which *Division Zero, Virtual Immortality, The Awakened Series, The Harmony Paradox, and the Daughter of Mars series* take place. Along with being an editor at Curiosity Quills press, he has worked in IT and technical support.

Matthew is an avid gamer, a recovered WoW addict, Gamemaster for two custom RPG systems, and a fan of anime, British humour, and intellectual science fiction that questions the nature of reality, life, and what happens after it.

He is also fond of cats.

Visit me online at:
    Facebook: https://www.facebook.com/MatthewSCoxAuthor
    Pinterest: https://www.pinterest.com/matthewcox10420/
    Goodreads: https://www.goodreads.com/author/show/7712730.
Matthew_S_Cox
    Email: mcox2112@gmail.com

OTHER BOOKS BY MATTHEW S. COX

Divergent Fates Universe Novels

Division Zero series

- Division Zero
- Lex De Mortuis
- Thrall
- Guardian
- Harbinger
- The Shadow Fixer
- Neuroshock

The Awakened series

- Prophet of the Badlands
- Archon's Queen
- Grey Ronin
- Daughter of Ash
- Zero Rogue
- Angel Descended

Daughter of Mars series

- The Hand of Raziel
- Araphel
- Ghost Black

Virtual Immortality series

- Virtual Immortality
- The Harmony Paradox

Prophet of the Badlands Series

- Prophet's Journey
- Prophet's Mercy

Divergent Fates Anthology

(Fiction Novels - Adult)

The Roadhouse Chronicles Series

- One More Run
- The Redeemed
- Dead Man's Number

Faded Skies series

- Heir Ascendant
- Ascendant Unrest
- Ascendant Revolution

Temporal Armistice Series

- Nascent Shadow
- The Shadow Collector
- The Gate to Oblivion
- The Queen of Discord
- The Burning Alchemist

Vampire Innocent series

- A Nighttime of Forever
- A Beginner's Guide to Fangs
- The Artist of Ruin

- The Last Family Road Trip
- The Phantom Oracle
- How Not to Summon Demons
- Ordinary Problems of a College Vampire
- A Vampire's Guide to Surviving Holidays
- An Introduction to Paranormal Diplomacy
- A Vampire's Guide to Adulting
- How to Stop a Vampire War in Six Easy Steps
- Ancient Vampire Death Cults and Other Annoyances
- Hunting Vampires for Fun and Profit
- A String of Seriously Unlucky Events
- The Summer of Completely Usual Strangeness
- Demonic Crisis Management for the Modern Vampire

Standalones

- Wayfarer: AV494
- Axillon99
- Chiaroscuro: The Mouse and the Candle
- The Spirits of Six Minstrel Run
- Sophie's Light
- The Far Side of Promise anthology
- Operation: Chimera (with Tony Healey)
- The Dysfunctional Conspiracy (with Christopher Veltmann)
- Of Myth and Shadow
- The Girl Who Found the Sun

Winter Solstice series (with J.R. Rain)

- Convergence
- Containment
- Catalyst
- Catacombs

Alexis Silver series (with J.R. Rain)

- Silver Light
- Deep Silver
- Silver Quarrel
- Silver Crucible
- Silver Heart

Samantha Moon Origins series (with J.R. Rain)

- New Moon Rising
- Moon Mourning
- Haunted Moon

Vampire For Hire series (with J.R. Rain)

- Moon Master
- Dead Moon
- Lost Moon
- Vampire Destiny
- Infinite Moon
- Vampire Empress
- Moon Elder
- Wicked Moon
- Moon Blade

Maddy Wimsey series (with J.R. Rain)

- The Devil's Eye
- The Drifting Gloom
- Dark Mercy
- Primal Wrath

Samantha Moon Case Files series (with J.R. Rain)

- Blood Moon

Immortal Operative (with J.R. Rain)

- Broken Ice
- Broken Wing

Four Elements series (with J.R. Rain)

- The Elementalist
- The Black Rose
- The Wakefield Curse

Witches series (with J.R. Rain)

- The Witch and the Hangman

Zeb Clemens series (with J.R. Rain)

- The Beast of Devil's Creek
- Wanted: Undead or Alive

Young Adult Novels

The Eldritch Heart Series

- The Eldritch Heart
- The Cursed Crown
- The Sapphire Soul

Evergreen Series

- Evergreen
- The World That Remains

- The Lucky Ones
- Nuclear Summer
- The Nuclear Frontier
- The World We Make
- The Threat Unseen

Progenitor Series

- Out of Sight
- Out of Mind

Diary of a Teenage Fey

(Short story series)

- Elder Horror
- The Hag of Barrow Falls
- Babysitter's Nightmare
- Lharakki
- Bauble for a Soul
- Simulacrum
- Amorphous
- Manticore

Standalones

- Caller 107
- The Summer the World Ended
- Nine Candles of Deepest Black
- The Forest Beyond the Earth

Middle Grade Novels

The Adventures of Ubergirl series

- My Dad is a Mad Scientist
- Aliens Ate My Homework
- The End of all Halloweens
- Dr. Infinity and the Soul Smasher

Tales of Widowswood series

- Emma and the Banderwigh
- Emma and the Silk Thieves
- Emma and the Silverbell Faeries
- Emma and the Elixir of Madness
- Emma and the Weeping Spirit

Standalones

- Citadel: The Concordant Sequence
- The Cursed Codex
- The Menagerie of Jenkins Bailey

www.ingramcontent.com/pod-product-compliance
Lightning Source LLC
Chambersburg PA
CBHW020052180626
46812CB00006B/2294